The MISTLETOE Problem

Contents

Content Notes

This book is a romcom, and you can expect to read a very cozy, lighthearted story here. With that being said, there are a few topics and events below that you may wish to be forewarned about.

In this book, you will find multiple scenes of explicit, consensual sex between two adults, and also a healthy heaping of profanity. More minor warnings include potentially excessive alcohol consumption in social settings, implied disordered eating (secondary character), and a *very* briefly mentioned miscarriage (in the past, to a secondary character who is at peace with the event). Our protagonist, Elle, also experiences two mild panic attacks as a result of her emotional journey through the book, but they are resolved quickly and she has support both times.

Other than that, this is still a romantic comedy. You are guaranteed a tooth-rotting, feel-good HEA at the end.

Happy reading!

To anyone who has felt unhappy with their life.
I hope you found your way to joy.

ELLE

S tanding in front of screaming children in a too-tight elf costume wasn't exactly how I thought I'd be spending my Saturday morning. And yet, here I was.

I wanted to stab whoever had decided that we needed to suffer for our art. Because in my case, I was currently sweating my tits off in an elf costume, passing presents to kids. My cheeks ached from the smiling, and my heeled shoes were killing me.

God, I hated my agent so much.

A kid snatched a gift bag out of my hand, and I didn't even bat an eye. I wished I had never taken this job, but the pay was so unreasonably good that I couldn't resist. It was an entire month's rent for three days' work. But my God, it sucked.

Why would someone want to do a Christmas community event in *November*?

I kept a smile pasted on my heavily made-up face and took another present from the pile, checking the line. I had to swallow a groan. There were still at least fifty kids to get through.

My fake eyelashes irritated my eyes, and I wanted to rip the elf hat off my head, but I was contractually obligated to smile and remain poised for the entirety of my shift.

So my smile never faltered, and I kept handing out those presents like my life depended on them.

❧❧❧❧ ❦❦❦❦

I loved Christmas. Honestly, I did. I loved the gaudy decorations—I loved the holiday food—I even loved the endless tasteless advertising. I wasn't particularly religious—I just loved the *idea* of Christmas.

But after the fifth straight hour of having to stand and smile and gift out little tote bags, I was getting tired of the whole damn thing. The line still wasn't getting any smaller, and my bladder was beginning to scream at me.

I put down my hamper and turned to Christine, the other elf on duty. "I'm taking a bathroom break."

She nodded at me with envious eyes. She'd already taken hers about an hour ago, and the company that hired us only permitted a single break over the entire shift. Assholes.

I kept my smile going all the way to the cubicle, trying to ignore the stares from the customers in the mall. I looked ridiculous, dolled up in my brightly colored costume, and I wasn't the only one who seemed to think I was out of place. Only when I'd shut the door and locked it did I relax the muscles of my face. They ached, and I gave myself a single moment to massage my jaw, careful not to smudge my makeup. Heaven forbid I look anything less than perfect. The entertainment company would have a field day. I did my business, then closed the lid and sat on the seat. Checking my watch, I did a rough calculation. I had about two more minutes, which was just enough for me to close my eyes and wish I was somewhere else.

The spirit of Christmas indeed.

When I'd decided I was going to be an actor seven years ago, I hadn't factored in *this*. Struggling, endless struggling, having to work two mind-numbing jobs and barely scrape by—sitting by the phone, waiting for my shitty agent to call and tell me I have to go to a stupid audition for another shitty commercial tomorrow at six am.

It was not the acting career I had hoped for myself. As I stared at the stall door, I winced. I used to think I would be the exception, one of those few lucky actors who got discovered, who got interesting roles, who got to do something other than extra work and mindless commercials and *this*.

Instead, I was here, dressed as an elf and the biggest joke in LA.

My watch beeped, and I stood. Slowly, excruciatingly, I built my smile back up, imagining all the times I had felt joy, felt excitement, felt anything other than what I was actually feeling right then.

My acting teachers would be proud of me. At least I'd got this job, beating out a dozen other girls who looked just like me. I tried to count my blessings and ended up with a bitter taste in the back of my throat.

I washed my hands and checked myself in the mirror. I was a girl with a megawatt smile and a ridiculous costume, ready to spread holiday cheer once more.

I had to swallow down my nausea at the thought. I had to go back out there—I couldn't afford to wallow.

So I turned and left the bathroom, ignoring the stares, ignoring the kids who pointed and laughed as I passed by. I walked swiftly, knowing I had only one more minute before—

I slammed into someone exiting a store and nearly lost my balance. A briefcase of documents fell onto the tiles, and I heard someone swear. I didn't think it was me.

"I—Sorry." I jerked myself back from the person—who I quickly realized was a very attractive man—and fluttered my hands. "Sorry."

The man gave me an annoyed look and kneeled down to gather his papers. His jaw clenched, and I felt my stomach flip. It was unfortunate he was so attractive, given how much he was frowning at me.

I hurriedly kneeled down next to him. I could fix this. "Let me help—"

"No." The man's reply was sharp. He sounded *really* annoyed. "Do elves like to run into people?"

My head reared back at his barb and I ground my teeth together. "I was just offering my help."

"The bare minimum, really, after you just ruined my day."

Jesus, this man had a serious grump issue. I stood and watched as he gathered the last documents and filed them away. Why was he looking at me like I'd just murdered a kitten in front of him? I took a breath and stood my ground. "You were the one who barrelled out of a store without looking."

The man straightened. He was tall, so I had to crane my neck a little to look him in the eye. "I couldn't see you—you were running too fast. Do elves make a habit of running around recklessly?"

"We do when we're on company time." I grumbled and gave him a bitter smile. "It's still your fault for running into me."

"I don't think so, princess." My spine straightened at the patronising word, and I flushed angrily. Damn him for being so attractive and so *infuriating*. He eyed my costume with distaste. "Do you usually like to dress like an elf in November?"

I really was going to kill my agent. Right after I'd killed the man in front of me for making me angry *and* horny. "Actually, I dress like this all year round. Keeps the cheer."

He narrowed his eyes. "Your hat is bent."

My hand flew up to my head, and it annoyed me to realize that he was right. It was crooked. I quickly fixed it and sent him a soft glare. "Some manners might help."

The man straightened his tie, and I got the feeling his suit had cost more than my whole wardrobe. He checked his watch. "You've made me late. Thanks for that."

"Not my fault." I quipped, clenching my hands behind my back. "You shouldn't blame others for your own problems."

He gave me a dark glare. "And I should listen to a girl in an elf costume because…?"

I realized my smile had completely dropped during our in-teraction, so I whipped it back up again, my sudden expression change throwing him off guard. "I hope your job pays well enough for how miserable it makes you."

He scoffed. "I can tell it pays much better than *yours*."

I grit my teeth, but couldn't muster a smart retort, knowing it was true. Even if my ridiculous elf costume gig paid well by my standards, I could tell that his paycheck was leagues above my own. So, I had to resort to a petty jab as I walked away. "Have fun living life as an asshole."

"Okay, elf girl."

My smile didn't falter as I walked away, but my left eye twitched a little. The only reason I didn't turn around and spit at him was because there were little children nearby.

After all, I was Santa's little helper. I was *full* of holiday cheer.

>>>>>> <<<<<<

Somehow, I made it through the rest of my shift. The first thing I did was call my agent, because I was only half kidding about my intention to murder her.

Leslie Knapp, agent to the stars and other various failures, answered on the fifth ring. "Elle, darling, I'm a little busy, so let's keep this quick."

I sighed, still smarting after the interaction with the asshole in the mall. My conversations with Leslie always began with some variation of '*I'm busy and you're not worth much of my time.*' "Leslie. I just wanted to talk to you about the elf job."

"Riiiight." There were rustling sounds in the background, and I knew I barely had half her attention. "I'm glad you like it. Good pay and easy work makes a happy actor."

"Leslie," I took a breath to keep myself rational, "it barely qualifies as acting work."

"Elle, darling, this is the first gig you've worked for me in months. I put effort in booking it for you, and you're telling me you don't even like it?"

Every day that passed, I became more convinced that Leslie was an incompetent agent. But she was the only fairly credible one who took a chance on me. I breathed through my nose. "It's not really the gig you described to me."

Leslie sounded like she was eating. "Well, Elle darling, you know these things can change. As long as they're not asking you to do extra work or take off your clothes, I wouldn't be too picky if I were you."

Something burned in my belly, and I tried to tamp it down. "When I signed with you, you promised me you would send me for real acting work. I specialize in *Shakespeare*, Leslie. I'm not a showgirl."

"Elle, it's not my fault that the jobs you want aren't the jobs you get. I'm trying really hard here," crunching sounds came from the speakers, "and if this working relationship is going to keep *working*, you need to respect that."

Basically, *shut up or I'll drop you, you dumb bitch.*

I swallowed the rage that seized up my throat and hummed. Leslie was right. Right now, as a young actor with no impressive credits behind me, I needed her a lot more than she needed me. I just hated it all so much. If only I could get a good acting gig—a real one where I could actually act—I wouldn't have to put up with this shit anymore.

Leslie made another rustling sound. "You know what, Elle? I've got just the thing for you. There's this job a client of mine has been trying to fill for a while—it's a remote location job for the month of December. Pays just as well as the costume work, and it has free board. I'll even sweeten it for you. You do this job for me, and I'll make sure you get an audition for a professional play early next year."

"Do I have to audition for this gig?"

"Not at all. They just want an actor with training, young and vibrant."

"Why me?" The job sounded too good to be true, and every actor knew to be wary of those.

"I don't have anyone else available for all of December."

I closed my eyes, knowing that I couldn't say no unless I came up with a foolproof excuse, and quickly. I'd already told Leslie that I was available for December, hoping she would snag me a holiday play, or something vaguely decent. There were always more acting gigs during the holidays. Unfortunately, my tired, angry brain couldn't come up with anything reasonable except... "You haven't told me where it is."

"Mistletoe Valley." Leslie paused, and when I didn't make a sound of recognition, she continued. "It's about four hours away, in the Sierra Nevada Mountains."

"Mistletoe Valley? Is that even a real place?"

"Google tells me it is." Leslie responded, sounding bored now.

"It's a four-hour drive? And it's for all of December?"

"Correct, darling." Leslie made a coughing sound, like she had choked on a cookie. "The town council wants to throw a Christmas play, and they want a young actor to come in and direct the kids. They got some funding from somewhere, I think."

My brain stuttered. "So, why aren't they just getting a young director?"

"Darling, I asked them that, and they said they wanted someone who 'knew how to act, too.'"

A job putting together a Christmas play for a small town, paying well? I thought about it, realizing how much better it would be than the elf costume monstrosity.

Leslie made the decision for me. "It's that, Elle, or I've got plenty more shifts as an elf."

I nearly vomited at the idea and shook my head. "Nope. No more elf gigs, thanks."

"So that's a yes, then?"

I looked at my calendar, mentally preparing myself. "Yes. I'll do it."

After all, anything was better than squeezing into that elf costume for another day.

ELLE

Mistletoe Valley was nothing like I expected. The town was nestled in the mountains, surrounded by towering pine trees. According to the information booklet I'd found, it was once a big logging town, but in recent decades had changed into a tourist haven for city goers to escape during the holiday months.

It was gorgeous.

Watching from the passenger seat of my taxi driving through a winding mountain pass, I shook my head. This was the place I got to spend all of December in? There had to be a catch. Cottages and BnB's sat against the hillsides, and there were several wineries on the way in. It was a town made to say '*come, welcome, stay for a while.*' The winding roads led me through the Main Street, a bustling area filled with little shops and restaurants.

It wasn't quite snow season yet, but I could tell the town would be gorgeous covered in white, the slanted rooftops and cozy shops perfectly set up for colder weather.

I checked the directions on my phone and guided the driver past the town center into a quieter street overlooking the river.

We pulled in front of a house with a brightly colored door, and I double checked I was at the right address: 21 Elderflower Lane. I paid, got out of the taxi, and stood on the footpath with my two suitcases. The house looked like a gingerbread cottage, and I half expected Mrs Claus to walk out at any moment.

But the moment passed, and I reminded myself of why I was here. Work. And there was almost certainly going to be some catch, some fatal flaw in the gig that made me hate it. I walked up the small path to knock on the door.

After a while, the door opened and a white-haired older woman smiled down at me. A feeling of vague familiarity overcame me as I looked at her face. Had I seen her before? I hiked my bag higher on my shoulder and gave her one of my practised smiles. "Hi. I'm Elle Sutton. Are you Deanna?"

She nodded and smiled even wider. "Elle! Lovely to meet you. And yes, I'm Deanna. Come in, come in!"

She pulled me into a warm hug, which I hesitantly returned, unused to such warmth. I blinked down at her. "My agent said you—"

"It's so good to have someone new to stay for a while." Deanna led me through her house, gesturing for me to sit at her dining table while she bustled around the kitchen. "Tea? Cookies? You must be hungry after the journey."

I nodded at her, getting the distinct feeling that I was being grandmothered. Maybe I wasn't wrong with the Mrs Claus thing. "Thank you, I'd love that."

As she made the tea and prepared some snacks, I got the chance to look around her house. It was cozy, a fireplace crackling in the corner, well-appointed furniture and rugs all adding to the warm atmosphere. It felt like the sort of place you'd want to stay for a long while, relaxing and reading a book.

It was a stark contrast to my shitty apartment back in the city, messy and unwelcoming and crowded. Deanna came round to the table and handed me a steaming mug. "There you are. How was the drive?"

"Peaceful." I gave her a quick smile. "The mountains are beautiful."

Deanna slid herself onto a chair, her face kind. "Once you hit the mountain range, I find the drive is wonderful."

I nodded and took a sip from the mug, grateful for the warmth. Now that I was here, I wasn't sure what to do. Was I meant to get straight into work? I hated not knowing what was expected of me, because then I couldn't give people exactly what they wanted. I searched around for something, anything to say. "It's colder here than the city."

Deanna pushed a plate of cookies over to me. "It's an alpine village, love. That'll do it."

I flushed, feeling stupid. "Right."

"You'll soon get used to the chill." Deanna leaned forward on the table, her eyes bright. "Now, I want to hear more about you. Leslie told me you're twenty-five, correct?"

"Yeah." I washed my mouthful of cookie down with some tea. I mentally prepared my little speech, wanting to make sure

I proved myself worthy of the job. "I graduated from LADA three years ago, and I've been—"

Deanna grabbed my wrist and smiled. "I know you've got the training, love. I want to know about who you are, not what you've done."

My brain stuttered to a stop. What did she mean, who I was outside of my career? Acting *was* everything I was. I threw everything I was at acting, my hopes and ambitions, my energy, and my spare time. "I don't... what do you mean?"

I don't think I imagined the way Deanna's eyes softened. "I mean, what are your passions? What drives you?"

I blinked at the woman in front of me. "Acting. I love acting, anything to do with it."

"Anything else? Everyone has hobbies."

Everyone except me, apparently. I struggled to find something, anything, to appease this kind woman, but I came up with nothing. "I guess... I just love acting so much, I don't have time for anything else."

Deanna gave me a shrewd look that I didn't particularly like—I was being seen far too easily. "Did Leslie tell you much about me?"

I shook my head. Leslie hadn't mentioned anything about my host and employer, only that she wanted someone young for the job. "Not much, sorry."

Deanna nodded. "I expected as much. I knew Leslie's mother years ago, which is why I contacted her, but bless her, she's not the most switched on agent that ever lived."

I coughed into my tea, silently agreeing with Deanna. "So tell me more about you, then."

Deanna smiled. "My name's Deanna Hooper. I was an actor in LA, just like you. I did a lot of stage shows back in the eighties and nineties."

I sat up straighter, suddenly more alert. "Wait, are you *that* Deanna Hooper? The one with the name plaque at the Magnolia?"

Deanna gave me a kind smile. "The same."

I had to stop my jaw from gaping open. Deanna Hooper, the actress, was an icon of the theater scene back home. Her *Hedda Gabler* had been revolutionary, as was her one woman performance of *Waiting for Godot*. I sat forward in my seat. "Oh my god, you're—why'd you quit, why'd you come here? What happened?"

Deanna ran a hand over the table, giving me a soft smile. "Contrary to common belief, I didn't fall ill or have a family disaster or anything of the sort. I had a moment of realization and just… quit."

I frowned at her, still confused. "But… why? Your career was going so well."

Deanna shrugged. "I got to forty and realized that I didn't like it anymore. I didn't like the city, nor did I like the people who were my friends. So I came here for a holiday… and I never looked back."

I sat back in my chair, blinking at her. "But… you could have kept going for another twenty years. You could have… formed your own theater company, you could have…"

"I didn't want to, love." Deanna smiled at me. "Whilst I appreciate your young enthusiasm, understand that I made the choice, and I've never regretted it."

I swallowed. "Of course. Sorry, I didn't mean to offend with my questions—"

"Don't worry, love." Deanna stood, smoothing down her long skirt. "I've had many people ask me similar questions over the years. It doesn't bother me much anymore."

I stood with her. A thought occurred to me, and I had to ask the question. "Why do you need me to direct the Christmas play if you have the experience?"

Deanna gave me a look. "It's my way of giving back, really. I can get the funding easily, and I love giving the kids exposure to new talent, new ideas. It's a small town—there's only so much I can give them. Every actor I've brought here has really enjoyed the experience, too."

I stared at her, not fully comprehending her words. She just… enjoyed doing this out of the goodness of her heart?

Deanna laughed. "You'll get used to it, love. This town is all about giving and sharing things around. It's one of the things I love about it. Now, I'll show you your room."

I followed her down a hallway and up the stairs to the second floor. She showed me to the first room on the right, and I stopped at the open door.

It was the loveliest room I'd seen for a long time. The large, soft bed was covered with fluffy blankets. A small fireplace sat in the corner, ready to be lit. A reading chair faced the window, with a beautiful view of the mountains surrounding the valley.

Deanna gestured to the furniture. "This is the closet, which is empty for your use. I've put extra towels and sheets in there, in case you want more."

She showed me how to light the fire, which added a comforting ambient sound of crackling logs to the room. I walked to the window and stared at the view. "This is… beautiful."

Deanna touched my elbow. "I haven't finished showing you everything, love. There's an ensuite through here—it's just yours to use."

I sighed with delight as she showed me. My own bathroom? I hadn't had my own bathroom in over seven years, always having to share with other flatmates. "Deanna… this is wonderful. Thank you."

"I'm glad you think it'll suit you. I've tried my best to make sure artists who come and stay have a nice space. There's another room on this floor that I occasionally use to sew, but if I'm not in it, use it for exercising, yoga, anything of the sort." Deanna gave a nod to the room. "If there's anything else you need to feel more at home, always ask me. I'll provide breakfast and dinner for you, and help yourself to anything in the kitchen. You don't have to eat with me, but I just ask that you let me know."

"I didn't know meals were provided." I thought of my bag of cheap groceries in the car, cans of beans and rice for meals.

Deanna raised her eyes to the ceiling. "Leslie's really letting herself go, isn't she?"

I couldn't help but snort, suddenly feeling that I could be honest in front of Deanna. "You could say that."

Deanna appraised me and smiled. "I want you to enjoy your time here, Elle. All we're doing is putting on a Christmas play for the families of this town, and it'll be great, no matter how it turns out."

I nodded. I could deal with that. "When do we start?"

Deanna raised a hand. "You get settled and relaxed first. We start rehearsals in three days, so you've got time to explore and prepare. Once you're settled, I'll give you the script to look over."

"Thank you. That sounds great."

Deanna smiled at me again. "It's supposed to be fun, Elle. For you, and for the kids. Nothing else really matters."

I nodded, and she left me to settle in. Fun. I could do that, right? I dropped my duffle bag on the floor and sank into the reading chair, blowing out a breath.

I looked around the room and took stock. It was gorgeous, like something out of a fairytale, all cozy and warm and peaceful.

And Leslie considered this gig a punishment? Spending a month in this delightful little holiday town, working with an icon of the stage? Not for the first time, I got the feeling Leslie didn't know what she was doing.

The fire crackled, and I closed my eyes. I allowed myself to dream, just for a moment, that I was going to live here forever, peacefully—

I jerked upright. I could not let myself entertain thoughts like that. Mistletoe Valley was a lovely town, sure, but I couldn't stay here forever. My acting career was too important.

I would enjoy this month, and I would return refreshed, with a much heftier savings account. It was all going according to plan.

So why did I feel so sad about the idea of leaving? I had only just arrived.

The fireplace kept burning and offered me no answers.

After unpacking, I went for a walk around town. Deanna gave me directions to follow the path along the river, which would take me straight to the town square. As I walked past pines and oaks and willows, I got out my phone. I needed to keep a record of the beauty of this place, of how peaceful it was making me feel. I felt if I blinked, it would all disappear.

The narrow river flowed through the town, winding down from the mountains. I wondered what it would be like in summer, people swimming in the icy pools to cool down from the heat. For now, the air held the promise of snow, and I wrapped my scarf tighter around my neck. I was glad I had packed well for the cold.

The path along the river ran past a tourist park, and I could already see it filling with visitors—early vacationers setting up their prime spots along the banks. It all looked so cheery, and some people waved as I walked by.

Eventually, the path landed me right into the town square, hemmed in with shops on three sides and the river on the other. A walking bridge led to the other side of the riverbank.

People were doing their daily errands and shopping, smiling and waving to each other as they went. Warm lights shone from storefronts, and I wandered around the square. There were clothing shops, an artisanal bakery and deli, several more retailers and a few cozy restaurants. It was a town made to be inviting, full of interesting places and wares. As I strolled, a brightly lit shop caught my eye.

It was a Christmas Holiday shop. Open year round, the sign said, tinsel and holly decorating every square inch of the windows. A neon sign shouting '*HAPPY HOLIDAYS*' emblazoned across the top of the oak door.

A smile grew on my face. I could already tell I was going to adore this town. They had a Christmas shop. It was perfect.

I pushed on the door and walked in.

꘏꘏꘏꘏

The smell was the first thing that hit me. Suddenly I was seven years old again, sitting at the breakfast table as my mother prepared food for Christmas. It was the smell of spices, of fireplaces and pudding and roast meats.

I nearly laughed in delight. I'd never seen an evergreen Christmas Holiday shop before, but was glad this was going to be my first experience.

A woman rounded the corner, curly haired with a warm smile. "Hiya. Can I help you?"

I took another look around the place. "I… mostly just came here to look. I've never seen a year round Holiday shop like this."

The woman chuckled. "Most people have a similar reaction when they come in. It's a real treat, especially for the youngsters."

I nodded and turned in a slow circle to admire the mountains of decorations.

"You here on holidays?"

I touched a small bauble made of glass in the shape of a reindeer. "Yes. No. I'm here to help put on the Christmas play."

The woman perked up. "Oh! You must be Elle Sutton, right? My Nathaniel's one of the kids in the play, Deanna told us about you. I'm Susan."

Suddenly I felt self-conscious, as though I needed to prove myself to this woman. All the quiet joy I'd found in the shop fizzled out. I swallowed. "Nice to meet you, Susan."

"How are you finding Mistletoe Valley?"

"I've only just got here, really. But it's so beautiful."

Susan gave me a lopsided smile. "That it is, but it's still probably a shock for a big city girl."

I eyed the floor. "I grew up in Lumley Cove, so small towns are much more my style."

"Ah." Susan nodded at me. "Well, the kids are sure glad that you're coming to teach them. They love the Christmas play, and the rest of us get a kick out of seeing our kids onstage. It's wonderful how Deanna organises you lot to come every year—it really brings new life into the town."

I picked up a gingerbread bauble that looked edible. "How long has Deanna been running the Christmas plays?"

"Nearly as long as she's been here—God, must be running on twenty years now." Susan shook her head. "Time flies."

I set down the decoration. "How long has this shop been here?"

"Oh… maybe ten, fifteen years? I don't own it, I just run it for Mrs. Paisley."

I took one last look at the dazzling display around me. "You're doing a wonderful job."

Susan smiled. "Thank you, darling. I hope you enjoy Mistletoe Valley."

As I pushed open the door, Susan called out to me.

"Elle, if you want a good place to eat lunch, the Hollyoak Hotel down the street does a lovely meal."

I waved and went back out into the cold winter air. What was it with this town? Everyone was so welcoming, so positive, as if the very water they drank was magical.

If I wasn't careful, I might fall in love with this town. Which was a problem, because I had to leave. No one can be a paid actor long term in a small town.

~>>>>⟩ ⟨⟨⟨⟨~

I arrived back at Deanna's house on dusk, after walking the streets for over an hour. I felt good, my legs were stretched, and I was eager to get back into the warmth. I sniffled, the cold wind making my nose run. I let myself in with the key she had given me and was drawn by delicious smells to the kitchen. Deanna stood before a steaming pot on the stove, and my mouth watered. She waved her wooden spoon at me as I walked in. "Hello, love. Did you have a pleasant walk?"

I smiled as I unwrapped my scarf. "Great, thanks. I met Susan in the Christmas shop, and she seems delightful."

Deanna stirred the pot and nodded. "Lovely woman, she is. Her son was having a hard time at school, but she sent him to me, and he's brightened right up."

"What do you mean?" I sat at the island counter.

Deanna cocked a hip against the bench and looked at me. "He needed something where he could express himself. Something with no right or wrong answers. Just so happens that thing was my acting classes."

"How many kids have you got at your studio?"

Deanna looked at the ceiling, counting. "About fifty, I'd say. I run classes for every age group, but really they're just theatre games for the youngsters most of the time, and only a little more structured for the teenagers. Not all of them will be in the play, though."

I straightened. "But… you don't run competitions, exams?"

Deanna smiled at me, something flinty in her eyes. "Nope. I didn't open my school to put these kids through a sausage factory. When I was a kid, theatre gave me joy. I forgot that, when I was a pro."

"What if a student wants to become professional?"

"Then I tutor them individually. But that's only happened a few times, and even then, they eventually decide to pursue something a little… easier."

I sighed. "Can't say I blame them."

"No." Deanna gave me a shrewd look. "I can't say I do, either. Go, wash up before dinner if you want. This'll be ready soon."

As I washed my hands, I allowed my thoughts to wander. I thought of my childhood acting teacher, endlessly pushing me to be a star. I thought of my parents questioning my career choice, worried about the long, hard road I had chosen. I thought of my motivation to pursue it regardless, driven by spite to prove I could become a star if I just *worked hard enough*.

Mostly, I thought about the little girl I was who had found a way to express herself all those years ago.

I realized how far removed my life was from her.

⟫⟫⟫ ⟪⟪⟪

The casserole was delicious, but my endlessly spinning thoughts soured the experience. The perfectly cooked chicken was like chalk in my mouth, but I expressed my thanks to Deanna, anyway. "Thank you for this. It's delicious."

She gave me a searching look. "My pleasure. But something's on your mind. Missing the city already?"

I coughed into my bowl and grabbed a napkin to wipe my mouth. I recovered and shook my head. "No. That's… definitely not the problem."

"Then what is?" Deanna smiled at me. "I know I'm your host, and technically your employer, but be honest with me. Remember, I was in the industry once. I know how hard it can be."

I inhaled, deciding to take the leap. "It's tough right now. But it beats being a lawyer, doesn't it?" I cracked my usual joke, the motto I repeated to myself every year since deciding to become an actor.

She gave a wistful smile. "My godson's a lawyer. He quite enjoys it, actually."

My face froze, and I worried I had offended her. "I—didn't mean that being a lawyer is… bad, I just—"

"I know, love." Deanna served me another slice of bread, urging me to eat. "There are many unhappy people working in jobs that seem impressive, and lawyers are no exception. But don't make the mistake of thinking all of them are miserable. Focus on yourself."

I took another bite of bread and nodded.

She tilted her head. "Did you want to be a lawyer?"

I let my gaze drift to the window. "I applied for undergrad, just in case I didn't get into LADA. I had an offer. But when I got into LADA, I turned it down."

"You didn't answer my question."

I felt strange, thinking about what my life could have been if I had made a different choice seven years ago. But I was a child then, and I couldn't change it now. I had to stay the course. "I don't know. I didn't entertain the idea for long. It was mostly to please my parents."

"You could always change careers."

"No." I shook my head vehemently. "I'm not taking on more student debt to fix some idle curiosity."

Deanna winced. "Fair enough. Student debt is a trap, it's appalling."

I made a sound of agreement around my forkful of food. I searched for another topic, to take the focus off myself. "Your godson, is he in town?"

Deanna waved a hand, a wry smile on her face. "Occasionally. He comes and goes, really. He's the unofficial town lawyer, but he's based in the city. Drives me crazy that he won't move back properly."

"Why doesn't he?"

"Not sure." Deanna laughed. "He keeps saying he will, but it's getting old."

"How old is he?"

"Thirty." Deanna stood and reached for my empty plate. I joined her to help clean up, and she sent me a grateful smile. "I've been desperate for him to move back ever since he graduated, but Nick keeps putting it off."

I chuckled. "I see."

"He said he was going to visit soon. You might get to meet him." Deanna passed me a dish to dry.

I grabbed a dishcloth and began wiping. "Cool."

Deanna gave me a sly look. "He's single, you know."

I baulked and changed the subject. I didn't need anything else to distract me while I was here. "You mentioned a script for the play?"

"I did." Deanna cleaned the bench. "I have an old friend from my stage days. He's retired now, but he pens a new play for us each year, something holiday themed. Family friendly."

"That's... incredibly generous."

Deanna gave me a look. "He does it for the joy of it, love. It keeps him going, writing."

"Does your studio keep you going?" I finished the last of the dishes and put them away, as Deanna opened the cupboards.

"In a way. I had lost the joy, back when I retired from the stage. The kids helped me get it back. This town helped me get it back. There are a lot of different artists here, you know."

"In such a small town?" I frowned, doubting her words. Small towns were not artistic hubs, in my experience.

"In this one, yes. Many have visited and stayed. Like me. Must be something in the water."

Funny. I'd thought the same thing earlier that day. I bid Deanna goodnight and headed to my room, suddenly exhausted.

I slid into the sheets and pulled the coverlet over me, sinking deep into my emotions. I hadn't even been here a full day, and I already felt confused. What would an entire month bring?

ELLE

T he eyes of about fifty children blinked up at me, and I swallowed my nerves. I had to direct all these kids?

I hadn't really thought about the fact that directing a Christmas play would involve actually wrangling *kids*. My only experience with kids and acting was my own childhood, and I didn't want to be anything like my strict acting teacher.

You are too sloppy, undisciplined, Elle, she had said. *You must try harder if you want to be a star.*

Telling a child they needed to crush their joy wasn't the way to go, but what was I supposed to *do* with them? There was a show to make. I would have to find the way to guide them through it with just the right amount of pressure.

"Elle?" Deanna nudged me and interrupted my panicked pause. "Do you want to introduce yourself?"

I clasped my hands and gave the kids my best approachable smile. "Hi. You can call me Elle. I, um….graduated from LADA three years ago and have been working in—"

Their eyes glazed over, and I could tell that approach wasn't going to work. Deanna had told me she played theatre games with them, right? So I should probably try to do a similar thing to get to know them.

I shook my head and grinned. "But that's all the boring stuff. What I'm here for is more important, which is to make a really enjoyable Christmas play with all of you. So, what I want to know, from each of you, is what do you love about the holidays?"

We formed a huge seated circle and I listened as they spoke in turn. Some responses were predictable—presents and sweets and yummy food—but others surprised me. One little girl, Celia, said her favorite part of Christmas was the smell of her grandmother's kitchen. A morose teenager mumbled that Christmas was one of the few times her parents didn't argue.

That one shook me. One by one, a picture began to form of these kids' lives, and what was important to them. I realized each one of them deserved to feel important, to feel heard. *This* was what I could foster for them.

After the exercise, I stood. "Now, I don't want to lie to you. There will be some of you in the play who might get a little more of a spotlight than others, but this is a team effort. Every single one of you will get a chance to do something wonderful on that stage, even if it's a single line of song or speech. I'm not really a big fan of leads and a chorus. That means everything will be shared a little more than you might be used to. Sound good?"

They all nodded, and I set them to work on their first job: sorting themselves into their favorite colors. It was a nonsense activity, but it gave me a chance to check in with Deanna.

"Well done." Deanna whispered to me.

I blew out a breath. "I see what you mean, about this being an important space for them to express themselves."

"I agree." Deanna gave me a side eye. "Far too many acting teachers neglect that, I think."

I pressed my lips together, trying not to think too hard about my own childhood experiences. "You're right."

"What was yours? A narcissistic egomaniac or a failed actor trying to live vicariously through you?" I realized Deanna was asking me about my old acting teacher, and my stomach clenched.

"A bit of both, I think." I sighed. I didn't like thinking about that time. "And it barely got any better when I went to LADA. They were just better at hiding it."

Deanna hummed.

I looked at the children as they sorted themselves into groups, shouts and laughter echoing around the town hall. I turned to Deanna, something still bothering me about the whole arrangement. "Why don't you hire young directors?"

Deanna shook her head. "Too high and mighty, usually. Most of them aren't actors, or at least haven't been acting long enough to really know the struggles of it. You, and the others, you do. You understand what it feels like to be poorly valued, to be dismissed and put under unnecessary pressure. I've been doing this for nearly twenty years and I've not yet had a year where one of the actors hasn't been able to create a beautiful experience. For the kids, and for the audience."

I turned back to the kids. "No pressure, then."

"Like I said this morning, just spend today getting to know them. The proper work can begin on Friday." Deanna squeezed my elbow and went to talk to a teenager who had withdrawn a little from the pack.

When everyone had sorted themselves into their color groups, I clapped my hands to get their attention. "Alright. Great job everyone. Now, these will be your groups for a little improv game. I want to see your outstanding personalities at work on the floor!"

The kids hurried to obey my directions, and I smiled.

Maybe this would be okay.

"I think I'll head to the Hollyoak tonight—I've been told it has decent food." I said to Deanna as we locked up the town hall after a few very successful hours with the kids. "And it's Friday. I could do with a drink."

Deanna stretched her arms above her head. "You know what? It's been a while since I've gone out. Let's go together."

After I bundled myself up in my coat and scarf, we set off. The short walk was going to be brutal in the evening air. A light dusting of snow fell around us, but it melted as soon as it hit the ground.

Deanna looked up at the sky. "It won't stick, not yet."

I watched as the snowflakes floated to the ground. "When does it usually set in?"

"Later in December, but it could be as early as next week, the forecast said." Deanna's breaths puffed out in clouds.

I blinked against a snowflake that landed on my eyelashes. "It's been ages since I've seen a white Christmas."

Deanna appraised me. "I imagine it's been a while since you've got to experience many things at all."

I gave her a look of reproach. If she was saying what I thought she was saying…

Deanna nudged me. "Don't look at me like that, love. I know what it's like to be a young actress, hungry and ambitious. You can miss a lot of ordinary life."

I huffed out a breath and watched it spread like a cloud around my head. "You're right. I just don't like being reminded of it."

"Fair enough, love." Deanna turned the corner and gestured to a large building. "Behold, the Hollyoak Hotel."

The establishment was one of the largest buildings in Mistletoe Valley, standing at two stories with a large frontage along the town square. From what I had learned from Deanna, it was one of the oldest buildings in town, dating back to when Mistletoe Valley was a logging village, and workers needed somewhere warm to stay with hearty food to eat. Over the years, the downstairs area was updated to a cozy bar for drinks and dining, and it became what it was today.

Deanna stopped before we went in. "Now—I need to warn you, it's Friday night trivia. It might get raucous."

"I can deal with raucous." I could hear laughter and cheering inside, and the bar looked packed. "Will there be room?"

Deanna looped her arm in mine. "There's always room for everyone in Mistletoe Valley, Elle."

The bar was a blazing furnace of warmth when we entered, and more than a few patrons raised their glasses towards where Deanna and I were standing. No one looked at me like I didn't belong. A few people even sent me a warm smile.

God, what was with this town? They were just so *welcoming*. Coming from LA where no one gave a shit if you lived or died, I was unused to this.

The man behind the bar waved Deanna and me over. He was wearing a flannel shirt, a silver scruffy beard covering his slightly grizzled face. "Deanna. It's been a while since we've seen you here!"

A burly woman sitting at the bar beside us gave Deanna a broad smile. She wore a tight tank top, showcasing her muscular arms, and she had a twinkle in her eye. I immediately liked her. "An entire month. We thought you'd died."

"Billie, you saw me at the farmer's market last week." Deanna squeezed the woman's firm shoulder, and turned to the barman. "Mike, this is Elle. She's directing the Christmas play this year."

"Nice to meet you, Miss Elle. You're a pretty one." Mike smiled at me, but I didn't catch any creepy undertones in his words. "I guess all actors have to be good looking, hey, Deanna?"

Mike winked at Deanna, and she gave him a pleased smile. "If you say so, Mike."

I looked at the two of them, and I didn't think I was imagining the tension between them. Billie caught my eye and winked before going back to her beer.

Mike focused back on me. "So, Miss Elle, what's your first impression of the town?"

"It's beautiful. I didn't even know this place existed before I got the job." I smiled at them, trying to make sure I said all the right things. "But I have to ask…why is it called Mistletoe Valley?"

Mike barked out a laugh. "One of the old mayors thought it needed to be renamed. Originally it was just called Pine Valley, and there's enough of those as it is. Certainly makes the town memorable, doesn't it?"

Deanna gave Mike an indulgent smile. "Not to mention the overgrowth of Mistletoe on the trees caused a problem for the loggers decades ago."

"Yeah. That too." Mike winked at her.

Deanna cleared her throat. I definitely wasn't imagining it—there was something going on. "Is there a spot for us to eat?"

Mike gestured to the left of us. "Always, Deanna. Round the corner, against the window there's a table. Drinks?"

We carried our drinks to the table. Mike waved us off, and I felt the friendly gesture clench at my heart. I might not be used to the easy familiarity of this town, but I could enjoy it all the same. It reminded me of where I grew up, many of those memories hazy and distant now.

We squeezed through several tightly packed groups to reach our table, but Mike hadn't lied. A small empty setting was waiting for us. We slid into our chairs, and I removed my coat, my limbs already defrosting in the cozy atmosphere. I shouted over the chatter and noise to Deanna. "When does trivia start?"

Deanna took a sip from her warm cider. "Not sure."

A woman leaned over from a nearby table, crows feet crinkling her kind eyes. "It starts in twenty minutes, so you better get yourselves signed up. Hi." The woman offered me her hand and a smile. "Linda Roche. I own the gelato shop that's down the way."

I shook her hand and couldn't help but smile back. Like almost everyone in this town, she had an easy, open energy about her, and I felt immediately at ease. "Elle. Can't imagine you'd be getting much business this time of year."

Linda barked out a laugh, looking at Deanna. "She's a good one. And no, I close it during the winter months, take the time off to rest, and spend extra time with my grandchildren."

I rested my chin on my fist. "How many do you have?"

Linda gave a sly smile. "Twelve. Several of them are in the play. Celia, the youngest, is probably the most memorable."

I thought back to the afternoon, only half of the kids' names set in my memory. "She's the one with red hair? Full of energy."

Linda nodded. "That's the one. Anyway, we're so grateful to you lot, always coming and helping the kids. I don't see a lot of theater anymore, but I daresay the Christmas play could outshine most amateur stuff across the country. Deanna's always done such a good job."

Deanna took another sip of her cider. "It's the kids that do it, Linda. And all of you who keep coming out to support it every single year."

Linda laughed. "That's the easy part. Alright, I won't bother you any longer. Don't forget to sign up for trivia!"

Deanna nodded, and Linda turned back to her own table. "She's lovely."

I sent her a soft, accusatory look. "Is there anyone in this town who isn't?"

Deanna thought for a moment, then shook her head. "I guess not. Everyone can have their moments, though."

I looked over to Linda's boisterous table. "This play really means a lot to the community, doesn't it?"

"It does. I've worked hard to make it that way, but it's become a tradition now." Deanna took a sip of her drink, a twinkle in her eye. "And small towns love their traditions."

I finally took a sip of my cider and closed my eyes. Delicious. "Where's this cider from?"

"Distillery a few miles to the north. They grow the apples themselves." Deanna raised her glass. "To art, and community, and brilliant, brilliant cider."

I touched my glass to hers. "Cheers to that."

Deanna stood. "Now, let's see about this bloody trivia signup."

I watched her weave through tables, waving at people and squeezing shoulders as she went. Everyone knew her, everyone loved her, and she loved everyone back. She was completely at ease here, moving through the crowd like the former actress she was. Except there was no artifice. I had only known her a few days, but I could tell Deanna never bothered being anything but herself, totally authentic.

Judging by the energy in the bar tonight, I felt like I could be myself, too.

Except I didn't know who that was.

I had a sinking feeling it had been a long time since I'd been myself. Did I even know what authenticity meant? Not the sort of authenticity actors strive for—the kind that is manufactured, all pretend. The kind of authenticity that Deanna had. I looked at her and wondered what it would feel like to walk through a room entirely as yourself, with no hint of performance, no hint of wanting to hide.

I took another sip of cider, and the brew sat strangely in my stomach.

⇝⇝ ⬳⬳

I slumped my head in my hands, laughing. "I have—never been so bad at trivia in my life! What—what are these questions?"

"They're Mistletoe Valley questions." Deanna was leaning back in her chair as we watched people slowly file out of the bar. We'd lost, badly, at trivia. "We do it so often, with the same groups, that the questions have to be really obscure to offer a challenge."

I shook my head wryly. "Well, I'm glad it's not just me."

"Oh, it's mostly just you, city girl." Deanna stood and smiled at me. "That's me done. I think I'm going to toddle home. Are you staying?"

I eyed an empty seat at the bar, and I had the sudden desire to nurse another beverage and… talk to someone?

Believe me, that's a very unusual urge for me to have.

I stood with Deanna. "I think I want another drink, so I'll stay for a bit. Will I disturb you if I come home a little later?"

Deanna shook her head. "Not at all, love. It's a Friday night. You do what you want."

She gave me a wave and sauntered out, chatting to people as she went.

I perched on a barstool and flashed a smile at Mike. He gave me a toothy grin, draping a cloth over his shoulder. "Drink?"

I glanced at the drinks board. "What sort of gin have you got?"

Mike nodded his head sagely. "City girl like you, I reckon you'd like the local gin. I've got a really interesting one."

I laughed. "How many distilleries have you got here?"

"Only the two, if you're only counting the valley proper. Although there is a guy further up who does a tasty craft beer—"

I laughed again. "I see. I'll have a gin and tonic, thanks. How long have you been here at the Hollyoak, Mike?"

I watched as he prepared the mixer, adding perfect cubes of ice to a crystal glass. "My whole life, Miss Elle. My parents ran it, and I took over once they retired."

"What did you do before you took over?"

Mike gave me a crooked smile, his eyes crinkling. "This and that. I knew I'd come back to this place, so I did a fair share of traveling."

"Where'd you go?"

"All over. I loved Australia the best." He slid my drink to me.

"Huh." I nodded. "I've never been. Never been traveling much, though."

Mike grunted, and I got the feeling he was restraining himself from making a comment. The bar was emptying now—only a handful of people remained. I looked around, able to see more of the bar's walls now that most people were gone. It held old photographs, men standing around huge trees, brandishing axes.

I pointed to one of them. "Are those of the town?"

"Sure are. We found them in the attic ten years ago, so my late wife told me I should use them for decoration."

"I like it." I gestured around the room, then belatedly realised he'd mentioned his *late* wife. "I'm sorry for your loss, Mike."

"Thank you, Miss Elle. But it was a long while ago, now." Mike wiped down the bar. "How do you like the gin?"

"I love it." I took another sip and eyed Mike, remembering the way he and Deanna spoke earlier. "So… how well do you know Deanna?"

Mike barked out a laugh. "You sure are a bold one, Miss Elle. No. It's just good, friendly fun, though she is a beauty."

I couldn't argue with Mike. Deanna—who was surely pushing sixty—had a regal, well-aged face, and she carried herself with style. I imagine it was a carry-over from when she had been an actress, the self-assurance and posture second nature to her now. "You're right, she is."

"Nick should be home soon. You'll get to meet him."

"That's her godson, right?"

Mike nodded. "He's a good lad. Been helping with the legal side of the Hotel for years, and he does the same for most of the businesses in town."

"There isn't another lawyer in town?"

"There's one in the next town over, but not here. We keep telling him to come back properly and set up his own firm here, but he says he's waiting."

Billie piped up from nearby. "I reckon he's waiting to bring back a partner, someone he can start a family with."

A few of the other patrons seated at the bar laughed at that. Mike flipped his towel over his shoulder. "He hasn't brought back a girl back since he left."

I took another sip of my drink, not wanting to pry on what was obviously common knowledge.

Billie gave me a sly glance from beside me. "You got a partner back in the city, Elle?"

I pressed my lips together and smiled wryly. "Nope. Being an actor doesn't allow time for a relationship."

Mike chuckled. "Funny. That's exactly the line Nick gives us whenever we ask him."

I sipped my drink and smiled, but my shoulders sank a little. I didn't like to think about my perpetual loneliness. It had been years since I was in a relationship. All my attention had gone to my so-called career.

One of the sacrifices was my ability to form and maintain meaningful connections. The only close relationship I had was with my sister Kat, and she lived in San Francisco with her fiance.

I didn't like this about myself. The only other friends I had were old ones from high school or professional ones from my time at LADA. I felt adrift in a sea of loneliness, unable to latch onto anything meaningful. And all for the sake of what? A career that was going nowhere, and promised nothing in the future.

I felt out of place in this town, with its easy familiarity and close knit community.

I looked up and caught Mike watching me closely, and I blinked. He gave me a shallow nod and took my empty glass. "Another?"

"Just water, thanks."

He looked up and down the bar and leaned in closer. "You right, kiddo?"

I bristled at the nickname, but I saw the look in his eyes and realized he was showing me *kindness*, not being patronizing. "I don't know. You're all so close here. It's lonely in the city."

Mike slid a clear glass of water to me, and I watched the condensation slide down the sides. He shrugged. "It's not all sunshine and roses, what with everyone knowing everyone's business."

I raised my eyebrows in agreement and took a large gulp of water. "I can imagine."

"But," Mike smiled at me, lines appearing around his eyes. "We get a lot of lonely city folk come here. So I recognize that look in your eyes. I hope it eases by the time you leave."

I rested my forehead on my fist. "God, you're all so nice... Is there something in the water of this town?"

Mike barked out a laugh. "Some folk believe in some old legend or whatnot. But I prefer the idea that we're all living peaceful lives here, so it's pretty easy to be nice, Miss Elle. Most of us are here because we love it, because we belong."

That would be nice—to feel like I belonged. But I didn't voice the thought aloud, just nodded and stood. "Thanks, Mike."

"My pleasure, Miss Elle."

I nearly turned and left, but remembered something I had forgotten to ask Deanna. "Hey—are there any good running trails here?"

Mike jerked his head towards Billie, who turned and smiled at me. "You bet there is, new girl."

Billie's grin was practically wicked, and I smiled back. I knew I liked her.

ELLE

B illie was right. Mistletoe Valley had the best running trail I've ever been on in my life. It wound through a forest of pine trees, along the river, and did a full loop of the town. Billie had assured me I didn't need to worry about bears if I didn't have food on me, so I could run relatively carefree.

The cold wind on my face was like a balm for the old city air in my lungs. My feet propelled me under tall trees, past deep gullies and through misty clearings, until it all became a blur of color and speed and feeling.

I had always loved running, because it helped to get my brain to shut up, but this felt different. This was like I was shedding something, escaping something that had smothered me for way too long.

I didn't like dwelling too long on it. On *what* I felt I needed to escape.

I ran on, the dusty colors of dawn giving way to a fully fledged sunrise, kissing the tops of the pines with golden light.

I turned a corner and reached the spot Billy had urged me to find: A hidden lookout accessible only by trail, overlooking the entire valley.

I stopped, my breaths coming out in quick puffs of cloud around my face. I had run four miles, further than my usual run, spurred on by the scenery and the excitement.

I looked at the view. It was magnificent, and I could see everything below with incredible clarity. I could see the river winding its way through the town. I could see the tall tower of the town hall, caught the steeple of the church, saw the paved expanse of the town square.

It was like a scene from a fairytale, smoke puffing out of chimneys, mist drifting through the valley, bringing the promise of snow.

I checked my watch. I had time to sit for a while and admire the view.

I chose a fallen log, sat and crossed my legs, and just existed. After a while, my brain went quiet, calmed by the beauty of nature around me.

It had been a long, long time since I had felt this peaceful.

>>>>> <<<<<

When I arrived back at Deanna's house, something was different. A black BMW was parked out the front, gleaming in the morning light.

I wasn't totally sure who the visitor was, but I had a suspicion. After all, Deanna had warned me her godson could arrive any day in the coming week, depending on his commitments. And the godson was a lawyer. The BMW checked out.

I subtly checked my hair in the front window, smoothing down the flyaway from my ponytail. I don't really know why I checked, but I did it anyway. Maybe because I knew how much Nick meant to Deanna, and I wanted to make a good first impression.

First impressions, as my acting teacher used to say, were sometimes the only thing that mattered.

The cold air had quickly chilled most of my sweat away, and my face was no longer red and blotchy from the run. Thank God for small miracles. I let myself in, hearing voices down the hall. One was definitely Deanna, the other distinctly masculine.

I closed the door with a thud, letting them know I was home.

Deanna poked her head around the corner. "Elle, love! Look who's here!"

I summoned my brightest smile and closed the distance to the kitchen. When I entered, a man had his back to me, facing out the window. I couldn't see his face yet, but I kept my smile bright and eyes friendly as he turned. When he faced me fully, my stomach dropped.

I had seen this man before. The way his eyes widened slightly— I knew he recognized me too.

Oh, my God.

He was the man I had crashed into at the shopping mall a week ago. He was the man I had sniped at for being an asshole—dressed as a motherfucking elf.

›»»⟩ ⟨««‹

We stood there for a moment, each of us clearly unable to process the fact that we had already met, and that it had been under very different circumstances.

I couldn't call him out, not while Deanna was standing there. By the way she had spoken about her godson, he meant the world to her, and I didn't want to disrespect her by being aggressive to him.

I turned my frozen smile towards Deanna, opting to act stupid. Deanna put a hand on his shoulder, and I felt my stomach clench again. "Elle, meet Nick, my favorite godson."

Nick broke eye contact with me to smile down at Deanna. "Your only godson."

My left eye twitched, and I focused on my breathing to maintain a serene expression on my face.

Nick reluctantly turned back to me, and his eyes were sharp. Now was the moment to see if he would acknowledge our previous meeting, because I sure as hell wasn't going to. He gave me a tight smile. "Hello, Elle. It's nice to meet you."

So he was going to pretend. Interesting.

A muscle tensed in my lower back with the effort of maintaining my smile. "And you. Did you have a pleasant drive here?"

He gave an even tighter smile in response, and I felt smug that my smile was more believable than his. I was a goddamn trained actor—I knew how to make a fake smile look like a real one. Somewhere in the back of my brain, my mind was believing this was a cool and fine situation, and I felt my stomach release.

It was just as well, because Deanna's eyes were flicking between us like she really wanted us to get along, and I couldn't disappoint the woman who had invited me into her town and home. I just couldn't.

Nick cleared his throat, and he smiled warmly with no trouble at Deanna. I was a little impressed he was maintaining the ruse. "Yes. It's always pleasant."

I nodded my head as a polite person would. "Right. Because you drive it often."

Nick looked at me sharply, and it suddenly felt odd that something so strong was going unspoken between us. I barely knew him.

But, as my old acting teacher would say—*that's the power of subtext, baby.*

"Yes." Nick nodded, his eyes burning into mine. "You know, I wonder… Have we met before?"

A muscle tensed in my neck before I could control it. Okay, so he was… giving me an opening to be a dick in front of Deanna? Absolutely not. I wouldn't allow it. "I don't think so. Although I've been told I have a memorable face."

I knew I had a memorable face, and I knew he knew that he'd seen me before. After a half-second pause, he nodded again, his jaw tight. "Right."

The subtext of that line? *You're a fucking idiot.*

Deanna touched Nick's shoulder again. "Nick's just told me he's going to stay for the whole of December."

I raised my eyebrows slightly to look surprised and delighted. Inside, I was screaming, but managed to respond. "Oh, really? I hope I haven't taken your room."

Nick gave a polite smile, his brown eyes boring into mine. "No. I have my own house here."

I'm a lawyer, you fucking idiot. Of course, I'm not staying in the spare room.

"What a delight for you," I said back. *I don't give a shit.*

His left eye seemed to twitch at that, and I had to hide a smirk. His eyes sharpened, he stood taller, and I got the feeling I was suddenly in court. I readied myself for battle.

"Tell me," Nick tilted his head at me, "have you had much experience with directing?"

A part of my brain was mildly impressed with the way he was sparring with me. He certainly didn't seem as grumpy as he was when we first met. I crossed my arms. "A little, with a theater group I formed with some people I studied with."

Deanna made an exclamation. "I didn't know that."

I gave her a little shrug. "It's not the thing I'm proudest of."

"What are you most proud of?" Nick's voice was deep—deliciously so. Damn him, but it couldn't hide the dig he was making at me.

I gave him a sweet, insipid smile. "You know, it's probably all the contract costume work I get to do for kids."

Deanna gave me a strange look. She knew that work was absolute bullshit, but she said nothing.

Nick clasped his hands in front of him. "Have you done much of that lately?"

"I have, in fact." I smiled at Deanna to keep her included in the strangely charged conversation. "Just last week I had the pleasure of working as one of Santa's little helpers."

There. His jaw clenched, and I knew I'd pushed him over the edge. He couldn't say anything else without making this conversation even weirder. He cleared his throat. "Right."

Deanna looked at me. "Nick and I were going to have brunch at Jo's Place. Do you want to join?"

Nick looked like he would rather die than sit next to me for the next few hours, and I had to agree.

It might have been fun to taunt him, but I couldn't keep it up forever. I shook my head at Deanna. "I don't want to intrude, and I've got some things to do. You have fun."

Deanna made a soft sound of disappointment, but she recovered and linked arms with Nick. "Let's go."

Nick dragged his eyes to mine, and my stomach tightened.

God, it really was a shame he was so attractive. If he hadn't exposed himself as an asshole who yelled at unknown women, I'd be having lots of hot fantasies about him right now.

But my first impression of him had left a lot to desire, so unfortunately, I would not be doing any flirting. I gave him a canine smile, knowing my dimple was popping. "It was lovely to meet you, Nick. I hope we see a lot more of each other while we're both here."

Subtext: *I despise you, and there's probably not much you can do about it.*

Nick gave a tight smile, but his eyes were burning into mine. "I couldn't agree more."

I clenched my fists behind my back as I watched them leave and then smiled to myself.

It was going to be fun tormenting him for the rest of the holidays.

NICK

God, I hated Christmas. It was one of the worst times of the year. The decorations? Disgusting. The incessant carols? Nauseating. But I hadn't expected my dislike of Christmas to come back and bite me like *this*.

It was the elf girl from the shopping mall. Except this time, she had smiled a fake smile at me, dressed in tight running gear, and every thought had left my head.

Deanna had always told me my impatient temper would have consequences. I just didn't expect consequences to be a five-foot-five woman with bright blonde hair and big doe eyes.

Unfortunately, Elle was absolutely gorgeous. And I'm sure she was both absolutely aware of that fact, and hideously insecure about her perceived shortcomings. I'd dated a few actors in LA, and all of them had been the same in that regard.

I regretted snapping at her that day the moment it happened, but there was something about the way her eyes burned at me, beautiful and fierce—dressed in an *elf* costume—that made me irrationally annoyed.

And now I had to deal with the very deserved consequences of my short temper for the rest of December.

"Okay. That's the third time you've ignored my question." Deanna sat opposite me, sipping coffee. "What's going on, Nick?"

I winced and took a sip of my long black; the bitterness soothing the residual regret curling in my gut. "It's Elle."

Deanna narrowed her eyes, and I knew I was about to get a lecture. "You've only just met her."

I held up a hand. "Nope. I've met her before. Briefly, and I was an asshole to her."

"What do you mean, briefly, and you were an asshole to her?" Deanna got that look in her eye that usually meant trouble for me.

"She ran into me and spilled all the documents that I needed for an important meeting with Anderson. I got angry, and I may have made a very poor comment about her clothing."

"Her clothing?"

"She was dressed as an elf."

Deanna's eyebrows raised. "Why didn't either of you mention it?"

I rubbed a hand against the back of my neck. "I imagine she didn't want to call me an asshole in front of you. So I didn't bring it up."

Deanna leaned back in her chair. "You really need to improve your bedside manner with people, Nick."

"I'm aware, Dee. But it's never been a strong suit."

Deanna cracked a smile, and I felt like I was ten years old again, running to her house after school for a cup of hot chocolate. "It used to be. But not since you started working for that devil Anderson. You need to apologize to her, Nick."

"I will. I intend to." I wasn't lying. I didn't want to go all of December avoiding Elle. I would apologize, and then I would keep my distance. Women like Elle were dangerous for me to be around, for many reasons. One of which was that she would be a distraction from my primary goal here.

Deanna looked out the window. "She's lost enough as it is. She doesn't need to feel you're judging her, too."

I leaned forward at that. "What do you mean, she's lost enough as it is?"

"She reminds me of how I was a long time ago." Deanna had a wistful look in her eyes.

I crossed my arms. "Don't tell me she's another one of your charity projects."

"I taught you better than that, Nicky." Deanna gave me a sharp look. "It's not charity; it's called paying it forward. And I need someone to take over my studio soon, because I can't keep doing it forever."

I stiffened. "You're only sixty. You've got time."

Deanna shook her head. "It's not about me. It's about the kids. They need someone fresh, someone vibrant, with lots of energy. Why do you think I've been luring actors here all these years for the Christmas play?"

I looked up at the ceiling, my lips twitching. "So that's what you've been doing. Why didn't you mention it?"

"I didn't mention it because none of them were the right fit." Deanna's eyes shifted to the window again, and I knew she was thinking about something far away. "But Elle reminds me so much of myself, and I've only known her for less than a week."

"She's a lot younger than you were when you came here." I reminded her. "She must be what, mid to late twenties?"

"True." Deanna shifted her shoulders slightly. "But I can see it in her eyes. I don't know everything, but I can feel she's not happy. I remember that feeling."

"Loneliness?"

Deanna gave me a sad smile. "Not lonely. Just… lost. What do you think happens, Nick, when someone works for so long on something but finds no genuine joy in it?"

I clenched a hand around my cup. "I wouldn't know."

Deanna patted my fist. "Just apologize and don't make this month any harder for her, alright? I need her to like this town."

I nodded. I could do that, at least.

⤜⤜⤜ ⤛⤛⤛

Finding Elle Sutton proved a much harder task than I thought it would be. It was a Saturday, and I knew for a fact that she wasn't working with Deanna. So I headed to the town square first, which turned out to be a big mistake.

I'd forgotten to account for how friendly Mistletoe Valley was, and I was their golden child, returned from the city. Susan stopped me on the street first and gave me a tight hug. "Nick! It's so great that you're back. How long are you here?"

I gave her an amiable smile. "All of December."

Susan put her hands on her hips. "Deanna'll love that. And how long until you come back here for good, huh?"

I ducked my head briefly. "I don't know, Susan."

She gave me a sly smile. "Have you met Elle yet? She's the one directing our Christmas play this year."

My hand twitched, and I gave Susan a tight smile. "Yes. Just this morning, actually."

Susan waggled her eyebrows. "And? She's quite a lovely young woman, isn't she?"

"Sure." Christ, I wanted to jump off the bridge to save myself from this conversation. "But that doesn't mean you should play matchmaker."

"Why not, Nick Corrigan?" Susan winked at me, and I smiled at her indulgently. "Hey, do you reckon you have time to look over something for me today?"

I checked my watch and decided. Elle Sutton could wait another hour, I was sure. "I've got time for that."

Except the moment I finished up with Susan, old man Harold found me. "Nicky! I heard you were back in town! Do you have time to look at my insurance contract? I don't understand it."

I sighed and followed him into his hat shop. Mistletoe Valley had a lot of small businesses, and all of them needed advice and help from a lawyer. That lawyer always happened to be me.

I enjoyed helping the people in my hometown. After all, I owed them a lot. As it was, Anderson, my boss, was frustrated at my insistence that I came back here every six months for a stint.

That was okay. I'd already decided he would not be my boss forever. It was always my intention to open my firm here. There were no other lawyers easily available here, and I knew I would make a good living being able to help my town.

I'd already set the wheels in motion to do just that, but I wasn't ready to tell anyone about it yet.

Harold's Hat Shop had stayed the same for fifty years, passed down from father to son. It was rare to find hand crafted hats these days, and I knew he still got good business from tourists during the holiday season. I eyed a bowler hat that looked straight out of the last century. "How's business been?"

Harold nodded, his whiskered face bobbing up and down. "Good, good. I'm getting ready for the Christmas rush, as you know, but my insurance company sent me this confusing letter."

He handed the letter to me, and I scanned the words. I caught a sentence that confused me, and I read it again. I frowned and nodded. "I'm glad you asked me about it. This is bullshit."

Harold's eyebrows raised. "Oh, boy. What do I do?"

I checked my watch again. It was only noon. Still plenty of time to find Elle Sutton before the sun went down. I sat down behind the counter and fished my reading glasses out of my pockets, gesturing for Harold to join me. "Okay. So, see this clause here? That means they are saying you can't…"

It was three o'clock in the afternoon when I got another chance to catch my breath. After sorting Harold out, Patsy from the Artisan Deli wanted to consult me on an issue she was having with one of her employees.

I had a hard time saying no when someone asked for my help. It didn't matter most of the time, because I got a lot of satisfaction from helping people. But today was one of the few days that it frustrated me.

Today, I had an elf girl to apologize to.

I was getting hungry and giving up hope of finding her, so I changed course. I went to the Hollyoak to say hello to Mike and grab some food.

Mike was wiping down the counters as I walked in, and he gave me a broad smile. "Well, if it isn't the town superstar."

I bypassed the counter and walked right behind the bar, pulling Mike into a powerful hug. I'd spent a good portion of my teenage years at the Hollyoak, first as a server and then as a bartender, when I came back during the summers from college. He'd been one of the first to encourage me to go to law school. He'd even set up a community fundraiser each year to help with the cost of my tuition. Mistletoe Valley was a giving community like that.

Knowing I had the support of my town behind me meant a lot to me, and I may not have got through law school without it.

Mike pulled back from the hug and gave me a critical once-over. He squeezed my shoulders. "You're looking sharp, son. New workout routine?"

I'd never known my father, but Mike had stepped up in my adolescence to fill the void, and he'd called me son ever since. He was a good man. I rolled my shoulders. "Something like that, yeah."

I had been working out more recently, but only because I was under a lot of pressure in my job back in the city. Anderson had been making me work doubly hard to make up for my absences to Mistletoe Valley, even though I still did a lot of remote work for him while I was here.

I couldn't punch Anderson, but I could hit the gym. The arrangement worked out well for me.

Mike gave me a wry grin. "You know, if you moved back here, you wouldn't have to deal with that asshole."

"That asshole is giving me the experience necessary to run a good firm here."

Mike waved his hand in the air. "You've been working for him for five years. I think that's plenty enough experience."

"Soon." I promised him. I wasn't lying. I'd already made the decision that this was the month to start seriously considering it, inspecting potential locations and crunching the numbers.

Everything had to be meticulously planned, because Mistletoe Valley deserved that. They'd already given me so much. I wanted to be the lawyer they deserved.

Mike gave me a doubtful look. "Nick, I love you, but I'll believe it when it happens."

"Fair." I inspected the countertops. "Anything new since I last came?"

"Well, if we're doing that…" Mike pulled out two glasses and some whiskey. "Drink?"

"I'll never say no to that." I helped him by pulling out some ice from the countertop cooler, a move that was second nature to me. "Think the kitchen could whip something up? I haven't eaten since breakfast."

"For Nick Corrigan, I reckon the kitchen would do a full spread." Mike winked at me.

I nudged him with my elbow and smiled. It was good to be home.

⟫⟫⟫   ⟪⟪⟪

When the food came, Mike and I sat at a table to catch up. "Brenda's son came back from college. He dropped out. Didn't like it, according to her."

I winced, imagining the poor kid's experience. "College in the city can be a shock when you're from Mistletoe Valley."

Mike shrugged. "Yeah. But it's all good. He's doing one of those remote degrees now, so he's here. A bit of a sensitive lad, but he's a hard enough worker."

"How's business going?"

"It's good." Mike rubbed a hand over his face. "I've got a bit of a headache going on with the gas company contract, but I only want to talk to you about it once you're settled."

I leaned back and spread my hands out on the table. "I'm settled. I've already solved three other problems today."

Mike gave me a baleful look. "You're eating, son. I'm not going to give you indigestion over my petty woes."

I dragged a slice of bread through the remains of my soup. Mike's kitchen made some of the best food in the world, and I ate it gratefully.

Mike cleared his throat. He had a gleam in his eye, and I knew there was going to be trouble. "Say, have you met Elle yet?"

I stopped chewing for a moment, then swallowed. "Why do I get the feeling you already know the answer?"

"Dunno what you're talking about." Mike shrugged innocently.

I glared at him, then relented. "Yes. I met her this morning."

Mike took a sip of his drink, and I braced myself. "She's a beautiful one, don't you think?"

"Sure." I clenched my hand around my drink. "She's also only going to be here for the month."

I gave him a pointed look, and Mike raised his hands. "I don't know why that means anything, since all I was doing was making conversation."

I swirled the whiskey around in my glass. "Making conversation. About the only other single woman in town near my age."

"The only one you haven't entangled yourself with already, you mean?"

I winced, remembering my stumbling attempts at relationships when I was a teenager and during college summers. "Thanks for reminding me."

Mike clapped me on the shoulder. "You're most welcome, son."

If he was going to make subtle jabs at my love life, I might as well rib him back. "How's Deanna?"

Mike grabbed his own drink. "Not sure why you're asking me that question, Nick. I know you saw her just this morning."

I gave him a pointed look but said nothing else on the subject. I'd suspected that Deanna and Mike had a… thing going on, but I'd never been able to confirm it. The two of them were more tight-lipped than the CIA. "Alright then, tell me about the business with the gas company."

Mike opened his mouth to begin, but he never got the chance. The door to the Hollyoak Hotel opened.

And in walked Elle Sutton.

I downed the rest of my drink and sent a quick look to the ceiling. This was going to be interesting.

ELLE

Nick Corrigan was here. I'd spent all day avoiding him, ducking in and out of shops when I saw him. At one point, I'd even resorted to hiding behind a bush. *A bush*. But eventually, my stomach had won out, and I'd come to the Hollyoak for some food.

I really didn't want to deal with him today. The first meeting this morning was enough, and I wanted to enjoy my day off, *sans* rude lawyer. But the universe had different ideas, and I refused to turn and run now.

I wasn't a coward. Most of the time.

My hands itched, and I clenched them in the folds of my long coat. There was no one at the Hollyoak this time of day—that strange time between late lunch and early dinner—and I thought for sure it would be safe for me to get a snack before I went back to Deanna's.

But no such luck, because Nick—the apparent golden son of Mistletoe Valley—was sitting at a table with Mike.

I could not have picked a worse time. They had seen me, and there was nobody else that I could pretend to greet. Only Mike and… Nick.

It was exactly my kind of luck.

I shot them a tight smile, and scanned the rest of the room like I was searching for something, my palms sweaty. Mike stood. I glanced at their table and realized they must have been talking business. There were some documents near Mike—this could be my perfect excuse to leave quickly. "I really don't want to interrupt—"

Mike waved his hand. "None of that. You want something, you get it here."

I couldn't help but laugh, nervous as I was. "I'm seeing that."

I forced myself to look at Nick, pasting a polite smile on my face. But it faltered when I really looked at him, at the assured way he sat in his chair, his suit jacket draped across the back of it, his shirtsleeves rolled up to his elbows.

Oh.

I mentally shook myself and nodded to him. "Nick."

He nodded back, a strange gleam in his eyes. "Elle. Busy day?"

I bristled at the strange question, sensing he was… annoyed? I couldn't quite place it, but it bothered me. Who was he to get annoyed by my presence? He was the one who had been an absolute asshole. I took off my scarf, and he tracked the movement. I frowned. "You could say that."

In fact, I had been busy hiding in bushes to avoid him, but he didn't need to know that. He slid back in his chair, and then I realized what I was so distracted by.

He was wearing *glasses*.

Oh no. He looked… delicious. Like a studious Clark Kent, hero of the town.

I swallowed and broke eye contact with him. He wouldn't ruin my afternoon, I wouldn't let him. I walked to the bar, slid off my coat, and eyed the barstools with trepidation. I would just have to drape the coat over the chair next to me.

A hand appeared out of nowhere, and I paused.

My gaze followed the arm up and I realized it was attached to Nick. He was… offering it to me. What the fuck? I blinked.

He cleared his throat. "There's a coat rack hidden in the corner. Let me."

I clutched my coat tighter for a millisecond. "You don't need to do that."

"I don't, but I'm offering. It looks like a nice coat, and the stool isn't the best place for it." He flicked up his left wrist, eyeing the expensive-looking watch that sat there. "It's approaching five, and soon there'll be a lot more people wanting seats in here."

His logic was sound, which was annoying. I eyed him with a touch of suspicion, but eventually concluded that if he wanted to pretend to be nice to me, he could do that. It was just a shame I knew what he was like on a bad day, like some performative white knight.

I'd had enough of those to last me a lifetime already.

I handed the coat to him reluctantly. "Alright. Thanks."

He draped it carefully in his arms and turned away. "Don't mention it."

Except I would mention it in my brain, and probably a lot, to puzzle out what the fuck this guy's problem was. He's an asshole, but then he pretends to be nice to me? I didn't want a bar of that, because I'd had enough of *pretending* and false kindness to last me a lifetime.

Mike cleared his throat from behind the bar, and I realized I'd been staring at the spot Nick had been standing in for three whole seconds.

I gave Mike a blinding smile. "Another one of those delicious gin and tonics, thanks."

Mike grinned, a little too knowingly. "You and Nick would get along well. He likes the gin, too."

"No offence, Mike, but you've only known me for a day." I forced myself to keep smiling easily.

"Ah, see, that's where you're wrong." Mike pulled out a glass and began mixing my drink. "I'm a bartender, and I'm very good at reading people based on what I see."

"Such as?"

"Such as, the drink a person orders, and how they order it. The way they sit at the bar, the way they leave. If they want conversation, if they don't."

I played with the hem of my dress. "And what have you learned about me?"

Mike pushed my drink to me and crossed his arms. "You wanna know?"

Tentatively, I nodded. I couldn't resist feedback on how I appeared to others, valuable information for an actor—even as part of me shrivelled at the thought.

Mike gestured to my drink. "Yesterday, you went for cider first, but only because Deanna ordered it first. That tells me you like to please people, like to be in their good graces."

"Guilty." I admitted, a little miffed he'd picked that so easily.

"But then, I saw that you're curious, adventurous, because you stayed after Deanna left and ordered something else. You're not afraid of asserting yourself when you can."

My eyebrows shot up. It was uncanny how accurate he was. "I try."

"You're a hard worker, too. I can tell because of the way you speak about your work."

"I could be lying." I reminded him.

Mike smiled at me, crinkled eyes. "I don't think so, Miss Elle. Strangely enough, you don't strike me as the sort of person who pretends when it matters."

When it matters. God, what did that even mean? I took a sip of my gin and looked up to see Mike staring at something behind me. To my shock, I saw it was Nick Corrigan. I presumed he would have… gone back to his work after he'd finished his strange performative chivalry, but no. He was standing right there.

I turned back to the bar, and Mike slunk away just as I tried to ask him another question. Now that everyone was out of earshot, I knew Nick was going to be an asshole to me again. I swirled my drink around in the glass.

"Can I sit here?" He asked from beside me.

"Why?" The question blurted out of me before I could stop it, and I turned to him. "Why are you bothering pretending to be nice to me? We established in our first encounter that you are incapable of that."

He winced.

I looked into my glass. "I'm fine with pretending to be civil in front of other people, but I'd rather not do it when we're alone. Thanks."

He cleared his throat. "I wanted to apologize for my unacceptable behavior when we first met, actually."

I wiped a droplet of condensation from my glass. Now I was going to get some weak excuse, and a request for us to 'start over' or some other trite bullshit. "Okay. Do it."

He sat on the seat next to me. "There's no excuse for it, and I always regret when I snap at people like that."

"So don't do it, then." I gave him a baleful look.

He nodded his head, and I realized he seemed almost… genuinely apologetic. "I try. That day was a bad one for me, and my boss…"

He trailed off when he saw the look on my face and got the hint. I was not interested in thinly veiled excuses or explanations.

"… And all that doesn't matter. What does matter was that I was an asshole to you, and I'm sorry. I don't expect forgiveness, or understanding. You didn't deserve someone taking their own frustration out on you."

I straightened slightly. As far as apologies went, that one wasn't as bullshit as I had expected. He had nearly gone on the wrong road, sure, but he had corrected and owned his mistake.

I stirred my drink with a small straw and decided to see how far his contrition went. "You called me *elf girl*."

He winced again, taking the reminder on the chin. "I did."

I swiveled in my chair slightly, so I could really make him squirm. "You made fun of what I was doing to earn a living."

Nick, to his credit, held eye contact and nodded again. "I did."

I crossed my arms, internally delighted at how much he was letting me needle him. "You also tried to blame me for your mistake, which was practically running out of a store without giving way to anyone."

He nodded. "I plead guilty to that one, too."

I narrowed my eyes at him, but felt my lips twitch. "This is just a court case to you, isn't it?"

"See, a court case I can win or lose. There's no winning here, just making amends." Nick shrugged, and I definitely didn't notice the way the fabric bunched around his muscles when he did it.

I was melting inside, and I knew it. But I didn't let myself smile, not yet. "You're still only apologizing because you have to be around me for a month."

"Alternatively," Nick leaned his elbows against the bar, "you were a stranger and I had no way of apologizing before. Fate gave me another chance."

"You could have done it the moment we met this morning."

"And I would have, if you had brought it up." Nick gave me a sidelong look. "But you gave me an alarmingly bright smile, which threw me off for a while."

I took another sip of the drink and casually quipped, "I get my teeth professionally whitened."

He made a soft sound, almost like a laugh. "I guessed. Most actors do."

"Correct." I leaned back and examined him again. "Alright. Here's my verdict."

He nodded and held my gaze. His eyes were a distracting shade of warm brown, and I had to master myself so I wouldn't get distracted.

I cleared my throat, clasping my hands together. "Since that wasn't the worst apology I have ever heard, I accept it. That doesn't mean I've forgotten it happened, but we have dealt with it. As long as you're not an asshole to me again, I'll permit us to be casual acquaintances for the duration of my stay."

He dipped his head, and I caught the glimpse of a smile on his lips. "A very fair decision. I appreciate it."

Curiosity got the better of me again. My hands itched for… something. "What were you doing with Mike when I walked in?"

He gave me a look of surprise and leaned back on his stool, crossing his arms. "I was helping him with some business contracts."

I hummed and took another sip. The alcohol slid down my throat, and I felt the warmth sink into my belly. "Is that what you were doing today, going around all those shops?"

Immediately, I realized my mistake. Oh, my God. I just basically told him I had been watching him all day. I felt a flush rise on my cheeks, but I stared straight ahead and kept my breathing even.

In my periphery, I felt him eyeing me. "You saw me, today?"

I jerked my head in a nod.

He laughed. "Jesus. I got caught in all those consultations because I was looking for you. Meanwhile, you were just following me around?"

I turned my head, indignation and something else burning in my gut. "I was avoiding you!"

"I was looking for you to apologize!"

"How was I supposed to know that?" I gesticulated. "I was just trying to run some errands, and you kept getting in the way."

Nick wiped a hand down his face and made a sound like a laugh was getting stuck in his throat. "This is the most ridiculous conversation I've ever been in."

I silently agreed with him there. I rested my forehead on my hand. Come to think of it, he *had* looked like he was searching for something, ducking into every shop along the square. "Were you seriously looking for me today?"

"Were you seriously avoiding me all day?" He countered, and I couldn't help but laugh.

"I can tell *you're* a lawyer." I quipped and took another sip of my drink.

He ignored my comment. "Don't avoid me next time."

"Next time, don't be rude to someone you don't know." I brushed a hand over my hair. "Believe me, I didn't like it. I fell into a bush."

Nick struggled to swallow his drink, and I hid my smile behind my glass. He coughed and recovered enough to say, "I imagine the bush came away with more bruises than you."

I gave him a saccharine smile. "Correct."

What was I doing? Was I… flirting? I was both mildly impressed and disgusted with myself. The man had barely apologized, and I was already batting my eyelashes at him. But God, it was fun sparring with someone again. I had done a lot of debate club in high school, and I had been good at it. Somewhere along the line, though, my verbal wit became much less important than my face and my ability to pretend.

Something soured in me at the thought. I had done that to myself, chosen that career path for myself.

I finished the last dregs of my drink and let the glass thunk down onto the bar. Suddenly, I needed to leave. I didn't want to stay here anymore with Nick Corrigan, with his warm eyes and sharp wit, in case I did something really stupid. Like properly flirt with him. "I'm going to head back to Deanna's. I told her I would eat with her."

"…Yeah." Nick gave me a sheepish smile. "She may have invited me, too. Let me walk you there?"

A muscle in my stomach twitched, and I desperately wanted to leave, just in case I actually started to like him. "You haven't finished your drink."

Nick grabbed his glass and finished it. I watched, mesmerised, as the smooth muscles of his throat rippled. He stood and grabbed his jacket from the nearby table. "Now I have."

Alarm bells went off in my head, and I scrounged for any reason to get away from this attractive, suddenly not-so-arrogant man. "It's barely a ten-minute walk from here. You don't need to come with me. I doubt Mistletoe Valley has anything more dangerous than an angry raccoon on the way."

Nick flashed a smile, and I got the distinct feeling he was about to tease me. "Yeah, but then I wouldn't get to ask you more about your bush fighting techniques."

Fine. I pursed my lips and stomped to the door. When I got there, I remembered my coat—I turned to get it, but Nick was quicker. He'd already retrieved it and held it out to me with a shameless smile.

I took it from him. "You can cut the contrite act now. You've already apologized."

Nick pushed the door open and held it for me. "What if I said I enjoyed helping people?"

He gave me an easy smile, and I wanted to punch him. Why was he so good looking, and now—apparently—a mostly decent person? I walked out the door and bit my tongue. "Here, you mean. You didn't seem to have much patience for *elf girl* back in the city."

We started walking towards Deanna's house, the sun just dipping below the mountains. Nick grimaced. "I don't like the city. I don't like the sort of person it turns me into. But here, everyone knows me. I'm part of a community."

I stayed silent, internally alarmed at how much his words resonated with me. He was describing the growing dissonance

I had noticed in myself, too. But he had one thing I didn't. "You can move back here whenever you want."

"And I will." Nick gazed ahead, his eyes distant. "Not just yet."

Part of me wanted to prod at that strange reasoning, but I said nothing. I barely knew him, and it wasn't the time to ask him to explain his motivations. I was only here for a month. I didn't need to know why he was doing something.

We were just casual acquaintances. And we would stay that way, because I was leaving at the end of the month. I kept my head forward and looked across the mountains.

Nick sucked in a breath. "Okay. I have a question for you."

I gave him a sideways glance. "… Alright."

"Why *were* you dressed as an elf that day? It was November."

I sighed. "My agent signed me up for the gig, and it was good pay."

Nick nodded. "Sorry for being a judgemental prick about it."

I laughed. "Yeah, you were. But you were kind of right. I *hated* that job. I rang her that evening and begged for something else. She had a bunch lined up for all of December, apparently."

Nick winced. "She sounds like a shit agent."

"She is." I was relieved I could finally be honest with someone about that. Back in the city, if I breathed a word of that to anyone and it got back to her, she would drop me. "But no one else will have me."

Nick gave me a strange look. "Hard to believe."

"Based on what?" I sent him a small head shake. "You haven't seen me act."

"No, but you're—"

He cut himself off, and I knew exactly what he was about to say. I raised my eyebrow at him, willing to tease him. "No, go on, say it, and I'll prove how wrong you are."

Nick sent me a look of soft reproach. "I'm just surprised that the best your agent can do is costume gigs."

I kicked a bit of gravel ahead of us, scuffing my black boots against the road. We were getting close now. "I wish the acting world worked the way you think it does. I wish that if you are pretty, and nice, and hard-working, you're guaranteed work. But young, hot actors are five a penny. That elf gig was the first thing I'd worked in *months*. I'm not valuable. Maybe in five, ten years, when I can be seen as an actor and not just some young, desirable piece of meat. But right now, I'm not valuable."

Nick was silent for a while, and I worried I had somehow offended him. I hadn't said anything wrong, had I?

He stopped walking. I looked at him with apprehension.

He glared at the sky. "I think that's fucked, personally."

Oh. I shrugged. "It's how it is."

Nick shook his head. "I don't really mean the industry. I mean, how it has made you honestly believe you are not valuable."

My shoulders tensed. "I'm just being practical."

"Bullshit."

I glared at him. "Careful. You're skating a little too close to asshole territory again."

Nick blew out a breath and shoved his hands in his coat pockets. "And you shouldn't let anyone make you believe you aren't valuable. That sounds like a terrible way to live."

It was, a voice whispered in my head. I ignored it and kept walking. "Not all of us can be the town's star lawyer, Nick Corrigan."

After a moment, he followed me.

NICK

I was fuming. No—I was so irrationally angry I wasn't sure if I wanted to punch a wall.

I barely knew her, but there was something about the numb way Elle had called herself 'not valuable' that got me seeing red. I had grown up in a town that always helped me feel my worth, and I had only experienced the feeling she was describing once I got to the city. I knew exactly what it felt like to feel worthless, when I'd gone to Stanford as a scholarship kid and found out that most of the other rich assholes looked down on me for it. I had worked, for a very long time, to never feel that worthless again, but having the support of my town behind me had always bolstered me.

So hearing Elle talk about herself in that same way had my fists clenching, a whole host of old emotions bubbling up. God, I wanted to send her useless agent a very scary legal letter.

This was why I had wanted to become a lawyer in the first place—a chance to help people, in business and in life, to avoid being ripped off and to have their rights asserted. Everyone, even people who had done something wrong, deserved the right to legal help, and too often in corporate law, I had seen big companies trying to rip off their customers.

Unfortunately, in the city, I was usually one of the schmuck lawyers who had to defend those big companies. I came back to Mistletoe Valley to help as penance.

But what Elle was describing was even worse. It was systemic, how worthless the industry made actors feel, just so that they would be desperate enough to take any job that was offered. I was sure there were lots of good people working in it, but like any industry with a supply and demand problem, it left too much power in the hands of corrupt people.

Elle sent me a wary look as we ascended the steps to Deanna's front door. Her cheeks were pink, flushed from the icy wind, and her pouty lips were soft and slightly down-turned. She looked way too adorable for someone who had just told me she 'wasn't valuable.'

I had an absurd urge to grab her face and kiss her until I'd shown her just how *valuable* she was. Christ, I barely knew her. And she was clearly struggling with something, so I really shouldn't be thinking of her that way.

But Elle Sutton had something about her that made me want to do unreasonable things to make her happy. Great.

This dinner was going to be fun.

I cleared my throat and rapped on the door.

Elle rummaged around in her pockets. "Wait—I have some keys—"

The door swung open, and Deanna stood at the threshold. Her eyebrows raised when she took us both in. "You're both here! Come in, come in."

Elle sniffed the air and smiled at Deanna. "Whatever you're cooking smells amazing."

"It's a roast tonight." Deanna waved us in and gave me a squeezing hug, even though I'd only just seen her this morning. I indulged her anyway—because I loved her. "How was your day?"

She sent me a subtle questioning glance and flicked her eyes over to Elle. The question was obvious. I nodded my head softly to her and jerked my head toward Elle. "I got a bit caught up with some business matters, but then I ran into Elle at Hollyoak. That's why we walked here together."

"I see." Deanna turned to Elle. "Did you find what you wanted?"

Elle pulled off her coat and smile coyly at Deanna. "I think so."

I tried not to spend too much time analyzing whatever that could be about and failed. I took off my coat, wishing I had a change of more comfortable clothes. A suit worked well for when I was consulting with people, but it wasn't comfortable for a casual dinner. "Hey Deanna, do you still have some of my old clothes hidden somewhere? I'd like to change out of this suit."

Deanna pointed up the stairs. "I keep them in the same place as always, you know that."

Elle sent me a look. "You should have grabbed a change of clothes from your place on the way. I told you, I was fine walking alone."

"But then I would have missed the chance to protect you from the deadly raccoons." I moved towards the stairs, but couldn't resist one last remark. "Or protect Mistletoe Valley's bushes from you."

Elle looked like she was trying not to smile, and Deanna snorted.

I turned around and went upstairs before Elle could form a response, and I was suppressing my smile the whole way.

I had always stayed at Deanna's whenever I came back from college. After my mom had passed when I was seventeen, I couldn't stand to stay in her house, but I couldn't stomach selling it, either. After college I sold it and bought another place for when I came back. If it wasn't for Deanna, I might never have come back to Mistletoe Valley.

I really would have become a soulless corporate lawyer working in the city.

I pulled the drawer open, revealing my old college sweaters and hoodies, all perfectly folded. I smiled and rifled through them until I found one of the larger, softer knitted sweaters. It was a far cry from my expensive Armani suit.

Anderson, the asshole, demanded all his employees over a certain pay grade wear 'quality'. Whatever the fuck that meant. And he insisted I do business in Mistletoe Valley in a similar manner, even though I wasn't working for him here. Something about credibility, or some bullshit.

I pulled my suit jacket off and let it fall over a chair, and pulled the sweater over my dress shirt. I checked my hair in the mirror and pushed it back a little, then glared at my reflection. I was fussing.

And that meant I was trying to impress someone. Fuck.

I gripped the base of the dresser and gave myself a stern look. I had to pull myself together. For Christ's sake, I was a goddamn lawyer. I was here to have dinner with my godmother, and someone else happened to be eating with us.

I had many more important things to worry about than a beautiful actress sitting across from me all evening.

⇥⇥⇥ ⇤⇤⇤

I came back into the kitchen to find Elle and Deanna leaning over a photo album, and my heart sank. I knew what it was.

Deanna was the first to look up, and she gave me a sly smile. "And what a difference thirty years make."

Yep, definitely the baby album.

Elle jerked her head up and pursed her lips, obviously trying to stop herself from laughing. It was adorable how readable her face was, every single emotion there like an open book. Her eyes darted between Deanna and me as if I had caught her doing something wrong. I crossed my arms and focussed on Deanna. "Of course I look different now. I'm not covered in bubbles."

Elle snorted and clapped her hand over her mouth. Christ, yet another adorable thing I had to endure.

Deanna slid the photo album away, smiling. "Wine?"

I leaned back against the kitchen counter. Did I imagine the way Elle's eyes flicked over me? "Sure."

Deanna filled three glasses on the countertop and we all took a sip.

Elle made a sound and examined the bottle. "Is this… from here?"

Deanna chuckled. "Arrowbeam Winery. You probably drove past it to get here. The higher altitude makes it a good place for the grape, Tim told me once."

I put my glass down. "How's his son doing?"

Deanna shrugged. "Better, I heard."

Elle glanced between us, and I could almost tell what she was thinking.

I hid a smile behind my glass. "Yes, we do."

Elle looked at me with alarm. "What?"

"We know everyone. That's what being in a small town is all about."

Elle fiddled with a delicate ring on her middle finger. "I'm aware. I was from one, too. It's just been a while."

Deanna cleared her throat. "Your family?"

Elle shrugged. "I'm very close with my sister, Kat, but she lives in San Francisco with her fiance."

"And your parents?" Deanna pressed.

Elle kept her eyes on the table. "They didn't like my decision to become an actor. So we're not…close, not anymore. They visit me sometimes, but it's too hard to go back home. Everyone there just sees me as a failure, which I guess is true."

Deanna and I stared at her, and I clenched my fist on the countertop. What had *happened* to this girl? Deanna beat me to it and looked at Elle sternly. "Are you, or are you not, currently being paid to be in artistic residency here?"

Elle swirled her glass of wine. "Yeah, but most of the people in my hometown think being in a blockbuster movie is the only mark of success."

"Why do you need to prove anything to them?" I ground out, feeling irrationally annoyed at people I didn't know.

"Not all of us can be impressive lawyers." Elle raised her eyebrows.

"I don't do it to be impressive." I paused. "Well, I might get some satisfaction from being good at it, but I don't care about how it looks to others."

Elle snorted. "It's easy to say you don't care about being impressive when you do something that is socially respected, like law."

My knuckles went white, they were clenched so hard. "Being an artist is just as noble."

"You really think being an *elf girl* is noble?" There was a brighter gleam in Elle's eye now. Good. Anything but the sadness that was there before.

I nodded, considering Elle's comment. "You know, I've thought about it, and I actually do. Bringing joy to the world through entertainment could be one of the noblest professions in the world."

Elle's eyes shuttered. "I think doctors, teachers, and cleaners might want a word."

Deanna cleared her throat. "Is this part of some conversation I wasn't privy to earlier?"

Elle answered before I could. "Yes. I made a joke about how horrible it would be if I had to spend my December dressed as an elf, like my agent originally planned for me."

Deanna put down her glass and examined Elle. "Did you want to do this work?"

"No."

Deanna got a flinty look in her eyes. "Did Leslie know this?"

"Yes."

Deanna was silent for a moment, then swallowed a large gulp of wine. "I think you should get a new agent, Elle."

Elle laughed, a fragile sound in my ears. "No one would take me. I haven't done enough."

Deanna set her glass down firmly, and I sensed a lecture coming. For once, I was glad of it, because all I was capable of right now was frowning and grunting in anger. Deanna leveled a look at Elle. "I want us to have a nice dinner, so this is all I'll say on the subject. This is your life, and I'm not an actor anymore, so I may be a little out of touch. But listen to this, Elle. Nobody will value you if you don't value yourself. The industry wants actors, especially young women, to be desperate. Because then they can take advantage of that. You don't have to put up with it, Elle."

Elle stared at the table with a numb expression, and I had the urge to pull her into a hug. Except I wouldn't, because it would be inappropriate. We'd only just met. Well—properly just met.

Elle twisted the stem of her wineglass and gave Deanna a soft look of reproach. "I don't think it's as simple as that."

Deanna looked like she wanted to argue, but I interrupted. I didn't want Elle to feel judged, and we were getting dangerously close to that. Christ knows she'd already been judged enough by me. Honestly, I could punch myself in the face for the way I acted when I first met her. I cleared my throat. "Do you need any help setting the table, Dee?"

Deanna caught my meaningful look and nodded. "Right. Yes, that would be great."

I started to collect plates and cutlery from the drawers, all places I had memorized from childhood.

Elle put down her glass. "Let me help—"

Deanna tried to wave her away but couldn't stop her, and Elle sidled up beside me and tried to take the cutlery I was balancing.

I stared down at her. "I promise you, I'm more than capable of carrying three plates and some cutlery."

Elle's lips twitched, and she grabbed the cutlery, anyway. "Yeah, but this way it won't rattle around or drop."

It was alarming how much of a reaction her words had on me. The way she said the words were so gentle, so lovely, and I winced at the effect she was having. I tried to act normal and shrugged. "Suit yourself."

When I glanced over Elle's head at Deanna, she was looking at us with a strange expression. I frowned at her and tried to tell her to mind her own business with my expression.

I angled my elbow toward a drawer that I couldn't reach. "Could you grab the napkins in that one?"

"Sure." Elle turned, and I could see a slight flush on her cheeks. Great. Another thing to think about.

While we set the table, Deanna was busy bringing the roast out of the oven. This was one of my favorite parts of returning to Mistletoe Valley, the warm, wonderful meals I shared with Deanna. She was the only family I had left, so I always soaked it up.

I snuck a glance at Elle as she arranged the cutlery with careful, efficient movements. I forced my eyes away, so I wasn't tempted to keep watching her. Fuck.

Deanna was battling with the roast, so I held out a hand. "Let me."

She gave me a grateful look. "My wrists aren't always strong enough."

"Must have been from the strain of holding up the arts in this town," I quipped.

Deanna let out a surprised laugh, and I smiled back. It was always nice when I could surprise her. "That must have been it."

"What was it like, starting from scratch here?" Elle spoke up, looking at Deanna with keen eyes.

I needed to stop looking at her, or I was going to chop my hand off with the carving knife.

Deanna brought a salad bowl from the fridge and set it on the table. "It was… interesting. Some folks didn't know what to think of me at first. But I volunteered for things, made friends as much as I could, and after my first year, I volunteered to put on the Christmas play."

"It sounds like it was hard."

Deanna shared a look with me, and I knew what she was about to say. She'd said it to me throughout my childhood. "I like hard. But only when it's the right kind. And moving here, starting anew, it was the right kind of difficult, because my life as an actor wasn't fulfilling me anymore."

I brought the plate of roast meat to the table and we all sat down, serving ourselves from the plates. I snuck another look at Elle and could almost see her thoughts ticking over. What was she thinking?

I put another slice of meat on my plate and silently shook myself. I didn't need to concern myself with what she was thinking.

I'd only just met her.

ELLE

Nick kept looking at me. I could guess why, but I still didn't like it. I was sure it was pity—pity for the poor struggling actor who wasn't happy. I never should have revealed my feelings to him. I didn't want his pity, not his or anyone else's. I also definitely didn't want Deanna's idealism about a world where an actress could have standards.

I didn't think a world like that existed.

On the bright side, though, the dinner was delicious. I smiled at Deanna and said as much. "Have you always loved to cook?"

The two of them went still at my question, and I worried I had said something wrong. I turned the question over in my head and came up with nothing, so that meant…There had to be something else going on.

Deanna looked at Nick, gave him a sad smile, and answered, "Nick's mother taught me when I came here."

I didn't need to ask another stupid question to know what had happened. Nick's mom had passed away. I gave him an apologetic look. "I'm sorry."

Nick gave me a tight smile and inhaled. "Thank you. It happened a long enough time ago."

Deanna reached over and grabbed Nick's hand, giving him a warm smile. She looked at me and nodded. "Lorelle, Nick's mom, was the best cook in town. She saw the way I could burn water if I wasn't careful and offered to teach me. It's how we became close friends."

Nick began eating again. His hand trembled slightly, and I felt rotten. "Elle is right. This is delicious, and mom would be proud."

I began eating again, desperately trying to find a better conversation topic. Unfortunately, the only ones I could come up with were asking Nick about himself, so I swallowed the awkwardness. "Where did you go to law school?"

"Stanford." He said it without a hint of pride. He just kept looking down at his plate and methodically cut his salad greens into pieces.

I slowly swallowed. "Stanford."

Deanna chuckled. "We were all very proud of him when he got accepted."

Nick Corrigan went to Stanford. I leaned my chin against the back of my hand, eyeing him suspiciously. "And you insisted that you're not trying to be impressive."

Nick laughed softly at his plate. "No, young me was absolutely trying to be impressive. And I certainly had a lot of peers at Stanford who were doing it for their ego."

I rested my fork on my plate. "So what changed?"

Nick gave me a bland smile. "I got one of the best-paying jobs right out of college, a job that people would kill for, and I hated it."

"The same job you have now in LA?"

Nick nodded. That explained why he was so grumpy the day I had run into him, if he hated his job that much. He seemed so different here, so much more content.

I was silent for a while, finishing my plate. Deanna made small talk with Nick about some town gossip, but I mostly ignored it. I had the sudden urge to move, to do something, so the moment they both finished with their plates, I leapt up to clear them.

Unfortunately, Nick stood too, holding his own plate. He looked at Deanna. "You go relax. We'll clean up."

Deanna stood and stretched. She gave both of us a look, then shrugged, grabbed her wineglass and moved to the lounge room. "Thanks, Nicky."

I stifled a sudden and strong urge to snort. The man walking next to me to the kitchen sink did not resemble a 'Nicky' in any form. "Nicky, huh?"

He huffed and began filling the sink with hot water. I stacked dirty dishes, working in tandem beside him. "A childhood name. But it's Deanna, so I allow it."

"So…" I smiled to myself, "if I were to call you Nicky—"

"You'd be getting a sternly worded 'cease and desist' letter in the mail." Nick sent me a wry smile to soften his words. He rolled up his sleeves, and I tried not to stare at his forearms.

I searched for a dishcloth so I wouldn't keep looking at him. I leaned against the countertop while I waited for the first dish and surreptitiously watched him work. "Is that why you like law? Getting to write all those sternly worded letters?"

Nick chuckled, and I tried not to notice how lovely and deep his voice sounded when he laughed. "Yes, and no. I like the rules, the reading, finding loopholes, and solutions to problems."

I took a wet plate from him. "Huh. I was expecting something like 'I enjoy fighting with people.'"

"Only the right people. I prefer fighting for the underdog, you know?"

I eyed him over the dinner dish. "I can't imagine you'd get to do a lot of that as a corporate lawyer."

"No." Nick kept his eyes on the task. "I don't."

I reached out to grab the next plate and felt his forearm brush mine. Warmth tingled up my arm, and I looked down. He did, too.

The moment hung suspended in the air.

He cleared his throat and passed the plate to me. "Thanks for drying."

I hopped up and sat on the counter just to get some distance between us. His eyes briefly tracked the motion of my thighs as I crossed my legs. My dress pulled up to reveal sheer black tights. His eyes didn't linger. But there had definitely been some desire there.

I'd spent a long time getting very good at knowing when someone found me attractive, and I would bet anything that

Nick Corrigan thought I was. I could see it in the way he swallowed, the way his eyes tightened just slightly.

Something raised its head inside me. That was… interesting.

"Did you always want to do law?" I asked him while drying the cutlery.

"When I was five, I'm pretty sure I wanted to be a fireman."

I snorted. I couldn't help it. But his words conjured up an image of what he would look like as a fireman… I shook myself surreptitiously. "I wanted to be a doctor, before I realized I fainted at the sight of blood."

That was a lie, but Nick didn't need to know that. My parents may have wanted me to have a 'real job' but my head had already been filled with nonsense about being a star. Nick nodded and drained the sink, wiping down the surrounding countertop. "I realized I couldn't be a fireman because I hated getting covered in soot."

I smiled. "So what changed?"

Nick grabbed the dry dishes I had been stacking and began putting them away. I started to climb down to help him, but he held out a hand. "You stay there. I've got it."

I shrugged, folding the dishcloth so I had something to do with my hands. "So?"

Nick reached up to a high cupboard, and his sweater lifted slightly. Just enough for me to see a sliver of taut skin on his torso. I flushed. "What changed… was the old lawyer who used to practise here gave me some work experience during my sophomore year summer. I got to see the sort of things he did, how he got to help the town, the problems he got to solve, and I realized I wanted to do that."

God, this guy was being serious. He genuinely enjoyed helping people. If I wasn't already warming up to him, this would've been the final straw. "Most lawyers I've met usually just like fighting people or feeling like they're the smartest person in the room."

"And then in walks a neurosurgeon." Nick shook his head. "A lot of my peers at Stanford were, honestly, idiots. For a lot of reasons, mostly because they thought that studying law made them better than everyone else."

"I mean, studying law is a lot more impressive than what I did, to be fair."

Nick leaned against the island counter opposite me. "Why do you always do that?"

"What?"

"De-value yourself and what you've chosen to do." Nick crossed his arms, but his face was open.

I fiddled with the end of the dishcloth and gave him a rueful look. "Well, you did it when we first met. You de-valued what I was doing to earn money."

Nick looked pained, and he opened his mouth to apologize again.

I cut him off. "And it's not just you. Most of my interactions with people, my whole adult life, they judge me. The moment they find out what I do, what I want my career to be, they judge me. It's subtle sometimes, and those are the worst, but almost no one finds out I'm a struggling actor and thinks I'm adding to the world."

"Do you think you're adding to the world?"

I leaned my head back against the cabinet, and my brain went silent. "No. I don't think I am."

"Bullshit." I looked back at Nick, and he was frowning. "Everyone, with a few exceptions, adds something to the world. You're just not valuing it—not seeing it."

I didn't like how insistent he was being, especially someone who had so easily judged me when he didn't know who I was. I crossed my arms. "I think we'll just have to agree to disagree."

Nick gripped the counter behind him with both hands, the movement stretching his sweater across his pecs. It was—God help me—a really pleasant view. He looked strong, like he might pick me up and—I bit my lip, feeling the flush of my cheeks.

Nick's eyes darkened, and he inhaled through his lips. "Stop looking at me like that."

I flinched, and shame curdled my stomach. Oh shit, have I made him uncomfortable? "Sorry. I'm not—"

Nick's eyes flashed. "I don't mean—Jesus, it's just that my godmother is in the other room."

Oh.

Oh.

I felt something slither in my belly, something warm and pleased. "I didn't mean to look at you like that."

"I know." Nick's hand clenched and unclenched on the counter. "But my godmother is here and I've only just met you."

"I'm leaving in a month." I reminded him, looking him up and down openly now.

Nick exhaled sharply, his eyes burning into mine. "Exactly."

I tilted my head. Most guys would see that as an *advantage*, not a drawback. "I'm leaving in a *month*." I repeated.

The implication was clear. A part of me almost couldn't believe I was making such a bold offer to someone I'd—properly—only just met today. Nick's eye twitched, and I could tell he was tempted. That I tempted him.

Good. About time I had some fun with something. I smiled at him, the role of seductress falling over me like water. "We're both interested. Why not?"

"You're employed by my godmother." The tendons on his neck stood out clearly. "There's a… conflict of interest."

I unfolded my legs slowly. "We don't have to tell anyone."

Christ, who was I? It had been ages since I had been this interested in someone, this eager, this *hungry*. And I could tell in his eyes that he was tempted, badly. So what was holding him back?

Nick tracked the movement of my legs with intensity, and my core clenched. "Elle—"

I hopped off the counter. "I've got a long day tomorrow. Why don't you think about it?"

I walked away, knowing he was watching. I had forgotten how intoxicating it was to be *desired*, to be wanted. I had spent too much time being a waste of space, one of many gorgeous women in a room. But when Nick looked at me, I felt exceptional.

Strange, really, considering how rude he'd been to me when we first clashed.

As I turned to walk upstairs, I looked back and flashed him a megawatt smile. "I hope you have a great night's sleep."

His eyes followed me as I walked away, and I smiled to myself. I might be in a small town, but at least I could have some *fun*.

NICK

Christ. The tendons in my hands were screaming, clenching the bench so hard. I wanted to run after Elle, grab her in my arms, kiss her and get her to make such pretty noises—

But I couldn't. Not because I didn't want to, or even really because Elle was here to work for Deanna. No, the real reason was that I could tell Elle was hurting. I tried to not fuck with women who were going through something. It felt bad, like I could accidentally take advantage of their vulnerability.

But Christ, I wanted to indulge in my desires so badly. It didn't help that I'd been overworking too much for a proper fuck for a while, and that did bad things to my libido.

I wouldn't be taking Elle up on her offer. By the time I got to know her better, she would have turned her attention to someone else. She might not have met them yet, but there were a few young bucks in the town who'd be able to show her a good time.

Not as good as I would, a voice whispered in my head. I batted it away. That wasn't my concern, for Christ's sake. I was here to do some work, to spend time with Deanna, and scope out a place for my future firm.

I had things to do. And unfortunately, Elle Sutton was not on that list.

I needed a strategy.

I took the coward's way out. I avoided Elle for days. I felt like an idiot, avoiding Deanna's place and the main parts of town, but I tried to justify it because I had work to do. Top of my list was an appointment with a real estate agent. Avoiding Elle—focusing on my work—was for the best. If I saw her again, I wasn't sure how I'd react.

I met Matt Sanders outside the old accountant's office at ten o'clock and we shook hands in greeting. I'd gone through high school with Matt, and he had been a good friend. Given our past, he was one of the few agents in town I trusted to find me the right place.

Matt gave me a sly smile and clapped a hand on my shoulder. "You're looking good, brother."

With almost any other man, I would've shaken his hand off. But I let Matt, because we'd been through a lot together. I sized him up, noticing the pristine gray suit, the perfectly sculpted beard, the bright blue eyes. "So do you. What's it been, half a year since I've seen you?"

Matt laughed. "Something like that. What's this? You been working out more?"

He squeezed my shoulder, and I shrugged him off. "My boss remains an asshole. Gotta stay sane somehow."

Matt grimaced. "You gotta get away from him, bro."

"I'm aware." I gave him a meaningful look. "That's what today's about. I hope you've got some good options for me."

"You know I do." Matt rubbed his hands together and winked.

As we walked in, I eyed Matt. He was looking good, much better than the last time I'd seen him, recently broken up with his long-time partner, Elise. "You doing okay?"

Matt gave me an easy smile, but I could see the leftover pain in his eyes. "Better, bro. Always better."

"You look sharp." I said it because it was true—his suit was crisp, and he looked much lighter in the eyes than six months ago.

Matt unlocked the building, and I looked around. He watched me inspect it, and I could have kissed him for the way he let me look first without saying anything. After a while, he spoke. "Getting any good vibes from this one?"

I eyed the musty blinds and yellowing walls. "The… *vibes* are mediocre with this one."

To his credit, Matt just nodded. "Alright. Wanna skip to the next one or hear the usual spiel I give others?"

"Just tell me what it has going for it." I could already tell there wasn't much to the place, just one large main room and a few side offices. The space was… depressing, just like I could expect a former accountant's office to look.

Matt took in a breath and slid his hands into his pockets. "The rent's way cheaper than anything else on the list."

"Great," I grumbled.

"And," Matt paused meaningfully, "the owner is fine with basically any renovations you want to do."

"Seriously?" Now that had my attention. I eyed the yellow wallpaper again.

"Seriously." Matt nodded. "But I showed you this one first because it's the worst candidate. The next one is over the river, next to the park."

"Alright." I took one more look over the place, knowing that I wouldn't go with this one unless the others were worse. "Let's go."

The second building, to Matt's credit, was better. It had clean white walls in the reception room, mixed with cool brown paneling that I liked. But this building was almost a little too new for my liking. I knew I was being picky, but it was... soulless. I let Matt give me the talk, because I knew he would have prepared a good one for me.

"The rent is more expensive than the last one, but the lease contract is good, and there's a nice bathroom and kitchen out the back."

I followed him into the back room and saw he was right. It was new and clean, but I still felt like the office was missing something. I looked around. "It's better. It's good, if this was the only option I'd take it, but—"

"But Nick Corrigan wants the best." Matt rubbed his hands together and gave me a smile. "Don't worry, bro, I think I've got that for you."

⟶≫≫⟶ ⟵≪≪⟵

Matt was right. The last one was the best. It was in a perfect central location, surrounded by trees and a beautiful exterior. The inside was elegant and clean, and I could immediately see myself working from here.

For a moment, it transported me back to my younger years, when I interned with the old lawyer. That office had been turned into a dental clinic, now, but this building reminded me of that one, and nostalgia gripped me. I was sixteen years old again, discovering that I could be good at something.

I slid my hands into my pockets and inhaled. This was a big step for me, finally signing a lease for my own firm. Matt gave me a sidelong look, but said nothing. Eventually, I exhaled. "Yep. It's this one."

Matt rubbed his hands together. "I was hoping you'd say that."

⟶≫≫⟶ ⟵≪≪⟵

A few days later, Matt and I met back at the Hollyoak to catch up properly, now that we were both done with our business. It was nearly dinnertime, and I knew the bar would fill up soon enough, but we scored a good table in the corner. We sat down with our drinks, and Matt let out a sigh. "Thank fuck for Wednesdays."

I took a sip of my own drink. "Thanks for all the work you've done this week for me on short notice."

"For you? Anything, bro." Matt looked off into the distance. "But anyone else? Fuck that shit."

I laughed. "What's been new with you? I know you said you were doing better, but…"

Matt cracked a grin. "But was that a lie, you mean?"

I jerked my head in a nod. "I just mean—we're both relaxed and got some drinks in hand. I'm all ears."

Matt dragged a hand over his face, and I could see the exhaustion there. "We finally sold the old house a month ago. But it was five months of talking to her, man. I would've been better off if I could've just blocked her, never seen her again. But I see her all the time."

I winced. "I'm sorry."

"At least we hadn't got to kids yet, y'know?" Matt chuckled darkly. "That would've been way worse."

I took a sip of my drink and nodded.

"She got a new boyfriend, too."

I sat up straighter. "Who?"

Matt waved a hand. "Some farmer prick from Mulberrydale."

I whistled through my teeth. Matt and Elise had been together for nearly ten years. To find someone else again after six months… "That's fast."

"Right?" Matt shook his head and dragged a hand down his face again. "I just…there's no one here, y'know? If I want to find someone new, I'm going to have to go to the city, one of the other towns. I thought I was done with that bullshit."

I tipped my glass up. "There'll be someone."

Matt leaned forward, a sudden gleam in his eyes that I didn't like. "Hey, what about that actor girl from the city? What's she like?"

My stomach dropped, and I remembered with clarity my conversation with Elle, when she basically offered herself up to me on a silver platter. "What do you mean?"

"I heard you two got talking when you arrived." Matt eyed me. "I heard she was pretty."

I leaned back in my chair and gave Matt a look. "Why don't you judge that for yourself? I'm sure you'll see her around."

Matt whistled. "That pretty, huh?"

I took another drink and tried to smooth out my scowl. I didn't want to talk to Matt about how pretty Elle was—I wanted to be bundling her up in blankets and cooing compliments to her face, just the two of us. It was scary, really, the intensity of my feelings towards her in such a short time. Had it really been less than a week since I'd properly met her? And I'd spent half that time avoiding her, like a coward.

Matt leaned back and chuckled. "Alrighty, then. So you don't have any designs on her?"

Because I was an idiot, I swallowed and said, "Nope. I've got other things to worry about."

I ignored the urge to punch Matt, even though I knew he was just asking out of idle curiosity. Every muscle in my body tensed, like I had some weird claim on Elle. I didn't. Women weren't something to put dibs on, and if Matt decided he liked the look of Elle, then she could get what she so clearly wanted: a holiday fling. Who was I to get in the way?

I wasn't the person to give that to her. I'd always known I was a commitment sort of guy. I'd spent too much time in the city dating casually. The appetite to do that shit was leaving me, and I had better things to focus on than finding pleasure temporarily.

If Matt wanted to pursue Elle, then I would have to deal with that. I ignored the sinking feeling in my stomach and took another sip of my drink.

⟿⟫⟫ ⟪⟪⟪⟵

Fate had other ideas for me, it seemed. Almost as if we'd summoned her, Elle entered the Hollyoak Hotel bar right on six o'clock, and both Matt and I turned to watch her walk in. My heart quickened, my stomach clenched, and I fought against about fifty different irrational thoughts when I saw her.

She was gorgeous tonight. Her tight green dress accentuated her soft curves, and her blonde hair fell in lovely waves around her face. She looked like a sexy Christmas tree, all sparkly green. Christ, I was already describing her with poetic language in my head. This was bad.

Even worse, I had to watch as Matt took her in. I saw the way his eyes sharpened, as if he'd sniffed out a new deal, and knew I was going to have a horrific night. He looked back at me. "You're telling me you have no interest in a girl like that? She's exactly your type."

Down to a tee, I wanted to say. Instead, I shook my head. "She's only here for a month. I don't want to get involved with someone so short term."

Matt adjusted his watch, a gleam in his eyes. "So you won't mind, then?"

"Only if she doesn't." I said darkly.

Matt gave me a look of reproach. "Bro, speak now or forever hold your peace. You know I don't pursue women who aren't into it. So if you have *another* reason to have an issue with it, I'd say it now."

I said nothing and took another sip of my drink. "Do whatever you want, Matt."

My friend looked at me for a moment, rapping his knuckles against the arm of his chair. I didn't like the awareness in his eyes, almost like they were seeing all the things I wasn't saying.

He pursed his lips and stood. He buttoned up his suit jacket again and set his eyes on Elle. "Alright then."

I had to watch as Matt approached Elle—I had to watch as her eyes turned from wary to coy—and I had to watch Matt buy her a drink. Finally, I had to watch in horror as he invited her back to our table.

The fucking asshole. He knew.

Matt gave me a smooth smile as Elle slid herself down in the chair opposite me. "Hello, Nick."

"Elle." I gave her a look that I hoped was a smile, even as I was dying inside. "What brings you here?"

Elle turned her warm eyes to Matt and gave him an extra wide smile. "I thought I'd come and see what fun there is in the Hollyoak Hotel."

"There ain't much, darling, but we'll try to be as exciting as possible for you." Matt winked at her. Christ, he was such a flirt. I'd forgotten the Casanova he had been in our youth, since he'd been in a relationship for the last ten years. And this was how I had to rediscover it, watching him stretch his muscles with Elle?

Part of me couldn't blame him. She was gorgeous, and I knew now she was interested in a… casual thing. I gripped the glass of my whiskey hard and glowered at Matt.

Elle noticed and sent me a prim smile. I felt trouble brewing. "Something wrong, Nick?"

"Nothing." I grunted out. Matt was taunting me with her and I hated it. I knew he wasn't doing it to hurt me, but he was trying to call my bluff. I would not give him the satisfaction. "Long day."

Elle sank back in her chair and smiled to herself, fiddling with the tie at her waist. I watched, entranced, before I had to look away. She angled her head at Matt. "What do you do for work, Matt?"

Matt gave her a dazzling smile back, and I barely restrained myself from kicking him under the table. "Real estate, baby."

I was going to murder him, slowly. And I would get away with it too, because I was a lawyer.

Elle rested her chin on her hand, leaning in to Matt. "And how do the two of you know each other?"

Matt opened his mouth, but I beat him to it. "He came over to my house one day when we were toddlers and has refused to leave me alone since."

"Cheers to that." Matt raised his glass and winked at Elle again.

She clinked her glass against his and they both drank. Elle leaned forward, and I couldn't help but notice the way the fabric across her breasts stretched, silky smooth skin pressed against it. Ugh. "I've been in town almost a week now. How come I haven't seen you around?"

Matt slung an arm round the back of his chair, looking confident and commanding. I knew that's what he wanted, because he'd given me a lecture on the art of body language and flirting over a decade ago now. Everything he did was calculated. Matt twirled his glass between his hands. "I think the universe wanted us to meet tonight."

Elle gave one of her delicate snorts as I tightened my grip on my glass and glared at Matt. He looked me in the eye, tilted his head, and smiled. He knew exactly what he was doing, fuck him. "Need a top up for that drink, Nicky?"

I narrowed my eyes at him. Why was he volunteering to leave, if he was trying to get into her pants so much? Why would he….

Oh.

He was trying to push me to admit that I had designs on Elle. Fuck.

I glared at him. "Yes, but I'm—"

"Let me." Matt stood up and gave me an easy smile. "I insist."

Which left Elle and I sitting alone, and I had no idea what to do with myself. Elle watched Matt go, then crossed her arms. "What are you doing?"

"What?"

She gave me a soft look of reproach. "You don't want to take me up on my offer. I get it. But your friend here seems more than game. So why are you sitting there, glaring daggers at him when all he's doing is talking to me." Elle leaned back and shook her head. "If you're uncomfortable with me because of what happened at Deanna's, now's your chance to say so."

Words caught in my throat for a moment, but that was too slow. She thought I didn't want to be around her?

Elle pursed her lips and got out of her chair. "Understood."

I watched her walk away, my body paralysed, until I finally jolted out of my seat. I followed her through the bar, out into the frigid night air. "Elle."

She turned around, crossed her arms and waited. "It's okay, Nick. I made a very bold offer to you. I understand you're not interested."

"That's not it." I breathed.

Her eyes were guarded, but I could see the vulnerability in them, hidden under layers of frustration and impatience. "Then what is it?"

The words almost came out of my mouth, but I was a coward. I rubbed the back of my neck in frustration. "Just… not Matt, okay?"

"Why?" Her eyes shuttered. She was right to question me. I was making absolutely no sense.

"I know it's none of my business, but…"

Elle tilted her head at me. "It is none of your business. But you've ruined my appetite anyway, so thank you very much for that."

And she turned, giving me a single glare, and walked away.

I watched her and realized something with a sinking feeling in my stomach. I was beginning to care about Elle Sutton, an unreasonable amount. The only question was, what should I do about it now? I took a breath. "Wait."

She paused, and half turned back to me. "What?"

I breathed out and tilted my head back. "I'm not good at this stuff."

"At… talking?"

I huffed out another breath. "Yes. About what I actually *want*."

Understanding came into her eyes. "Right."

I shoved my hands in my coat pockets. "You know, I'm here because I'm finally thinking about moving back here. Something I've wanted for a while."

"That's good." Elle murmured.

I levelled her with a look, throwing caution to the wind. "But you're the first person I've *wanted* in a really long time. Just for myself. It's not rational, and it's not helpful."

Her lips opened to a silent 'ah,' and she nodded. "You've spent a lot of your life carefully planning everything, haven't you?"

"I've had to." I said simply. "Since I left town, I haven't given myself a chance to want something that doesn't work with my grand plan."

Elle gave me a sad smile. "That doesn't sound like much fun."

I shook my head, unable to stand how gorgeous she was, bathed in the streetlight. "You're something else, Elle Sutton."

Her lips curved into a smile. "You barely know me."

"Yeah, but I'd love to get to know you." I took a step towards her, suddenly feeling free to be honest. "I'd love to get to know every inch of you, every habit and thought, what's going on in that gorgeous head of yours."

She inhaled, and her eyes went soft. Her lips parted, ever so slightly, and I wanted to kiss them. I didn't.

I bent my head until we were just a few breaths apart. "I can tell you don't want that. You just want something physical, something temporary, and I can't give that to you. I would want more of you than that."

Elle closed her eyes, her mouth down-turned. "Because I'm leaving in a month."

"Because you're leaving in a month." I confirmed.

"Why can't we just enjoy this, as finite as it is?"

I stepped back, shaking my head. "Because then I might like you too much—might like you enough to disrupt my plans. And I won't do that."

Her eyebrows puckered, and she looked so adorably frustrated I wanted to kiss it away. Dammit. She shook her head. "I don't like this."

I shrugged. "We're adults. We'll be fine."

As I walked away from her, I doubted whether that was true. I felt this way after only a few days of Elle Sutton's existence in my life. What would happen after a month?

ELLE

"Miss Elle! What do you think of this?" Celia, a young girl of five, ran to me and showed me her red costume.

I grinned down at her and shared a look with Deanna. Celia was the most energetic of the younger kids, and she practically bounced off the walls at any opportunity. "I like it. But I think we'd better focus on working with the group to make the sled first, don't you?"

Celia ran away almost as fast as she arrived, and I laughed. God, some of these kids were a handful.

Deanna crossed her arms beside me. "It was a good idea of yours to do set construction first. Get their energy out for the afternoon."

I watched as some of the older teenagers acted as the leaders, guiding the younger ones through building the sled for the play. We'd already cast the play, were well into rehearsals, but I still wanted them to have fun. It was going to be collaborative and casual, so that's why I started them off with something physical, something to involve their minds and bodies.

The script for our play was called Much Ado About Christmas. It involved several meddling elves and reindeers trying to help the members of a small town pull off two weddings during Christmas.

The moment I read the script, I had been delighted. Shakespeare references, delightfully quaint characters and a happy ending? A perfect story, if you asked me.

Life needed more perfect stories, because God only knew how imperfect my life had been so far. But I didn't need to think about that, because the only thing that was important was my job. We had a play to make.

I looked at Deanna. "I think we should start, don't you?"

⤜⤜⤜ ⤛⤛⤛

Three hours later, the sun had set, and the kids were packing up their stuff to go home. I think I was doing okay. Most of them were jumping up and down, excitedly talking to each other about how amazing it was going to be.

The door to the town hall creaked open, and everyone turned. Nick Corrigan stood there with three takeout cups and a sheepish smile on his face.

My breath hitched in my throat.

The kids screamed and ran towards him. Celia launched herself at him and he barely avoided spilling the drinks. Within seconds, the other kids surrounded him, embracing Nick and giving him cheerful greetings.

I huffed, trying not to be too impressed with the way he interacted with the kids. "Should we save him?"

"Give him a minute." Deanna said wryly beside me.

I watched, stomach clenching, as he talked to the children, chatting and hugging them. As if I didn't need another reason to want him. He was great with children, too. Heat flushed up my body, and I took a breath. "They really love him."

Deanna crossed her arms. "They really do."

We watched as he gently extricated himself from the horde and held out a hand. "Excuse me, but I've got to deliver these to the ladies over there."

My lips threatened to stretch into an overly pleased smile, but I suppressed it. It wouldn't be right for me to be smiling too hard at Nick Corrigan. It might undermine me in front of the kids. Or something like that.

Celia bounded over to me before Nick did. "Miss Elle! Have you met Nick yet?"

I met his eyes and felt something in my stomach melt. Why did he have to be so good-looking and *unavailable*? I broke eye contact and smiled down at Celia. "I have, actually. Last week."

Only he and I knew that was a lie, and that we had met long before that, but that was our secret to keep.

Nick pulled a cup out of the carry tray. "I brought hot cocoa. Thought you both might want some after your long day."

Great. Another reason to want to jump this man into to-morrow. He brought me hot cocoa. I gingerly grabbed the cup and peered at him from under my lashes. "You didn't have to do that."

"I wanted to." Nick flashed me a quick smile and passed the second one to a grateful Deanna. "I may have heard on the pipeline that it was a big day for both of you."

He'd heard that from Deanna, undoubtedly, but I didn't call him out on it. I had a feeling if I opened my mouth right now, I would beg him to fuck me in front of everyone. A girl has to have *some* dignity.

Luckily, Deanna spoke up. "Thank you, Nick. I'm sure the kids loved to see you here, too."

"I love seeing them." Nick gave Deanna a quick nod, but he set his eyes on me. "But I'm actually hoping to ask Elle something."

"Ask away." I answered breathlessly.

"Come for a walk with me?"

Dammit, that was not at all the words I wanted to come out of his mouth. Something like… *I've changed my mind and we can fuck on every available surface in town*, or *would you like me to feed you hot cocoa tomorrow morning and then fuck you on the breakfast table?* Why was he wanting to walk with me? I thought he'd decided that he wasn't interested.

My mouth was a traitor, because I said, "Sure. I need to stretch my legs."

That wasn't a lie, but it was the only thing I could say in front of the kids and Deanna that wasn't inappropriate or unintelligible panting.

I grabbed my bag and waved at Deanna. "See you later."

Deanna was smiling smugly between the two of us, and I didn't like that one bit. She wasn't blind—she could probably guess that something was going on between us, she just didn't know that the something was a lot of unfulfilled sexual tension. "Be seeing you."

I walked out the door, the remaining students watched me and Nick with wide eyes. I tried not to speculate about what the kids thought, seeing us leave together. When we got outside, the wind bit my cheeks enough to make me snuggle further into my scarf. Nick slipped his free hand into his coat pocket and pulled out some gloves.

I looked at them and back up at him in question.

He nudged them further towards me. "For the cold—while you drink."

Something warm unfurled in my stomach. I wanted to punch him, or kiss him, or a combination of the two. How dare he be this thoughtful and yet wouldn't fuck me? I didn't know what to do with a man like Nick Corrigan. Usually, when I liked a man, I made myself available sexually, and that was it. But not with him, because he was saying… no? I snatched the gloves up. "Thanks."

He held my cup for me while I slipped them on, and I examined him. He raised his eyebrows. "What?"

I fiddled with the gloves. "You're… very prepared."

Nick gave me a small smile. "Experience. I know how brutal it is in this weather."

I looked up at the sky, if only just to stop looking at his stupid, handsome face. It was dusk, the cloudy sky barely lit with the last touches of the sun. "Will it snow soon?"

Nick eyed the sky. "Soon. Maybe tomorrow, maybe the day after."

I took a breath. Why had he asked me here, giving me fuzzy gloves and warm cocoa and the invitation to spend time with him? I couldn't work him out.

"Okay. So you've asked me to go for a walk." I took the cup back from him. "And you've brought me cocoa. Some people might call this a date."

"Does it have to be?" Nick gave me an unreadable look.

"I don't know." I shrugged. "You're the one who decided you couldn't *get to know me*."

The insinuation in my words was clear enough. But Nick winced and smiled. "Maybe I just want to get to know you. As friends."

I groaned. "Jesus, you really want to do this?"

"I have my reasons." Nick rolled his shoulders. "But I think we can be friends, especially while you're here."

I took a sip of my cocoa and watched him over the rim. "Why?"

Nick side-eyed me. "I would think my motivation was obvious."

A flush built on my cheeks, but I ignored it. I couldn't understand this man. What did he want? He wouldn't fuck me, but he wouldn't stay away, either. He just wanted to dangle himself in front of me like a delicious four course meal that I'd never be able to taste. I cleared my throat. "That still doesn't explain it."

Nick began walking along the footpath, and I followed. "Can't we just… enjoy each other's company?"

I blinked. "Yeah, that's what I'm saying. Why do you want my company if you don't want sex, or a relationship, or whatever?"

Nick stopped walking and turned to me with a hard look. "I don't know if you've heard, but men *can* sometimes like the company of women for the sake of it."

I gave him a shrewd look. "But we *both* know you're attracted to me."

Nick's throat bobbed. "Your cocoa's getting cold."

I took a vindictive sip, but the sweet chocolate quickly mellowed me out. I grumbled, "Fine, but I'm only indulging your weird, self-flagellating habit because of the cocoa."

"Are you ever going to believe that you're an interesting person to be around, and someone doesn't have to be getting something from you to justify your worth?" Nick's words came out casually, but I could hear the steel in them.

I stopped walking and felt the words bounce around in my head. But… people were only interested in me when I could give them something. That was something I'd known my whole life, that if I smiled and performed and gave them something fancy, they'd smile at me and clap. And then later, when I became a woman, I learned I could hold a man's interest in me with my body, with the things I could make them feel. But it was never about me, never about who I really was.

There was a bottomless abyss of *something* inside me, but I had been keeping the lid tightly screwed over it. With Nick's words, the lid rattled and threatened to come off.

Nick made a regretful face. "Elle, I didn't mean—"

I shook my head and shoved my cocoa into his hands. "I don't want your cocoa if you're just going to criticize me."

Nick's face was regretful. "I'm sorry. I shouldn't have said that."

"No. You shouldn't have." I started forward on the path again and angled myself towards Deanna's house. I walked fast, trying to put as much distance between us as possible.

Nick, the bastard, caught up with me quickly on his long legs. "Elle—"

I angrily wiped tears off my face. Great—I was crying. "What right do you have to lecture me? What right do you have to tell me how I should be? I was fine before I came here. I was absolutely *fine*, and when I go back to the city, I'm going to keep being *fine* for the rest of my life, and you won't be able to change that!"

The lid had opened, and a flood of emotions rushed through me. Somewhere along the line of my speech, I realized 'fine' wasn't really fine at all.

Because I wasn't fine. And I hadn't been for a really long time. Only coming here—to this beautiful, welcoming town—had I realized. I felt it, that endless abyss inside my skin that I had bottled for so long, because I had convinced myself that my happiness didn't matter for *success*. And I hadn't even managed that.

Nick said nothing at first—he just let me process. My breathing wasn't slowing down. I could feel the panicked hummingbird of my heart beating in my chest. I pressed a hand against my chest, feeling the start of a panic attack. My breath shuddered out of me. "Why did you say that? *Why did you say that?*"

My chest squeezed and I backed away from him. I wanted to run. I wanted to run far away from Nick, from anyone, so they wouldn't see the rotten core inside me.

Except Nick didn't let me run away. He put the cups of cocoa on the pavement and put his face at my eye level. "Can you count the freckles on my face?"

I blinked up at him, my breaths still uneven. "You—You don't…"

But as I looked at him, I noticed the tiny freckles across his cheeks, tiny marks that I hadn't even seen before. Slowly, gently, I counted them in my head and felt my panic come under control.

How had he known to do that?

Nick gave me an encouraging nod. "Good."

I put a hand over my face. "Oh God, I'm so sorry—"

"Don't apologize." Nick's eyes were soft, calm. "I got them too, in college. I know what it feels like."

That explained why he knew what to do so quickly.

Nick gave me a calculating look. "Would a hug help?"

I whined, turning away, and wiped my face with my sleeve. "Yes. But I've got snot on my face."

"I really, truly, do not care." Nick jerked me back into him and pulled me into a hug. I immediately relaxed, feeling safe and comfortable. God, he smelled *amazing*. He cleared his throat and wound his arms around my shoulders. "I'm sorry. I'm sorry I upset you."

I sniffed into his chest, brushing my sleeves against my nose to save his lovely sweater from the snot. "I know."

He rocked us gently from side to side, and I listened to the reassuring sound of his strong heartbeat. "Do you want to talk about it?"

I was silent for a while, thinking. I didn't really know what to say, and there were some parts of my panicked emotions I didn't feel ready to face yet. But with Nick, I felt safe. He was showing me already that I could be authentic around him—that he wanted my honest, raw self. What a weird feeling.

I sighed into his chest, still unable to look at him. When I finally spoke, it came out of me all at once. "I feel like I'm lost."

"Yeah?" Nick's chest expanded and contracted, a reassuring rhythm I latched onto. There was no judgement in his question.

"Yeah." I sniffled again and felt around the abyss in my stomach. "God, what is it about this town?"

I heard Nick huff, his breath ruffling my hair. "I know what you mean."

"Do you?"

"Yeah." Nick's hand pressed between my shoulder blades, applying just the right amount of pressure to keep me grounded. "But the opposite way. It shocked me when I went to college and saw how all these city kids lived. They were miserable, chasing some lost dream of success—so lonely and soulless."

"Do you think I'm like that?"

"I don't think anyone's really like that." Nick's breath tickled my ears. "But I think it's easy in a city to get caught up in the superficial, caring about things that don't really matter. I've done it for the last decade. It's why I need to move back here."

The abyss stirred inside me, and I squeezed my eyes shut. My next words tore out of me like a confession. "I don't want to go back."

Nick's hand tightened against my shoulder. He said nothing for a moment, just kept holding me. "Then don't."

At that, I pulled away. I looked at him, this perfect man who seemed to be drawn to me just as much as I was drawn to him. But I shook my head, shoving the feeling down, and returned to reality. "I couldn't."

"Why not?" Nick was calm, but his voice was insistent.

I curled my arms around myself. "I have nothing, no skills beyond acting. What could I possibly do in a town like this?"

"Deanna would hire you in a heartbeat if you stayed."

I blinked. He couldn't possibly know that. "She told you that herself?"

"Trust me." Nick slid his hands back into his pockets, and I felt guilty that he had given me his gloves. "I know she would. She loves you."

I looked up at the dark night sky. "What is it with you and Deanna? You barely know me."

"Elle, you're an open book." Nick gave me a fond smile. "Every emotion is written on your face at all times."

I felt my stomach clench in alarm. "That's… But I try to hide it."

"And maybe you do it with other people. I saw you do it in the bar the other night." Nick shrugged. "But you're honest with us. That's enough to see who you really are."

I clutched my arms tighter around myself. "But I don't even know who I am."

Because that was the crux of it. I'd spent almost my entire childhood, my whole *life*, learning to pretend. Pretending got me praise, got me attention, got me a ticket out of my own small town. But what it hadn't got me was contentment or even fulfillment. Just an empty, empty life, feeling lost and alone.

"I think you do." Nick's voice broke me out of my spiral of thoughts, and he looked at me solemnly. "You've just forgotten."

God, what a horrible thought. But even as Nick said it, I knew it rang true. Somewhere, buried deep inside me, was who I really was, without all the artifice and pretending and people pleasing. But how did I get to her?

I stared at him for a while, thinking. "That was good advice."

He nodded, and his lips quirked up.

"You dealt with that surprisingly well."

"No, I dealt with that like any decent human would."

"Decent." I let out a dark laugh. "I think your definition of decent is different to mine."

"Yeah, I'm seeing that." Nick nudged his head in the direction we had been walking. "Let's get you home."

I was so exhausted and emotionally wrung out; I didn't even bother to correct him. Mistletoe Valley wasn't my home, as much as I might dream it was.

Because a place this perfect, this welcoming, didn't belong to a girl like me. I didn't deserve it.

NICK

Fuck. Fuck. Fucking fuck. I'd made her *cry*.

That was the thought that occupied most of my brain space as I left Elle at Deanna's and walked back to my car. It was the thought that occupied me as I drove back to my home in the hills and parked in the garage. It was the thought that had me wincing as I showered and watched the water go down the drain.

Elle Sutton was dominating my every waking moment, and I worried I would never let her go. Especially not after she said that she didn't want to leave Mistletoe Valley. Until now, I'd been able to convince myself that sleeping with her was a bad idea because she was leaving. But what if she didn't have to?

But fuck it all, I still fucked it up. I'd made her cry.

I know it wasn't all my fault, that there was more under the surface that I'd dredged up for her. Except, if I hadn't said such a provoking thing, it wouldn't have pushed her over the edge. Christ, I was so bad at dealing with people sometimes.

I let the scalding shower water run down my back. My mind turned over every fact, every detail that I knew, trying to work out the best course of action. I had less than three weeks with Elle in Mistletoe Valley, if she left after Christmas.

What if... what if I didn't care if she was leaving? What if I just let myself enjoy being around her and damn the consequences? I couldn't ignore the gravity I felt around her, like it was pulling me into her orbit the more I got to know her.

But maybe, just maybe, Mistletoe Valley was pulling her in, too. I was a soppy idiot, really, for entertaining that hope, but I couldn't help it. I was an adult, I could deal with disappointment and possible heartbreak. But could I deal with it if I remained a coward and just let Elle slip through my fingers?

I turned off the shower. I got out and looked around my enormous bathroom, luxury fixtures exposing the money I had earned as a lawyer. As a corporate lawyer. But did any of that matter, really? I thought I cared about that stuff when I was younger. I didn't anymore. When I wiped the steam off my bathroom mirror, I looked at myself and made a decision. I wasn't just going to keep living my life like this, holding everyone at bay for some distant future where I could finally pursue what I wanted.

For once, I was going to do something simply because I wanted to. I was going to pursue Elle Sutton, because I couldn't get her out of my head, anyway.

The next morning I rang Matt. He picked up on the third ring. "What's up, brother?"

I put him on speakerphone as I fiddled with my hair. "Where do you usually go for dinner when you want to eat out?"

"What sort of dinner?"

"The nice kind."

Silence from the phone, then a sound that was almost laughter. "You mean the date kind, don't you?"

I glared at the phone. "Just answer the question."

Matt howled in response. "I fucking knew it! You're sweet on Elle, aren't you?"

"Matt, if you're not going to be helpful, piss off and go do some CrossFit or whatever." I played with a piece of hair that wasn't behaving and winced. I really was fussing with my appearance.

"First, I don't do that anymore." I could tell he was still sniggering. "Second, you can't blame me for giving you a bit of shit after the way you behaved the other night."

I sighed. "Yeah, I know. I was an idiot."

"Damn right you were, bro." A pause. "But Christ, she's a fucking looker, isn't she?"

"Matt." I warned.

"Alright, I get it. I won't interfere again." Matt chuckled. "That's going to be a real mess if you get involved, though. And you always do. I hope you know what you're doing."

I grumbled to myself as I picked out what clothes to wear. I wanted to look good, but casual. "Seriously, Matt, just answer my first question. I can deal with the rest."

A laugh. "Pierre's Bistro is where you want to go. It opened up a year ago in a cottage near the winery. Got some great views. All that cozy vibe shit that people love."

"Christ, dude, you kiss your mother with the mouth?"

"Sure as hell do, my man." A sniff came from the other line. "Best of luck with that one, bro."

I grunted and hung up. A quick google search gave me Pierre's number, which I saved on my phone. I checked my watch. It was mid-morning, and I was going to ask Elle out to dinner.

And yes, I was going to make it a date. A date with Elle Sutton. Because I wanted to, and I didn't need any other reason.

Deanna let me into her house an hour later, and I gave her a hug. "Nicky. Everything alright?"

"Is Elle here?"

"… She's in the reading room." My godmother gave me a shrewd look.

I turned towards the stairs, but Deanna's hand on my elbow stopped me. I looked down at her with a questioning glance.

Deanna cleared her throat. "I know it's not really my business, but she's been off since you delivered her home last night. What happened?"

I sighed. "Nothing. Everything. She's going through some shit, but I want to help her."

"Nick." Deanna said softly. "She's only here for the month."

I pressed my lips together and gave my godmother a smile. "I know. But I still want to help her. She needs it."

"She deserves more than just being another charity case of yours."

I cut an offended look at Deanna. "I enjoy her company. I'm spending time with her because I want to."

Deanna's eyebrows raised slightly, then she gazed at me proudly. "Alright. I just wanted to make sure you knew what you were doing."

I slid my hands into my pockets and looked up the stairs. "Actually, I've got no idea what I'm doing, but I'm okay with that. I'm trying out this thing where I don't plan too much."

Deanna gave me a look of approval. "I'm happy to hear that, love. I'm going to go for a walk."

And Deanna was gone, leaving me to look up the stairs. There was a strange feeling that my destiny was waiting up there. I didn't need to be thinking like that. I just needed to focus on the moment in front of me.

I climbed the steps and took a breath before I knocked on the door to the reading room.

Elle's soft voice came through the door. "Deanna?"

I opened it and saw Elle curled up in an armchair, facing the window, bathed in morning sunlight. She was in fluffy pajamas, and she still managed to look like a goddess. My heart wrenched a little in my chest, but she hadn't seen me yet. "Not Deanna, unfortunately."

Elle jerked upright and turned her head to face me. "Nick? What are you doing here?"

I swallowed. "I came to check you were alright after last night."

Elle breathed out and sank back into her chair. A faraway expression came over her face, and she looked so vulnerable.

I wanted to hug her. I wanted to crawl to her and beg her forgiveness for upsetting her. I wanted to do a lot of ridiculous things. My fingers twitched.

Elle looked out the window. "I'm alright."

There was vulnerability under her words. My hand clenched involuntarily. "You've got the day off, don't you?"

Elle smiled. "Yeah. I was just going to wallow and read a book. I'll be fine."

I leaned against the doorjamb to stop myself from going to her and pulling her into a hug. "Do you have room for something else?"

Elle's eyes darted to me, and I was relieved to see something other than quiet sadness in them. "What do you mean?"

I crossed my arms, suddenly scared. "Come to dinner with me?"

Elle straightened slightly, and she blinked. "You want… dinner, with me?"

I nodded slowly. There wasn't any distaste in her eyes yet, just disbelief, and I gave her a moment to process.

"Dinner," she repeated.

"Yeah." I huffed. "Dinner. Just you and I."

"So, like a—" Elle's eyes widened slightly.

"Yeah. One of those." My lips twitched and my stomach clenched. If she said no, I'd have to be okay with that.

Elle's fingers fiddled with the blanket on her lap. She shook her head in disbelief. "What's changed?"

I looked out the window for a moment, wanting to choose my words wisely. This moment, and how I spoke, mattered. "Last night helped me realize something."

"You mean when I was crying all over your nice sweater?"

"Yeah." I smiled at her. "I've spent a lot of my life since college holding everyone at a distance so that I could achieve my goals. But I don't want to do that here. Not with you."

She settled back into the cushions and waited, knowing I had more to say.

I cleared my throat. "I think we can help each other."

"With what?"

"Let's work out who Elle Sutton is." I said, the words falling off my tongue. "You said you didn't know who you were. We've got till Christmas. I reckon you and I could work it out."

"And what do you get out of it?" Elle's eyes were so big, I almost lost my train of thought.

I shrugged, feeling the anticipation of spending more time with her running through my body. "I need help too."

"With what?"

"Working out who Nick Corrigan is if he's not a big city corporate lawyer." I gave her a wry smile.

Elle eyed me with something that looked like suspicion, but her lips were curling into a smile. "You make a convincing argument."

"Baby, I'm literally trained to be good at arguments." I noticed the way she flushed slightly at the endearment, and suddenly all I could think about was the ways I could make her flush like that again, whispering delicious things into her ear. I swallowed.

She gave me a reproachful look. "You really want to go to dinner with me?"

"Absolutely." I clenched my jaw, hoping she was about to say yes.

Elle chewed on one of her fingers and then decided, smiling softly. "Alright. Where are we going?"

"I think I'll keep it a surprise, if that's okay with you." I crossed the room to her and handed her my phone. "Put your number in there, so I can text you when I'll pick you up."

Her eyebrows raised. "We're driving somewhere?"

"Not far." I took my phone back and gave myself a second to gloat that I had her number. "But we can't walk there."

Elle bit her lip, and I got immediately jealous that her teeth got to do that whenever they wanted. "What should I wear?"

I shrugged. Christ, it was so hard to act casual around her. "That's your choice. Wear what Elle Sutton wants to wear."

She laughed dryly. "Right. And what if Elle Sutton wants to wear pajamas?"

"Then she could wear that." I shrugged and gave her a once over. "If they're anything like what you're wearing right now, I'd be thrilled."

Elle flushed and settled back into the cushions, her eyes amused. "Hilarious."

"It's not really a joke." I shoved my hands in my pockets to stop myself from reaching out and playing with a strand of her soft hair. "I don't want you to do anything just because you think it'll please me or anyone else."

Her face sharpened slightly, and my stomach clenched at the sultry look in her eyes. "Really? Nothing at all that might please you?"

I clenched my jaw nearly tight enough to break a tooth. "Dinner. I'm taking you to dinner."

Elle rested her cheek on her hand. "Don't tell me you're trying to be chivalrous."

"No." I retreated to the door, suddenly aware that if I didn't put distance between us, I might try to fuck the sad look out of her eyes. And that wasn't the right way to play this situation at all. "But I am trying to be kind, and doing what I want with you isn't exactly in the spirit of kindness."

"What do you want to do with me?" She breathed, her lips parted slightly. Christ, I was getting hard just looking at her. My brain created images of her splayed out on my bed, of finding all the ways I could make her moan, and I inhaled quickly.

I shook my head and calmed myself down. "See you tonight."

I felt her eyes follow me out the door, and my stomach clenched again. Dinner. My focus had to be on dinner and getting to know her better. I couldn't hope for anything more, no matter how much my dick wanted to.

ELLE

I was going on a date with Nick Corrigan. Of all the plot twists the universe could have given me, this one truly took the cake. After he left, I stared at the door in disbelief. After last night, I thought I might have scared him off, or even worse, made him realize I was just too much of a mess. But no, he'd asked me on a goddamn *date*.

I knew that I was a mess, the more I looked inside myself. Somehow, though, that wasn't scaring Nick Corrigan away. He wanted me to be myself, wanted to help me figure out who I was. What an odd thought.

I spent the morning reading, but couldn't get comfortable in my chair after Nick left. What would I wear? What should I expect?

Most importantly, how the fuck was I meant to be myself?

By lunchtime, I had tied myself into knots in my mind, imagining what the evening would bring. I was equal parts nervous and excited, and I hated it.

But something had come awake inside me, and I couldn't help but feel a little… pleased. Someone had seen how much of a mess I was… and was still interested in a date with me? As a woman who had spent most of her adult life caring deeply about her appearance, I couldn't help but panic. I didn't know how to not care.

I was rooting through my wardrobe when Deanna knocked at my open bedroom door. I froze, half enveloped in my clothes, and gave her a smile.

Deanna crossed her arms, but didn't have any judgement on her elegant face. "Everything alright?"

I pulled myself out of the pile and grimaced. "Yep."

"Going somewhere?"

I sat down on the bed in a huff. "Why—Why would you ask that?"

"No reason." Deanna nodded her head at the bed. "Except for the fact that you've thrown half your wardrobe onto the bed. Particularly the nice dresses."

I looked down at the bed, then back at Deanna. Something choked up my throat, and I put my head in my hands. "I can't go anywhere if I don't know what to wear."

Deanna hummed and sat next to me on the bed. "I haven't seen you struggle with decisions this whole week. What's changed?"

After taking a breath, I let it go. "I don't know how to be real. I don't even know who I am," I mumbled into my hands.

"Okay." Deanna shifted on the bed. "Has Nick had anything to do with this crisis of faith in yourself?"

"What do you mean?"

Deanna gave me a sly look. "I let him in this morning."

"Yes. No." I groaned and stared at the ceiling. "It's not him. Not really."

I felt the bed move and looked up to see Deanna standing, looking over the dresses. "I'm guessing this is for some sort of dinner?"

I side-eyed Deanna. "Possibly."

"I wasn't born yesterday, love." Deanna tilted her head at the bed. "Would it help if I chose?"

I got up off the bed and stared down at my options with Deanna. "I don't know."

"The purple is lovely."

I covered my face with my hands. "I hate it."

"Why do you have a dress you hate?"

"My agent said I needed a party dress in every color." I deflated when I said that, realizing just how many of my life choices were influenced by someone else telling me what to do. God, how had I not seen this before? I leaned back against the wall and glared at the purple dress. It became a symbol of my own stupidity, of my own desperation.

Deanna saw my expression and, gratefully, said nothing about my obvious existential crisis. Instead, she examined the dresses one by one and looked out the window. Finally, she said, "It took me twenty years into my adulthood to realize that all I had been doing was pleasing other people. I had done very well pleasing them, got many awards and accolades and adoration, but I was not doing it for myself."

I stared at her, the cogs in my head turning. Was Deanna saying that she was... like me? But that couldn't be right.

Everything I'd seen of her, how people talked about how she had been… unless that was all an act too? I swallowed. "How did you know? How do you stop it?"

Deanna exhaled. "I achieved something I thought I had always wanted, only to realize that I didn't care at all. So I stopped doing it, all of it. It was slow, and it was painful. I washed up here, looking for community and purpose and joy. And I found it."

"I don't know how to do that." I whispered.

Deanna came up and clutched my shoulder. "Habits might be hard to change, but it is much harder to wake up and realize that you have lived your life for other people."

"But… how?"

Deanna nodded down to the pile of clothes. "You start. Start with simply making a choice, and getting rid of all the voices that judge it inside your head…"

Start. I looked down at the dresses, representing a lifetime of pleasing and pretending, all for other people. God, it would be so much easier if Deanna just told me what to wear. But that was the problem, wasn't it? I'd been listening to people tell me what to do so much that they became voices in my head that governed every decision I made.

Deanna took in a breath. "I'll leave you to it."

I stared down at the dresses, touching each one as if they were relics of my attempts to dazzle everyone around me away from who I actually was. How did I work out what I wanted?

I closed my eyes and chose the first dress my eyes landed on. It was an emerald green a-line, floaty and free. It wasn't much, but it was a start. Voices that sounded like people I knew tried to tell me what was wrong with the choice, but I held firm. I might not know what I actually wanted, but I could at least train myself to ignore those critical voices.

I picked up the dress and breathed out. For the first time in years, all I had was myself, and the rest of my head was silent.

I smiled.

⇝⇝⇝ ⇜⇜⇜

My phone buzzed two hours later, while I was curled up reading again. I'd finally been able to settle myself, and I was enjoying the book a lot. It was a holiday romance, one of those delightful books you could get lost in for a few days and feel better about the world afterwards.

My eyes were reluctant to be dragged away from the page, because the heroine and hero were just getting together to admit their feelings for each other.

That was always the best part.

But my phone buzzed again, and I looked at it.

Unknown number: I'll pick you up at 7. Nick.

I grabbed my phone up and unlocked it. My lips twitched a little as I noticed the way he punctuated every sentence like he was writing an academic paper. I saved his number under Nick in my contacts.

ME: Sounds good :) You know, the text bubbles usually work at punctuation for the end of sentences...

NICK: Force of habit. My boss hates it when we don't properly punctuate our messages.

ME: Ah

NICK: But just for you, I'll try a new thing

ME: Look at you go :)

NICK: Thanks. It makes my eye twitch now to not use full stops.

ME: I hear eye drops are good for those things

NICK: Thanks for the recommendation. I've got a zoom meeting for the rest of the afternoon. I'll see you at 7.

ME: Okay :)

NICK: By the way, you might want to look outside if you haven't already.

I sighed and sank back into the armchair. I turned my face to the window, then sat up straighter. Whiteness fell in delicate flakes from the sky.

It was finally snowing.

⫷⫸⫷

It took me less than three minutes to throw on my long puffer coat and boots and race downstairs to the front yard. The snow fell gently, and it was just beginning to stick to the ground and bushes.

I tipped my head up to the sky and closed my eyes. I had memories of being a kid, playing in the snow during rare holidays in the mountains. It had never snowed in my hometown, not even in the coldest winters.

Suddenly, all I wanted to do was run, shrieking through the streets again, making snowballs and pelting them at people. I wanted to lie in the snow and make an angel. I wanted to make snowmen and drink hot cocoa huddled under a tree.

I wanted to feel joy—unfettered joy again—like I had when I was a child. I was allowed to want that, and I was allowed to do what it took to feel it again.

I stuck out my tongue, and a snowflake landed on it. I could do this, I thought. I could find a way back to joy, a way back to my true self.

⋙ ⋘

When Nick showed up at seven, I was ready. I had spent a bit of time on my appearance, curling my hair and applying makeup. It brought me pleasure, the idea of looking good for Nick. Not because it was an expectation, but because it was fun. He didn't even make it to the door, because I saw him from upstairs and beat him to it. I nearly tripped down the stairs, waving to Deanna as I went. She sent me a grin and a wave.

I was excited to see him, excited to explore who I was, excited because I was doing something just because I wanted to.

I opened the door and watched as his eyes took me in. His lips curved into a smile. "I'd say I'm disappointed you didn't go with pajamas, but that one looks just as fun."

Because some long hidden joy had unlocked beneath me, I gave him a twirl. The green velvet skirt ruffled around me, and I caught his eyes as they trailed my legs. I sized up his clothes. "You're dressing... softer than you were when we first met."

He leaned against the doorjamb and fiddled with a cuff of his black coat. I took a moment to appreciate the way his cream turtleneck sweater sculpted around his body. It looked great, but it was a stark contrast to the sharp three-piece suits he wore in the first days of his arrival. The man could *dress*. He cleared his throat. "Let's just say being back home helps remind me to be a little more... relaxed."

I leaned against the door and crossed my arms. "I like it."

"Yeah." A laugh rumbled out of him, like he was surprised at my brazenness. "I can tell."

I gave him a coy smile, pleased to realize that it wasn't an act. With Nick, it was almost like he wrung honesty out of me without meaning to. "Do you want to stand here forever, or shall we go?"

Nick cleared his throat and pulled himself away from the door. "You got a coat?"

I pulled my white wool coat from behind the door. "Now I do."

"I know I said that it was going to be a surprise, but if you hate it, we can go somewhere else." Nick flashed me a smile as we walked to his car.

I beat him to my door and opened it myself. God, that felt good. Sometimes, I liked men opening doors for me, but sometimes, I hated it. Nick just gave me another smile and shrugged. "Don't like doors being opened for you?"

"Only sometimes."

"Noted." He didn't look at all bothered.

I slid into his car and took a moment to appreciate it. The seats were heated leather, and I snuggled into them, realizing I'd never been in a car this luxurious before. I was once again reminded that Nick had worked as a corporate lawyer for the last five years of his life. When he got in, I eyed him. "Nice car."

Nick chuckled, but his face was dark. "Yeah. I guess when you work for the devil, you've got to get some payoffs."

"You really hate it, don't you? Working for them." I said softly.

Nick gave me a pained look. "It served a purpose."

"That makes it sound even worse."

"Yeah." Nick turned on the engine. "But I always knew it wasn't forever."

"So you're doing it, then? Moving back?"

He kept his gaze on the road, but his lips twitched. "I'm negotiating a lease. Matt found a good place for me, and it will be mine in January. I've got all the business paperwork for the firm."

"You've been keeping it a secret." I realized.

Nick made a small nod. "I'm telling everyone in town during the Christmas Ball."

I felt my jaw drop. "Sorry, there's a Christmas ball?"

Nick laughed, and I loved the way it lit up his face. "I'm sure Deanna has a ticket for you. She always buys extras."

"Where do they hold it?"

"The big old bank building to the north of the town square?" When Nick saw my nod, he went on, "Council owns it, and they decorate the whole thing. People travel for it."

"I'm sure they do." The car slowed, and we turned the corner to a small road winding up a hill, manicured trees running on either side. At the top sat a two-story cottage, festooned with strings of lights and a sign that said *Pierre's Bistro*. "Oh."

"Oh?" Nick parked the car in an available spot and turned off the ignition.

I exhaled, feeling something inevitable land in my stomach. "Just when I think this town is done being something out of a literal *storybook*…"

"I've got a confession to make." Nick gave me a contrite look, and I frowned.

"What?"

"I've never been here either."

I burst out laughing, relieved that was the only thing he was telling me. God, I thought he had been about to say he had a *wife* or something. That really would have been a plot twist.

Nick gave me a questioning look. "What?"

I waved a hand at him. "This place is gorgeous. Why haven't you been?"

Nick shrugged. "I was always busy on visits. It's been a while since I've had time to relax."

"Good." I gave him a soft look. "I think you deserve to enjoy nice things."

His face twitched like he was about to do something, but he twisted around and left the car. I smiled to myself, pleased to have stirred such a powerful reaction with just my words.

I got out of the car and looked up at the sky, the snow still falling gently around us. Nick stood at my side and slid his hands into his coat. The surrounding air was frigid, but I didn't mind a few seconds savoring the snow after the toasty car.

I felt Nick watching me as I smiled up at the sky. "You like snow?"

"I haven't seen much of it in my life."

"It suits you."

I raised a single eyebrow at him. "Snow suits me?"

Nick just kept looking at me, his eyes dark with intensity. "Yeah. You look like you belong in it."

"You saying I'm cold?" I smiled at him softly and took a small step towards him without meaning to.

He angled his head down with a small smile. "No."

"Then what?"

"It's nice seeing you smile like that."

I blinked at him, confused.

"Your smile changes when you think no one is watching." Nick's eyes roved over my face, and I held my breath. "It's brighter, and real."

I held still as he reached out a hand and brushed some snow from my hair, the white clumps almost blending in with my blonde hair. I wanted to ask him to do it again, to drag his hands softly through my hair until I was asleep. I wanted to move closer and hug into his warmth like I had last night.

I wanted a lot of things, but my stomach rumbled. I needed food. After that, maybe I could finally do some of those things I wanted so badly.

I took off towards the door of the restaurant, quiet chatter coming from the building. "I'm starving, so I suppose we need to go inside for that."

I looked behind me to see Nick watching me with an unreadable expression, the ghost of a smile on his lips.

Something burned inside me—a fire had been lit since I'd arrived in this town, since I'd met Nick Corrigan. I wondered how I'd ever put it out.

⤙⟫⟩⟩⟩ ⟨⟨⟨⟨⤚

I moaned softly for the third time in as many minutes, savoring the flavor of ginger pudding in my mouth. Nick watched me with sharp eyes and a smile, and I held my hand up in an apology. "I'm a sucker for desserts."

"I've gathered that." Nick drank from his glass of red, but had barely touched his own plate. "I think I'm getting more enjoyment watching you eat yours than I ever could eating my own."

The last hour had been one of the most enjoyable dates of my life. Even better than that, though, was that it didn't even feel like I was on a *date*. I cared more about what Nick had to say than if I was sitting just right, or if I had angled my face the prettiest way. He made me feel comfortable, and I could tell he felt the same around me.

But I was leaving in less than a month.

That thought cooled all of the enjoyment of my dessert, and I looked down at the table.

Nick noticed the change. "Alright?"

"Nick…" I clenched a hand in my napkin. "I'm leaving in a few weeks."

"I know."

"And you have to stay." I said firmly. "You can't—"

"And I won't." He promised. "But what's wrong with doing something a little stupid, for once?"

"This isn't stupid for me." I shook my head. "But it's…"

I couldn't finish the sentence, but Nick pushed me anyway "Say it."

"It's a lot." *I feel a lot for you already*, is what I really wanted to say.

Somehow, I got the feeling Nick understood the subtext. Of course he did. He always had with me. He just nodded. "What do you want to do?"

The question could be about so many things. What did I want to do with the evening? What did I want to do with Nick? What did I want to do with my *life*? "I don't know enough about Elle Sutton to answer such a big question."

"Tonight, then. What does she want to do?"

I looked at Nick Corrigan, at his sharp eyes, his soft hair, the way his sweater stretched across his chest, and I knew the answer to that. I didn't have to question it, because my insides were on *fire*. Even if my head lied, I knew with no uncertainty that I wanted Nick Corrigan. I wanted him in whatever way I could, for however long I could. "You said you had a house here, didn't you?"

"I did." Nick's eyes held mine, and a moment passed between us, sexy as all hell. He knew what I was about to say, but was waiting for me to say it, for me to make the request.

I tilted my head at him. "Care to show it to me?"

Nick's answering smile was almost predatory. "I'd love to."

ELLE

The car ride was almost unbearable—the most deliciously tense ride I'd ever taken. I squeezed my legs together, taking quick breaths to still my thundering heart. Thank God it was a short trip, and soon we were driving up a winding driveway to a house that was tucked into the hillside—solid brick with massive windows. Nick's house. It was gorgeous, just like almost every other building in this town.

I didn't spend long admiring the building because I leapt out of the car the moment it stopped. Nick followed me, and I could tell his eyes were tracking my every movement. I trailed up the path to the front door and spun around to Nick once I was at the top of the stoop stairs. "Nice house."

Nick walked towards me slowly and stopped on the step just below me. It brought us almost to eye level with each other, and I felt heat warm my belly. "Seen all you need to see?"

I heard the hidden question in his words, knowing he was giving me a reason to back out. He was always giving me a choice, always. Another piece of me thawed, and I shook my head. Anticipation curled in my belly.

Nick's eyes darkened, and his breath puffed around me in a cold cloud. "I need to hear you say it, Elle."

I held his eyes, caught in them. "Take me inside, Nick."

I'm not sure who moved first, but we exploded into action. He stepped up into my space and curled his fingers around my jaw, bringing my face to his. I grabbed the collar of his coat and closed my eyes just as his lips met mine.

His lips were warm and soft and *everything*. Nick backed me into the front door, using his arms to cushion the blow. His hands came down around my hips, under the backs of my thighs. I jumped up and wrapped my legs around his waist, desperate to press my body closer to his, always closer—

God, we fit so well together, and I parted my lips slightly to let him in. Our tongues danced together, and I wanted so much more.

I felt him fumble with the key, and I arched my back to help him. He broke away from me for a moment so that he could fit the key inside and grumbled in frustration that he couldn't do two things at one. I laughed into his jaw.

I had never been more relieved than when he finally unlocked the door.

Nick carried me inside and set me down briefly to rip off his coat. I did the same with mine, and then we crashed together again, like gravity pulled us together. The fire was burning so hot inside me now, and I was panting like an animal in heat against his lips. Nick wasn't doing much better, and he nearly ran us into his sideboard as he guided us towards the stairs.

In hindsight, we were never going to make it up the stairs in one go.

My foot stumbled against a step, and we fell down together. Nick broke our fall with his arms.

I tipped my head back and laughed, and he trailed searing kisses down my neck. My laughter turned to soft pants quickly after that. I could already feel myself getting wet—could feel the hot desire curling in my core growing.

I shoved my hands under his sweater, roving them over the gloriously warm skin I found— sculpted and thick. I pressed my fingers into his skin, gripping and pulling him closer.

Nick pulled back. "Elle—"

I chased his lips and pulled him back down for another kiss, humming in my throat. I didn't want to talk; I wanted more—

He broke away with a huff and gripped my scalp to keep me still. Somewhere—in a dark corner of my brain—I started purring. I bit my tongue and let him speak. "Do you want the bedroom?"

I arched my back to push against him. "I want you."

Nick closed his eyes and nudged my forehead with his nose. "Elle—"

"Soon." I reached my hands up his neck and tried to pull him back to me. "Not now."

That seemed to be enough persuasion for him, because he kissed me again with ferocity and pulled one of my legs up to wrap around his waist. The movement brought us closer, and he sank further between my legs.

My still-unfortunately-clothed legs, because I wanted to be naked five minutes ago. I ripped one of my hands off Nick's body to flutter around the hem of my dress, but I couldn't pull it up while he was between my legs.

His hands skirted up my hips, helping me. He pulled away from the kiss and thumbed the dark fabric. "This dress—"

"Do you like it?" I whispered, desperate for him to tell me he liked it, to tell me I had pleased him. It wasn't a requirement, it was a want.

He groaned against my mouth. "Yes. But I'd like you in anything."

I huffed out a laugh, and he trailed his lips down my neck again until he reached the sweetheart neckline of my dress. He mouthed at the edge of the fabric, and I whined. "Nick—"

"Can I?"

"Please." I begged so easily for him, and I didn't mind at all.

He didn't keep me waiting, and pulled my dress and bra down, revealing my breasts to him. "Christ, baby."

I preened under the attention, no self-consciousness to be seen. No—tonight, I was burning too hot to care about anything but the man in front of me. "Nick—"

I didn't need to ask him twice. He bowed his head against my sternum, his hands coming up to circle my breast. Slowly, he laved kisses over my flesh, working towards the hard peak of my nipple. I panted, waiting and waiting, and then he finally closed his lips over the tip in a luscious kiss that had me whining. He gripped my body so I couldn't writhe away, and gave equal attention to the other. He left a wet trail over my chest, and my skin prickled into goosebumps from the pleasure and the cold air.

I groaned, and he chuckled. In a distant corner of my mind, I was amused by how easily Nick had turned me into a panting, needy mess.

But a larger, louder part just wanted more and more and *more*.

I think I must have said the last part out loud, because Nick groaned and slipped a hand down my thigh. "You want more, baby?"

I locked eyes with him and nodded, my brow creasing together.

He held my gaze as he gave me a sly smile, and pushed my dress up around my hips, revealing the top of my stockings, garter and panties. He groaned when he saw them. "You've been wearing these all night."

A coy smile spread across my face. "Yeah."

Nick spread my legs further apart and trailed a hand up my inner thigh. My legs shook from the anticipation, and Nick made a sound that was almost a groan, almost a laugh. "Want me to touch you?"

"Please."

"Want to hear you say it, baby." His voice was firm, but held the hints of his own desire, his own desperation.

I whined, and he shushed softly into my ear. A flush broke out over my chest, my face, like I really was about to burn up. I inhaled and swallowed. "Please, Nick. Please touch me."

"That wasn't so hard, was it?" He whispered into my ear.

And then his fingers, his clever, clever fingers, finally pushed aside my panties and dragged along the core of me, right where I was hot and wet and waiting for him. It was—I clutched my hands into his sweater and squeezed my eyes shut for a moment.

"Christ, you're so wet." He sounded almost pained.

"Uh-huh," was all I could manage.

Slowly, agonizingly, he slid a finger into me. Then another. The stretch made me gasp, but I was wet enough that he slid in easily. His thumb found my clit, and I felt my internal walls flutter around him. He inhaled. "Good?"

I nodded, trying to hold his gaze and failing because my eyes kept squeezing shut. "Y-yeah. More. Please."

He huffed and slid his other hand back into my hair, gently pinning me in place. I could move if I wanted, but it was the suggestion of control—the hint of his ability to keep me pinned—that had me clenching around his fingers. His eyes tracked my face and his lips curved up. "Like this?"

I hummed in confirmation, unable to say anything more because his fingers were moving, delicious movements inside that had me clenching, had me gasping, had me flushing from head to toe.

His fingers filled me up, while his thumb pressed gentle circles into my clit, and it was—

I was going to come. That realization, coupled with the intense, passionate way he was watching me, built me up even further—until I was squirming—until I was crying out softly, and Nick was muttering little words of praise to me.

He held me so beautifully, played my body so well, and it caught me up in the current and took me away. The pleasure was almost overwhelming, given how quickly it had come on. "Nick, I'm gonna—"

"Good." Nick pressed a kiss into my temple and kept going. "Let it happen, baby."

My leg muscles tensed first, then my abdominals. My toes curled, and I held my head up, trying to hold his gaze as he brought me to climax. His eyes were so beautiful.

His thumb brushed against my clit just so, and I was gone, panting and writhing and sobbing through my orgasm. I squeezed my eyes shut, and could see white all around me.

Nick slowed down his hand and worked me through it, dragging it out and soothing me with kisses to my temple. I clutched at his shoulder, weak tremors running through my body, and I squeezed my eyes shut. In less than five minutes, Nick had already worked out how to make me come.

No other guy I had slept with had managed that, *ever*. I thought it would be impossible to find someone who understood my needs, who understood what I wanted and how to give it to me, without me having to coach them through it.

When my body relaxed, I laughed. Nick gave me a questioning look. "Alright?"

"Alright?" I repeated, covering my face with my hands. "That was more than alright."

"Good." Nick slowly slid his fingers out of me, and my legs twitched at the movement. Aftershocks of my sudden orgasm ran through my body. I nearly whined at the emptiness, but

Nick gave me a look that said he wasn't anywhere near done with me. He kissed my knee. "Do you need a minute?"

A smile curled over my lips. "Nope."

Nick flashed me an answering smile that was downright wicked. "Good."

And then he was kissing down the flesh of my inner thigh, and my jaw dropped. "N-Nick?"

He stopped a few inches from my core. "May I?"

I nodded—a little apprehensive. He looked…eager, like he wanted to devour me whole. With another smile, he went straight in, pressing hot mouthed kisses right against me, and I couldn't help but squeak and flop back onto the stairs. His lips sealed around my clit and *sucked*—

His mouth was so hot, pressing right against where I needed it. It was like he was starving, and I was the meal he had been waiting for. My thighs shook, and I choked on my breath, my chest splotchy from the pleasure.

When I started writhing against him, he groaned and clutched my thighs further apart. He spread a hand across my pelvis and held me in place, and I was pinned against his mouth, helpless against the onslaught of pleasure.

He brushed his lips just so over my clit, and I threw my head back and whined—

I was going to come again, mere minutes after my first. The thought was washed away quickly in waves of pleasure, and I was tensing again, my toes curling. "Nick—"

I grabbed his hand and clutched it in mine, squeezing hard. He moaned into me, and pleasure wracked my body. This orgasm was even more intense than the first, and I writhed and cried out from the pleasure-pain of it.

As I crested and came down from my second climax, I dragged my free hand down my face. "Jesus."

Nick rose from between my thighs and brushed the back of his hand against his mouth. "Not quite."

I closed my eyes and tried to laugh at his joke, but it ended up sounding like a breathy whine instead. "I—"

"Bedroom?"

"Please." The stairs were digging into my back, and I wanted to be somewhere comfortable. My body felt wrung out and sated, but nowhere near over. I tried to sit myself up and failed. All the muscles in my body were twitchy, shaky things. "H—help?"

"Of course." Nick leaned down and picked me right up, cradling me to his body. He was so *strong*. I loved it. I nuzzled into his neck and hummed, half my brain still refusing to work from the bliss of *two* orgasms.

I was vaguely aware of him walking, and then I was being laid against a soft mattress. I stretched out on the silky coverlet and smiled. Nick stood over me, and he looked at me like he wanted to destroy me. In a good way.

Despite two orgasms, I was hungry all over again. I sat up and reached for the belt of Nick's pants, but he stopped me with a firm hand. "You sure you're good to keep going?"

I gave him an amused look. "Why wouldn't I be?"

Nick shrugged, a sly smile rising on his face. "I don't know. Maybe it's that I made you come twice in a row."

I looked down at the obvious hard-on he was sporting in his pants and met his eyes again. "You have had none."

"Yeah." Nick gave me a look. "That doesn't matter at all if you don't want to keep going."

Something seized in my heart. None of the other men I had slept with had stopped to check if I wanted to keep going. None of them. I had always just assumed that once I had started sex it was unthinkable to stop—at least until the guy had come.

My brows drew together. Yet another thing to add to the list of things I had learned that was wrong, yet another thing that I had never done just for *myself*.

Nick caught the change in my face. "We can stop. If that's what you want."

Except I didn't want that. I wanted to keep going, even more now that he had given me the option, had given me that agency. It was like him respecting my boundaries made me *need* to fuck him even more.

I sat straighter, sending him a stern look. "Trust me. I really, really don't want that."

Nick's lips twitched. "Good. Roll over."

I cocked my head at him. "Why?"

"I want to undo that pretty dress so I don't rip it off you," he said simply. "Roll over."

I narrowed my eyes slyly and did as he asked, rolling onto my belly. "So bossy."

Nick leaned over me and grazed the shell of my ear with his lips. "I think you like me being bossy. Or was I wrong?"

A shiver ran up my spine and I arch back into him slightly. I had to hide my face in my elbow to answer him. "No."

"Didn't think so." Nick chuckled and slowly unzipped the back of my dress, sliding his fingers over my skin as he pulled the sleeves over my shoulder. He undid my bra, too, and then tapped me to roll over again.

I did so, and watched him with hooded eyes as he pulled the dress down my body, as he dragged my bra down my arms. It left me in my underwear and stockings, but I stopped him by sitting up.

I gave him a canine smile. "I think it's time you did some undressing."

Nick flashed a smile at me. He gestured down at his sweater. "Want me to do the honors, or will you?"

"I will." God, I loved how much he kept checking in with me, and it sent more pleased flushes down my spine. I got up and kneeled on the bed before him, and pulled his sweater over his head.

When it was gone, I took a moment to revel in his beautiful body. It was clear he worked out, all of his muscles toned and flexing with his breath. I wanted to nibble on his pecs, wanted to sink my hands into his hips. I trailed a hand down the center of his chest and watched as his muscles twitched in response. He caught my hand as I trailed it down. "Like what you see?"

I gave him a smug look. "If I'd known you were this pretty under your clothes, I would have jumped you ages ago."

"You tried." Nick chuckled, reminding me. "I didn't let you."

"Lucky me, then." I pulled my hand from his and started on his belt. I eyed the bulge in his pants with eagerness, knowing that he and I were about to get much better acquainted. I undid his zipper and then brushed my hand over his erection, still trapped in his boxers.

Nick inhaled, and I did it again. He grabbed my hand. "Not right now. I want to fuck you properly."

I sidled closer to him on the bed, me kneeling and him standing on the edge. I leaned my head up to his ear and said, "Then why don't you?"

Nick curled a hand around my jaw and pulled me in for a deep kiss. I could taste myself on his lips from minutes ago, and I moaned a little into his mouth. I trailed my hands down to his hips again, but he growled in warning and pushed me back to lie on the bed. He finally pulled off his boxers, and I fell back with a pleased laugh.

I stared, and stared a little more, a smile curling onto my lips. He looked like he was going to fit perfectly, like he was going to fill me up just right. I bit my lip and spread my legs for him, begging him without words to just fuck me already.

He kneeled between my legs and unsnapped the garters of my stockings, and I helped him undo the garter and throw it away. Then, he slid my panties off my legs, but he left my stockings on while he grabbed a condom from the nightstand, leaning over me to do it.

I snatched the condom from his hands, eager to get my hands on him in any way I could. I tore the foil and finally got to touch the length of his cock as I rolled the condom on him. I looked up at him and grinned.

Everything was ready.

He gave me a wicked smile back, and pushed me back onto the bed, covering me with his body. My legs perfectly cradled his hips, and he swiped a gentle hand through my core, checking I was wet enough. After coming twice, I definitely was, and began panting in anticipation. "Nick—"

"I know, baby. Just gotta make sure." Nick pressed a kiss against my forehead and something clenched in my stomach. I felt so soft and burning inside, and I just wanted him to—

The head of his cock pushed against my entrance, and my jaw fell open. Slowly, slowly, he pushed himself into me, and Nick gripped the side of my face to keep me looking at him.

As if I could look anywhere else but his eyes, alight with the same fire that burned in me.

He kept pushing in and in, inch after inch, my body stretching and pulling to accommodate him. My neck flushed, my legs shook, and I gasped a little when he pushed the last inch in. We fit perfectly together.

Nick dropped his forehead onto mine, giving me a moment to adjust to his size. "Good?"

I nodded, brows puckering. Good wasn't even the right word, it was everything.

Nick kissed my forehead. "Good."

And he pulled out and pushed himself back into me. My eyes squeezed shut against the friction, and my inner muscles clenched around him. He started a slow, punishing rhythm, easing me into it and making my thighs shake.

I whined, and his hand holding my head tightened. He groaned lightly "You like that, baby?"

Of course I did, and I tried to show him how much I liked it by wrapping my legs tighter around his waist, deepening the angle just slightly. Nick groaned and thrust harder into me.

I mewled at that and clutched at his back to hold on. Every thrust unmade me, every thrust set fire to the thing in my belly, every thrust had me panting and begging and pleading for more.

"More what, baby?" Nick's lips brushed against my ear.

"Harder." I hiccuped around a moan. "P-please."

Nick obliged, and threw his body into his thrusts, until I was seeing stars behind my eyes and crying out. God, it was so good.

He pulled out and rolled me over onto my belly, and I scrambled with my hands to get my bearings, but he just pulled my hips up and thrust back inside.

I sobbed at that, sobbed at the glorious stretch and power he put behind each thrust. He just kept giving and giving and giving, and slowly I felt something build inside me.

I was going to come again. I was going to come around him.

My hands clutched at the sheets and I bit my teeth into the fabric. My body was a maelstrom of sensations, building and building into an unknown crescendo of pleasure I'd never felt before.

I'd never orgasmed with a man inside me before. But with Nick, I realized that anything was possible. My body began tensing and my mouth began babbling. "Please—"

"I'm not going to stop, baby." Nick's grip on my hips was hard, and his pace was unrelenting. He would not stop, wasn't changing his rhythm, just going and going and going until—

My internal muscles seized, and I came around him. Everything went white for a second, and then I was crying out, squirming. My body wasn't sure if it wanted to get away or beg for more. Nick kept going through all of it, pulling more sounds and sensations out of my body.

Eventually, Nick leaned over me, pressing me down into the bed. He quickened his pace, and I could tell he was close to coming. My brain turned feral, and all I wanted was for him to find his release with me. I lifted my head and tried to look back at him. "Nick, please, please, give it to me—"

"You want me to come?" His question came out in a breathy grunt between breaths.

"Please, you've fucked me so good, please, just this one last—"

I didn't need to finish my sentence, because he buried himself to the hilt and grunted against my hair, and I whimpered as he did. I could feel him pulsing inside me, could feel the moment he relaxed into pleasure.

Nick slumped on top of me, but used his elbows to keep most of his weight off. He nuzzled my hair, and we both caught our breath for a minute.

I blinked against the flurry of feelings racing through my body. I wondered if I'd ever actually been *fucked* before. My breath slowed, and I was the first to recover. "Nick?"

"Yeah?"

"When can we do that again?"

Nick laughed into my neck and gave me a gentle kiss. "Soon, baby. Soon."

⤜⤜⤜⤜ ⤛⤛⤛⤛

I woke up an hour later—cuddled up on Nick's chest—and smiled. We'd both dozed off a little while after we'd finished, and I'd only moved from the bed to pee. I brushed my cheek against his chest and wrapped my arm closer around him. I felt so comfortable, so safe, and I couldn't imagine being anywhere else.

Oh.

I couldn't be thinking like that.

I slid myself out of Nick's arms and crept off the bed. I grabbed the nearest thing on the floor, which was Nick's sweater, and pulled it over me. I wasn't even sure what I was doing—where I was going—but I wandered out of the bedroom and into the hallway. Our coats were still lying on the floor when I looked down the stairs.

This was dangerous. I liked Nick Corrigan too much, wanted to never leave this house again, wanted to stay in bed with him forever. Life, the one I'd chosen for myself, didn't allow someone like me to have nice things like this. I would never get to keep it.

Clarity seeped into my brain. I needed to leave before he woke up and I saw his eyes and we did it all over again. So why weren't my feet moving?

I dragged myself over to the hallway window, looking out over all of Mistletoe Valley. Nick's house, perched as it was on the side of the valley, had the most magnificent view. It was like the town was taunting me, showing me everything I could belong to—be a part of—if I only gave in.

But I couldn't. I couldn't stay here forever, no matter how much I may have fallen in love with this place; no matter how strong my sudden feelings were for Nick.

"Penny for your thoughts?" Nick's voice startled me out of my reverie, and I found him standing at the door to the bedroom, wearing sweatpants.

I looked at him and swallowed. I had nothing, no idea how to lie to him.

Nick, as usual, knew exactly what to say. "If you want to leave, I understand."

"It's not that." I didn't want to leave. But I could see the tragedy unfolding, the pain coming ahead of us.

"Then what is it?"

I wrapped my arms around myself. "I *have* to leave."

"And?" Nick shoved his hands into his pockets. "We already agreed we would do what we wanted for a while."

"I don't want to be selfish for a while." I shook my head at him. "I want to be selfish forever."

"Okay." Nick didn't react to my words, and his voice was calm. "It's midnight. Do you *want* to leave?"

"No," I whispered.

Nick gave me a soft smile. "Have a shower with me, then. Stay the night."

Stay the night. I would stay forever if I could, but I couldn't seriously entertain thoughts like that. Staying just one night? I could do that.

I took Nick's outstretched hand and followed him to the bathroom.

NICK

She was going to stay. The fist that had gripped my heart relaxed a little, and I could breathe easier. I had meant it when I said Elle should leave if she wanted, because I only wanted her to be happy. But I would be lying if I said I didn't want her with me, happy.

Christ, it was scary how fast I was falling for her. Especially after tonight, because I've never had better sex in my life. She was everything I ever wanted in a woman. She was witty, and sensitive, and kind, and she was already getting under my skin.

Except, I couldn't let myself get ahead of the situation. Elle was adamant she was leaving, even though I could see in her eyes that she wanted to stay. I could feel the conflict tearing her apart, and I didn't want to be the reason to cause her more pain.

I only wanted to be around Elle if I caused her joy.

Her eyes were soft and wide as I led her into the bathroom and turned on the shower. There was more than enough room for both of us, but I wanted to check that was what *she* wanted. "Do you want to be alone?"

I asked because I knew that the wary look in her eyes could be from indecision, and I didn't want to be confusing her even more. I couldn't—wouldn't—do anything she didn't wholeheartedly want. Even the thought made me feel slightly ill, especially after everything I knew about her. Elle blinked at me, and she slowly smiled. "I really like that you do that."

"Do what?" I asked, even though I had a good idea what she was talking about.

"You ask." Elle uncurled her arms from around herself. "You ask if I actually want to do something."

I leaned against the sink. "I think you've had enough of pleasing other people. I really don't want to be another name on that list."

To my delight, Elle stepped into the space between my legs, and I curled a hand around her hip, just to touch her again. "You're not. You never were. I think because of how we met, it gave me the freedom to act *myself* around you."

"Then I'm selfishly glad I was rude to you that day." I gave her a rueful smile. "Because I'm so lucky I got to see that."

A light flush crept up her cheeks, and I wanted to lean in and kiss her. But I could tell she had something more to say, so I waited. She brushed her fingers in circles on the flat expanse of my stomach. "Okay."

"Okay?" I needed to hear her say whatever decision she'd come to.

"I'll shower with you." She paused and then went on. "I *want* to shower with you."

A smile broke out on my face. "Good."

I gently pulled the sweater—my sweater, I realized with a possessive pang—off Elle, and stepped out of my pants. The water was steaming, and I guided her onto the tiles. There were two streams of water, perfect for two people. Not that I'd had anyone else in this shower before, but I was glad of the design for this very moment.

I caught myself admiring her naked body again, but I tried not to be too lecherous. This moment was about more than just sex, because I wanted her to stay. I wanted to care for her and show her I valued her for who she was, not what she could give me.

Elle looked up at the shower-heads. "I don't think I've ever been in a shower this big."

"Perks of the damned, I guess." I shrugged and nudged her under the larger of the two streams.

Elle laughed, and her gorgeous laugh bounced around the tiled space. "And has it been worth it?"

"It is now." I grabbed some cleanser off my shelf of products. "Do you need this?"

Elle looked down at the cleanser and then back at me. "Did you… get this for me?"

I laughed. "I wish I could say yes, but no. I use it."

Elle held up the white bottle. "*You* use this."

"I like to take care of my skin." I shrugged. "The salesclerk told me it was the best one."

Elle shook her head, smiling. "I don't even use a cleanser this fancy."

"Use it."

Elle gratefully lathered some on her hands and cleaned her face, and I sorted through which of my body soaps I could offer her. "You keep surprising me, Nick."

I stepped back into the stream of hot water. "I mean, that's pretty easy to do when your first impression of me was '*asshole*'."

Elle giggled, and began wetting her hair. "Do you have some soap?"

I stepped into her space and gestured to the body wash in my hand. "May I?"

She flashed her doe eyes at me and smiled. "You may."

I began lathering her back, her arms, her shoulders, and handed her the soap for any other places I couldn't reach. I wanted to touch her, wanted to be close to her, but I could tell that her mind was preoccupied right now. I didn't want to push anything onto her, and kept my hands efficient and gentle. She leaned back into me and closed her eyes peacefully. I kissed her temple. "Sleepy?"

"Mmmm." Elle hummed, and I felt the vibrations in my chest. "But I like this."

"Want me to wash your hair?"

"Please." She leaned further back into me, and I could tell she was exhausted.

I poured some shampoo onto my hand and rubbed it into the roots of her hair, massaging her scalp. She went limp against me, and I smiled smugly to myself.

Some men, the stupid ones, thought the way to a woman's heart was by buying her shit, or fucking her hard in bed, or some other egotistical idiocy. They always got it wrong. This, right here, was the best thing in existence. A woman, relaxed and at peace in my arms because she felt safe. It was something I had missed out on for a long time because of my work.

But not anymore. I would do everything in my power to care for Elle because I didn't want to let her go. I swallowed, banishing the thought.

I rinsed her hair out, applied the conditioner, and then Elle turned around. She tried to reciprocate, but I stopped her by closing my hands around her own. I stared down at her sleepy eyes and brushed a hand over her cheek. "I've got it. You relax."

She gave me a gentle smile. "Thank you."

After a few moments, I had finished washing myself and shut the water off. Elle made a noise as I bundled her up in one of my fluffy towels. "Don't you—do you want to?"

I dried myself off. "I need a bit more information than that."

Elle shuffled over and dropped her head onto my chest. "Did you want to go again?"

I huffed at the ceiling and wrapped my arms around her waist. "You're sleepy. That's more important, I think."

"You take care of me." She grumbled into my skin, and I inhaled quickly.

"It's cause I like doing it." I answered simply. "Do you need something to sleep in?"

"Maybe a shirt?" Elle raised her head and blinked at me. "One of yours?"

"I can get that for you." I smiled fondly at her and brushed some wet hair out of her face, aware I was looking far too smitten. "There's a new toothbrush under the sink. I'll be back."

I extricated myself from her arms and went out into the bedroom, then grabbed pajamas and an old shirt from my closet. I looked down at the clothing strewn across the floor and tidied that up while I was there.

Elle was brushing her teeth when I returned to the bathroom, and my stomach clenched a little at how normal she looked there, like she belonged. I joined her and brushed my own, and I tried not to revel in the domesticity of it. I'd never done this since college, never had someone care enough to be vulnerable around me. But Elle had changed that. She was everything.

After we were done, I offered her an old cotton college shirt, which she slid over her head with a smile. I put my sleep pants back on and guided her back into my bed. The moment I slid under the sheets, she was curling into my side, like she belonged there too.

I stared down at her and took a breath, settling in for sleep.

My last thought before I drifted off was that I never wanted her to leave, either.

ELLE

I woke up the next morning with a warm man curled around me, and a deliciously sated body. That was… unusual. I stretched, rubbing my face into the pillow as memories filtered through my sleep-addled brain. Nick, and the stairs, and the bed, and the shower, and the softness when he'd tucked me into bed.

It really happened, and I was still here. In his bed. I cracked open my eyes, taking in the room, and saw that it was mid-morning.

It was mid-morning.

I jerked out of the bed and scrambled to find my clothes. Someone had folded them neatly on an armchair sitting in the corner, and I realized Nick must have done this during the night. I smoothed a hand over the fabric of my dress, which had been carefully draped over the back of the chair to prevent any creases. Something seized in my heart just looking at it.

I quickly found my phone in one pocket. Several missed messages, a fairly relaxed one from Deanna asking if I was coming home and if she could turn the porch light off. I swore. I sent off a quick apology text and a promise that I would be back home before the rehearsal this afternoon.

I looked back to the bed, only to find Nick already sitting up, looking at me with an unreadable expression in his eyes. I startled slightly, awkward and unsure. "Hi."

The sheets pooled around his waist, and I got a view of his muscles in the light of day. Magnificent, really—and super unfair for a *lawyer* to have such a toned body. He inhaled, and his chest moved with the movement. "Morning."

A flush crept up my throat. "Thank you for folding my clothes."

"Don't mention it." His eyes tracked mine, and another memory from last night flashed in my mind, one where his eyes were above me as he—

I cleared my throat. "I'm—"

"I was going to make breakfast." He interrupted, talking slowly, like I was a deer about to bolt. "If you wanted."

My stomach clenched, wanting him to feed me more than anything else, wanting him to care for me, wanting him to *love* me—

"Only if you wanted." Nick could see my slight panic, and kept his voice even.

"I…" I reflected on why I'd even jumped out of bed, why I'd hurried as if I had somewhere to be. Why? The answer came to me suddenly, and I wanted to smack myself.

I was scared.

Last night had been the most enjoyable, selfish thing I'd done for myself for a while. But old habits die hard, and I felt the need to go straight back to pretending, to playing the game that I'd played for so long. But that wasn't what I wanted to do.

"I want that." I admitted softly. "I'd love that."

Nick got out of bed, and walked over to me. He was only wearing a pair of soft sweatpants, and I swallowed again. Damn him for being so... He smiled at me and shoved his hands into his pockets. "Do you want to eat now?"

And because I knew what would happen if I said no, I said, "Sure." Like a coward. I twisted my hand in the hem of the old shirt Nick had lent me.

Nick shoved a hand through his hair, which was deliciously mussed up, and walked out of the bedroom. "Follow me, then."

Nick's kitchen was enormous. I hadn't got to see it last night, for various reasons, but it was almost too large to be practical for one person.

Not knowing what to do with myself, I jumped up and sat on the island counter, cool marble biting into the bottom of my thighs. "Do you cook much?"

Nick shook his head at me. "I'm only really good at breakfasts and pasta."

I swung my legs slowly as he collected ingredients from the fridge. "Pasta is a good staple to be good at."

Nick laughed softly. "Yeah. It is. What do you like?"

I looked at the ingredients he had before him. "Eggs. Mushrooms. Is that—sourdough?"

Nick nodded and popped some in the toaster. "No bacon?"

I shrugged. "I could go either way with bacon. I don't mind."

"I've never met someone so ambivalent over bacon. Usually they either love it or hate it."

"What can I say—I'm a little weird."

Nick cracked eggs into a hot pan, and sizzling sounds filled the room. "You said it, not me."

I laughed, surprising myself. I really enjoyed his dry humor. "Do you have to do anything today?"

He shrugged, flipping the eggs and sauteing mushrooms. "A few things. They can wait."

My lips twitched. He said it so simply, how he was rearranging his schedule for me. "Are you sure Mistletoe Valley can survive without the guidance of their hero?"

"I'm sure they'll be fine for half a day." His lips twisted into a sarcastic smile.

"Why are you single?" The question blurted out of my lips before I could stop it, and I sat still, incredibly embarrassed.

Nick froze for a moment, then leaned against the opposite counter and gave me a wry look. "I could ask you the same question."

Curiosity burned through my embarrassment. "It's not the same. I'm an actor, and you're a lawyer."

"Our careers don't define who we are, though." He said softly. "You're much more than just an actor."

I sent him a muted smile. "So you're telling me you don't identify as a lawyer in your head?"

"Being a lawyer is what I do." Nick shook his head resolutely. "It's not what I *am*."

"So you're telling me you don't get any joy out of it?"

"I never said that." He turned and stirred the pan. "But if I made my job my identity, I'd be a really unhappy person. Particularly with the work I've been doing the past few years."

Another wall crumbled inside me, another falsely held idea about the world tumbling down. I tucked my hands under my thighs, and my shoulders curled into themselves. "That sounds a lot healthier."

"Look," Nick started, but he sounded hesitant. "I don't want to… tell you how to do anything, or what is best for you. Only you can work that out."

"But?"

"But… I know what Deanna told me about her experience. I know what I've heard from you, about the way you talk about your life in the city. And I don't think calling yourself 'just an actor' is doing you any favors. It's making you miserable."

I stiffened. "You barely know me."

Nick turned the burner off and took the pan from the grill. He placed it down on the countertop beside me and leaned against it with his hands. "We're working out who Elle Sutton is, aren't we? That was just an observation."

I deflated and put my head in my hands. "I'm sorry. I just… get defensive around the actor thing. It's an old habit."

"You're probably used to people dismissing you, right?" Nick crossed his arms and winced. "I did it, too."

"Yeah." I sat up straight. "But you're right, I think. Back in the city, all my actor friends... acting is everything. It's all we allow ourselves to be. Dedicated to the craft and all that bullshit."

Nick put a plate down next to me on the counter and loaded it up with toast, mushrooms, and eggs. "Sounds a little unhealthy to me."

"And being a lawyer is renowned for work/life balance." I rolled my eyes.

"I didn't say I was immune." Nick gripped the counter. "We're talking about you."

"You never answered my question."

"Which one?"

"Why you're single." I picked up a piece of toast and took a bite. It was really good sourdough, better than I'd had in a long time.

Nick exhaled. "You're going to have to elaborate on the question, I think."

I gestured around me. "You have a house like this? And you're actually pretty nice."

Nick chuckled and shook his head. "And?"

"You clearly don't understand how rare that is." I took another bite of toast.

Nick looked up at the ceiling. "I could have a wife locked in the attic."

"And you've read Bronte. You're just proving my point." I gave him a deadpan look.

"I'm really not sure what your point is." Nick smiled softly at his plate.

What was my point? It had started out as an innocent comment, but I didn't feel like that was all it was. Why was he still single? Was there something I didn't know about, some demon of his past that I could use as a way of reassuring myself when it ended? "I'm just curious. How old are you?"

"Thirty."

My eyebrows raised slightly, and a surprised huff came out of my mouth before I could stop it. I vaguely remember Deanna mentioning that, now, and I felt stupid I'd forgotten. "Oh."

Nick's eyes flashed, and he angled his body towards me. "Oh? What's that supposed to mean?"

I laughed under my breath, my cheeks heating. "It's nothing."

"Elle… how old are you?"

I looked at the ceiling and kicked my legs out. "How old do you think I am?"

"Twenty-seven?"

"No money, no prospects…" I mumbled under my breath. "Close enough."

"Okay, Charlotte Lucas." Nick smiled at his plate. "Aside from the Austen reference, how old are you, actually?"

I turned my head to look at him, my brain doing somersaults. "You've watched the 2005 Pride and Prejudice?"

Nick shrugged, chewing on a piece of sourdough. "My girlfriend in college was a literature major. I liked the movie."

"You're just proving my point!" I gestured vaguely at him. "Look at you."

"Fine." Nick chuckled and raised his hands. "I've dated a lot. But the last few years, I've been working too much, and I knew I was coming back here, so I didn't want to get committed to anyone in the city. See? I've answered your question. Now answer mine."

I blew out a breath and hesitated before answering. "I'm twenty-five."

Nick blinked at me, then shook his head. "And you reacted that way when you heard how old I was because…?"

"That's like five, six years." I laughed at the ceiling. "When I was leaving high school, you were graduating from law school."

"You think I'm too old for you?" Nick's eyebrows were raised. "I'm thirty, not exactly geriatric."

I burst into laughter, a flush coming back onto my cheeks. "Cradle-snatcher."

"Right." Nick grinned. "Lemme get the bassinet for you. It's fine, Elle."

My lips twisted into another smile, but I shoved in a mouthful of eggs and mushrooms. We were silent for a few moments, both eating. I closed my eyes and nodded. "You're right."

"I usually am." Nick said dryly. "But about what?"

"You do know how to make breakfast." I nudged him with my ankle.

Nick looked at my bare legs, eyes tracking over my skin. He finished chewing his food. "When do you finish tonight?"

I nearly choked on my food, the directness of his question catching me off guard. "Eager, are we?"

Nick placed down his plate with a resolute thunk. "It's Sunday."

I blinked at him, confused by the dissonant train of thought. "Correct, Nick. It is Sunday."

He exhaled and gripped the counter next to me, his hand landing right next to my bare thigh. "I'll pick you up and we can watch a movie. Here?"

I finished the last of my plate and put it aside. "Are you asking me to Netflix and chill?"

"Netflix." Nick's eyes crinkled slightly. "The chill part isn't a requirement, but I wouldn't have any objections."

I hummed and brushed my ankle against his leg. "I thought you had stuff to do."

"I do." Nick looked down at our plates. "But it can wait."

"You sure?"

"Elle Sutton's only in town for a little while." Nick gave me a soft smile. "I'll take as much as I can get."

I softened and beamed back at him. "Alright, then."

Nick didn't move, just kept looking at me with an open, unreadable expression on his face. I felt flayed open, and I squirmed a little. I could tell what the heated look in his eyes meant, and I was sure I was giving him a very similar look back.

My ankle brushed his leg again, and we both froze. My heart began hammering in my chest, and I waited—

Nick's knuckle brushed against my thigh. I turned my face and found him much closer to me than I expected. When he finally spoke, it was a rough whisper. "I think my favorite Elle Sutton is the morning one."

My eyes darted between his. "Why?"

"You look perfect, sitting there in my old shirt. You're relaxed. You're real."

I twisted my fingers in the hem and brushed my ankle against him again. "I like this version of me, too."

"Good." Nick pressed his knuckle against me again. "Do you want—"

"God, yes." I interrupted and pulled him into me.

Making out with Nick Corrigan on his kitchen bench in the morning after he'd fed me? Add it to the list of my new favorite things. He stepped into the space between my knees and pulled me flush against him.

I groaned softly into his mouth, roaming my hands over his chest, his back, his abs. He nipped at my bottom lip, and twisted his hand into my hair, pulling just enough to send a thrill through me.

I tightened my legs around him, pulling my centre against his growing erection and grinding—

He broke off from the kiss with a grunt and looked distracted.

"What?" I asked.

"Stay here." Nick brushed a hand through his hair and pulled away from me, and I blinked.

But he was gone, walking out of the kitchen and rummaging through something in the entrance hall. I heard him swear once before finding something and he returned. I tracked him, noticing something in his hands. "Where'd you go?"

He threw a foil packet on the bench next to me and stepped back into the space between my legs. He curled a hand around my waist. "I really didn't want to interrupt us during to find one."

I blinked down at the bench, then looked at him. "That's… very prepared."

"Law school hammered a lot of habits into me that are hard to forget." His thumb brushed under the hem of my shirt.

I burst out laughing. "And you said you don't think being a lawyer is a part of your identity."

"Nope. Just one perk." Nick gripped my jaw, his large hand curling all the way around to the back of my neck.

I looked up at him, and desire curled around my torso until I was on fire. "Care to show me another *perk*?"

Nick's lips twitched. "That was a horrible joke."

"That's Elle Sutton's specialty, I think."

"I like it." Nick leaned in and brushed his lips against mine. His other hand danced up my thigh, and goosebumps broke out on my skin. "Allow me to show my appreciation?"

"Permission granted." I breathed against his lips. He leaned in until our lips were barely touching, and he used his hand to leverage my face up, finally, finally kissing me, pressing our lips together. I moaned and wrapped my arms around his neck, pulling him further into me.

His other hand pushed the hem of my shirt until he could grip my bare hip. He leaned over me, bending me backwards and arching my back into him, until every inch of our torsos were melded together, pressed up against one another.

I was teetering on the edge, held safe only by his hands, keeping me firmly against him.

Nick's hand that had been holding my waist shifted and brushed against my inner thigh. I shuddered and opened my thighs wider apart, silently begging. He chuckled against my lips, and I bit his bottom lip in retaliation. He responded by deepening the kiss, and brushing his tongue against mine and I melted again.

His finger stroked the skin of my inner thigh again, taunting me. I *whined*.

"Patience." Nick whispered against my lips.

"It's not one of my virtues." I panted back.

He chuckled again and rewarded me with a swipe closer to where I wanted his fingers, but not quite. I inhaled and dragged my nails lightly down his back, and he groaned into my mouth.

I did it again, and I felt his erection twitch against my inner thigh. Interesting.

Nick broke off from the kiss and pressed our foreheads together. "Behave."

A flush came up in my chest at his command, and I ignored it. "Make me."

He inhaled sharply at that, and I smiled smugly at him. Also interesting. "Not today, baby."

He finally, finally brushed his fingers where I wanted them.

NICK

Elle Sutton was going to destroy me. Completely, utterly destroy me. I couldn't get enough of the sounds I could wring out of her, of her gasps and pants and whines. I wanted to have her mornings—I wanted to have her evenings—I wanted to have her every day, forever.

If I'd thought the sex last night had been some sort of fluke, I was wrong. Every time I touched Elle—every time she touched me—I couldn't get enough. Sparks shot up my hands when I touched her, and I was addicted to the feeling of touching her, of being near her, of being *inside* her.

I finally brushed my fingers through her core, and I watched her gorgeous face stutter, her eyebrows puckering. She was gorgeous all the time, but especially like this, wide eyed and shuddering with pleasure. I kissed her again, unable to stop myself, drinking from her lips. I hadn't felt feelings this strong for a woman in a long time. Maybe it should have alarmed me, but I didn't care.

She ground down onto my hand after I pressed a finger into her. I tugged slightly on her hair with my other hand and watched as her eyes went glassy and unfocused. I hid my grin in a kiss to her temple, to her lips. She was so easy to read, so easy to please and toy with.

Inside, she was wet and warm and waiting, and I drove my fingers into her depths, wanting to hear her moan, wanting to hear her cry out again. The sound of her coming around my fingers last night—coming on my tongue, coming around my cock—was not something I would easily forget, and I wanted to hear it over and over again, as many time as I could get before she left.

My cock jerked in my pants, but I ignored it.

She tensed under me, and I knew she was close. She was so responsive, this woman. I adjusted the angle of my hand so my palm swept against her clit, and she keened. I kept going—a steady, steady rhythm—until her face flushed, her legs shook, and her toes curled.

She was silent for a single second, and I swore I could have seen salvation in her eyes. But it was gone when she shuddered, her internal muscles fluttering around my fingers, and she jerked in my arms. I held her close, helping her ride her way through it.

My erection was almost hurting now, and I had to squeeze my eyes shut and focus on Elle. I wanted to make sure she was okay, that she was—

Her delicate hands shoved under my waistband, and I tensed. She grasped my cock and brought it out, giving it a few desperate pumps in her small hands, and I shuddered over her. "Elle—"

"Now." She mumbled and fumbled around for the condom. "I want you inside me now."

Thank *God*. My hands shook as I took the condom from her.

I ripped open the packet and rolled it over onto my cock. I was desperate—jittery and hungry to be inside her. I didn't even bother pushing my pants off or pulling her shirt off—we were both too eager for that.

I notched my cock at her entrance, and we both groaned when I pushed in. She felt like everything, and I had to take a moment to close my eyes. I pushed her softly down, so she was laying flat on the bench, and pushed up the t-shirt so I could suck on her perfect tits.

She moaned when I latched my lips around her nipple, and I closed my eyes as she dragged her nails down my back again.

Inside her, my cock twitched, and I pulled out, slowly, slowly, and pushed back in just as slowly. She might still be sore from last night—I might not have prepared her well enough.

"Nick," she whined from under me. "Please."

I kissed my way up her neck and replaced my mouth over her nipple with a thumb, flicking lightly over the tender peak. She rewarded me by clenching around me. She panted and tried to kiss me, tried to move her hips to get some friction, but she didn't have enough leverage. I smiled against her neck. "Patience."

I kept my rhythm slow, pushing into her, and was rewarded when her internal walls fluttered around me again. She bit my earlobe. "Fuck patience."

I smiled to myself. I'd teased her enough. Time to give her exactly what she needed. "Alright."

I pulled out and slammed back into her, quick and dirty and fast. I set a punished rhythm, and Elle threw her head back, panting on each thrust. I straightened myself up for better leverage, and gripped her hips tightly. Christ, the sight of her underneath me, her whole body shuddering with each thrust—it nearly undid me.

But I held on, through sheer determination, because I only wanted to come once she had, once I got to feel her pulsing around me.

Her delicate hand grabbed mine on her hips, and I adjusted my grip so I could hold her hand. She was gripping my hand so hard; I knew she must be close.

Her back arched, and her chest heaved, and I kept thrusting into her. God, she was everything.

I used my other hand to flick against her clit, a soft touch to help push her over the edge. I wanted her to come; I wanted to feel her pulse around me; I wanted to hear her cry out—

Her whole body seized, and I grit my teeth and kept thrusting. Her orgasm pulsed around my cock, and I closed my eyes and felt my own climax roll over. I buried myself to the hilt and came into her, vaguely aware of her still writhing underneath me.

As I came down from the high, I had no idea how I would ever let her go.

After a minute, I cleaned myself up, threw away the condom, and helped Elle off the kitchen bench. She looked just as destroyed as I felt, and she rested her head against my chest and sighed.

I smiled into her hair, running a soothing hand against her back. "That was a big sigh."

"Yeah." Elle did it again and grumbled into my chest. "I have to go."

"I figured." She wrapped her arms around my waist as I pressed a kiss into her hair. I didn't want to move, but I didn't want to keep her if she didn't want to stay. "Get dressed and I'll drive you."

Elle hummed into my chest and nodded. "Yeah. In a minute."

I didn't want to go either, so I stood with her, the moment stretching out. Our breathing synced up, and I could feel her heart beating just under mine. I wanted to stay like this forever, but I quickly squashed that thought. That wasn't relevant. I frowned out at the window and steeled myself against the future. I knew it was coming, that one day she would be gone and I would be alone again.

When she went back to the city, I knew I couldn't follow her.

But right now, she was here. My hand tightened around her back.

"You look weird, bro."

It was mid-afternoon, and I was sitting in a cafe with Matt. Sheets of paperwork were spread around us. I pushed a hand through my hair, which was messier than usual. "Weird?"

I knew I probably looked weird, because my knee had been bouncing under the table for the past ten minutes, and I kept grimacing at the contract in front of me, finding more clauses to re-read so I could delay signing. I didn't want to be here. I wanted to be wherever Elle was, and ideally in a place where I could bury myself in her perfect body again. Christ, I was so gone for her already.

Matt crossed his arms and scoffed again. "There. You just winced again. What the hell's going on, man?"

I took a sip of water to delay my response. "Nothing."

I wasn't convincing enough for Matt, because he shook his head and rapped his hands against the table. "Is there something wrong with the contract?"

"No." I blinked my eyes down at the paperwork. "I'm just making sure it doesn't have any hidden clauses in it."

"Yeah." Matt said pointedly. "For ten minutes."

I sent him a dirty look. "I'm being thorough. This is one of the most important contracts I've ever signed."

"It's a lease agreement, Nick." Matt's eyes searched my face. "Surely it's pretty straightforward."

I brushed a hand down my face. "I'm just... making sure."

Matt was silent for a moment, then crossed his arms. "Alright. What's changed?"

"I don't know what you mean." I deadpanned.

"I mean, last week you were impatient to sign. Something's changed to make you... this." Matt gestured to all of me.

The snow fell softly outside as I looked out the window. I thought about Elle rehearsing with the kids in the Town Hall. I checked my watch. She'd be done soon. I wanted to make sure I was there, wanted to make sure she didn't have to walk home in the cold. Something seized my heart when I looked down at the paperwork in front of me.

If I signed this, I would damn any possibility that I could follow her back to LA, that I could follow her wherever she wanted to lead me.

And suddenly, I couldn't sign the contract. I put my pen down on the table. "I can't sign this. Not yet."

Matt frowned at me. "You'd better tell me what the fuck is going on with you."

I leaned back in my chair and pinched the bridge of my nose. "Things have... changed slightly, since we last spoke."

Matt tilted his head at me, his eyes sharp. "How?"

"I slept with Elle last night." I ground out.

"Holy shit, bro."

I said nothing, but took a sip of my water.

Matt's eyebrows shot up. "That good, huh?"

He got a dark look from me. "I'm still going to sign. I just don't want to, not yet."

"Bro, I say this with love, but the blonde's going back to LA. And you hate it there." Matt shook his head at me. "You shouldn't get involved with that. Have a fling and stick to your plan."

"Thanks for the advice," I responded dryly. "Still, I want to hold off signing."

Matt scratched the back of his neck. "You'd need to do it by New Year's. I can't draw out the process longer than that. There was someone else enquiring about the place the other day, and I can't hold them off forever if you're not… certain."

"I am certain." I replied, knowing my gut said otherwise. "I just need a bit more time."

Matt stared at me for a moment, then nodded. "Alright, bro. I hope you know what you're doing."

Secretly, I hoped I did, too. I pushed out my chair and stood, getting ready to leave to see Elle. "It's Christmas. What could go wrong?"

Considering how much I usually hated the season, probably a lot.

ELLE

"Why is he trying to scale the chimney?" Nick asked from beside me, looking vaguely horrified at the TV.

I chuckled and nudged his thigh with my own. "It's a Hallmark movie. Don't think too much about it."

Nick gave me a suffering look. "Remind me why we chose this?"

"I chose this one because you told me I could." I leaned over him and grabbed a handful of popcorn.

"Right. How could I have known you have such poor taste?" His hand played with a strand of my hair, and I tried not to preen too much under the affectionate touch.

I made a sound around a mouthful of popcorn. "Art is subjective. I like this sort of stuff. Don't tell me you're a snob."

Nick's nose wrinkled, and I resisted the urge to lean in and kiss him. For now, at least. "I guess so."

I paused the movie and looked at him closer. "You *are* a snob!"

Nick laughed a little and shrugged his shoulders. "I've never really thought about it. I don't watch a lot of stuff."

I pressed my lips together. "Oh, my apologies. Do you usually pull out your Tolstoy on a night like this?"

Nick tilted his head back on the couch and pinched the bridge of his nose. The column of his throat looked delicious, and I wanted to run my finger up it. "I'm happy with the movie if you're happy with it, Elle."

I shifted myself so I was facing him more, my curled knees against his thigh. "If you really hate it, I'd prefer you to say."

"I don't hate it." Nick gave me a sheepish smile. "I just… rarely watch a lot of stuff. I need time to get used to the—"

"Genre conventions?" I added playfully.

"I was going to say style, but that sounds fancier, so sure." Nick twirled my hair in his hand again.

"I'm a trained actor. I know all the wankiest words for things." The sarcasm was deep in my voice.

Nick inhaled. "I feel like the law profession might have a leg up on you for that."

I leaned further into him. "Try me."

"If I got a dollar for every time I reviewed a document that had either 'aforementioned,' or 'we note that' in it, I would be even richer than I am." Nick made a face. "I die inside every time I have to write the same bullshit."

"You know, I feel like the snobbiest thing in that sentence was you calling yourself rich, actually." I crinkled my nose at him, a gleam in my eye.

Nick gestured around his house in a deprecating manner. "I know what it's like not having money growing up. This is money. Ergo, rich."

"Oh, *ergo*, is it?" I teased.

Nick smiled. "See? I'm proving my point about the lawyer thing. We're all snobbish idiots."

I laughed, but remembered one of the other things he had said. "What did you mean, you didn't have a lot growing up? If you don't mind me asking."

Nick inhaled and his eyes went distant, unfocused. "I don't mind. My mom didn't have a lot. Single mother. She was… I don't know. I loved her, and she loved me, and she sacrificed a lot so that I could have a better life than her."

I rested a gentle hand on his knee. "What was her life like?"

"Hard. I still don't know who my father is. She never spoke about him." Nick focused on a lock of my hair as he twirled it in his fingers. "She raised me herself. We got the house when my grandparents died, but we didn't have much else. She worked so hard to pay for extracurriculars, so I could get into a good college. She was desperate for me to go, because she never got to—she was only nineteen when she got pregnant with me."

"She sounds like an amazing mother." My heart broke for him, for the sadness I could see in his eyes. It was amazing he had got as far as he had.

Nick smiled, a sad one, full of grief. "Yeah. My biggest regret is that she never got to see me graduate from law school, even though I know she's proud—"

He broke off and pressed his lips together. I rested a hand against his cheek and looked into his eyes. "She'd be so proud. Look at you. Look at the life you've built."

Nick nodded and flopped his head back onto the couch. I could tell by the tightness in his jaw that he was trying to hold in the sadness, the unimaginable grief at losing a loving parent. I didn't want to make him sadder by asking more questions. Instead, I wanted to make him feel better again.

I shifted again, nearly sitting in his lap to face him. "To quote someone earlier, this is a very rich lawyer's house."

Nick huffed, his head still tilted back at the ceiling. His hand dropped to my waist, tracing idle circling underneath my thin knit sweater. "Doesn't really matter, though, does it?"

"As someone who's been a starving actor for seven years, I disagree. You like law, right?"

"Yeah."

I smiled and nudged him with my hand. "There you go. That's better than many people in this world."

"And what about you?"

"What do you mean?"

Nick lifted his head upright, staring at me. "Do you like acting?"

I wanted to curl into myself to avoid answering the question. But Nick was staring at me, and I knew he wanted me to be honest. "I don't know."

His hand tightened against my waist. "Is it worth it, then?"

I shrugged, my turn to look at the ceiling and swallow my emotions. "I don't know. It's been so hard that I think I've forgotten why I love it."

"I'm sorry." Nick's hand squeezed me again. "I'm sorry it hasn't been what you wanted yet. You deserve more than that."

I chuckled, a horribly bitter sound to my own ears. "I don't think deserving has anything to do with it."

Nick was silent for long enough that I looked back at him and tried to give him a reassuring smile. I thought I did an okay job, but he shook his head at me. "Don't pretend. You don't have to do that with me. It's shit. You don't need to sugarcoat it."

I flopped my head forward against his chest, and his hands came around me. "I don't like how this has become about me."

"Too bad." Nick's chest rumbled with his words. "My mom is old stuff, mostly healed. We're talking about you now."

My lips twisted, though I knew he couldn't see. "I thought we were watching a movie."

Nick shifted and pressed play on the movie again. I couldn't see anything, but heard the main hero swear as he tried to climb further up the chimney. "Now we are. We can do both."

He pulled me further onto his lap, and I let him. I nestled my face into the crook of his neck and breathed him in. He smelled like cozy fireplaces and fresh snow. He smelled like everything I'd ever wanted.

I swallowed that thought as soon as it bubbled up.

"Nick?"

"Yeah?"

"I don't want to watch the movie anymore." I mumbled into his neck.

His chest tightened, and I sensed that he was holding back a laugh. His arm moved around me and the TV switched off. "What do you want to do, then?"

I sat upright and gave him a look. "Take a guess."

A barely concealed smile twitched across his lips. "Sorry, I don't have a brain."

I tapped his temples. "He went to law school without a brain. Remarkable."

"I have one." Nick smiled at me, and I smiled back. "I just have to put it in a jar for safekeeping whenever Elle Sutton's around."

I pushed back on his chest to put a bit of distance between us. "Are you saying I make you stupid?"

Nick's shoulders shook, but he pressed his lips together in a valiant effort to not laugh. "No. No—I'm trying to make a clever joke."

"It mustn't be working because you've locked your brain away." I flicked his shoulder. "What the hell was the joke?"

Nick shrugged his shoulders again, his lips twitching upwards. "I have to put it in a jar because I tend to *lose it* when you're around."

I stared at him for a second. I blinked. Then I tipped my head back, laughing harder than I had laughed in a long time. My stomach clenched, and I dissolved into a fit of giggles. This man was so ridiculous—

Nick started laughing, too. "I thought that was kind of good—"

"You went to law school!" I accused, wiping my eyes. "I can't believe *that's* the joke you come up with."

"I already told you I don't have full use of my brain—"

I waved my hand in front of his face. "You are not trying to use that again—"

I couldn't finish my sentence, because Nick slid his hand around my jaw and kissed me. His lips were soft, and it took me a second to soften against him. He must have taken my pause as hesitation, because he pulled back slightly. "Yes?"

I chased his lips with my own. "Yes."

I shifted myself so I was fully seated on his lap, straddling his thick thighs. His hands gripped my waist, pulling me flush against him. I don't think I would ever get sick of kissing Nick Corrigan. He was so… tasty.

Which gave me an idea of something I hadn't had the chance to do yet.

I ground my core down into his lap and felt him harden underneath me. Good. He groaned softly into me and used his hands to move me over him again. I gasped against his lips, and let him move me for a moment. It felt amazing, the hard zip of his jeans dragging against the seat of my leggings.

Nick kissed down my neck, and he found a spot that had me jerking my hips in his lap.

I whimpered. None of my clothes were off, and it already felt so good, so overwhelming. I just wanted more and more and more—

Nick skimmed his hands up my sides, brushing against the bralette I wore under my sweater. Impatiently, I ripped off my sweater for him.

Nick chuckled and leaned back against the couch. "Eager are we?"

"Don't pretend you're not." I rolled my hips over his erection for emphasis. His eyes traced my body, heat in his gaze.

"I like this." He said softly, brushing his fingers over the lace of my bralette.

I flushed at the compliment, but I wanted things to move quicker. I shrugged off the straps and reached my hands around to undo it.

Nick leaned forward and pressed a kiss to my sternum. "Let me do it."

I relaxed my arms, and his hands came up behind my back to deftly, swiftly undo my bra. He took it off me reverently and placed it carefully beside us on the couch.

His hands clutched at my waist, pulling me flush against him. Now, my tits were at perfect face level for him, and I flushed a little at the way he was looking at me, at my body.

He surged forward and captured one of my nipples in his mouth, sucking gently. I keened, pleasure racing through my body, and ground my core against his, seeking more stimulation. It was like his tongue, softly lapping at my nipple, was connected right to my clit, and I could already feel the pleasure building.

Jesus.

Nick pulled off my nipple with a soft pop and wasted no time lavishing the other with the same attention. This time, he brushed his teeth ever-so-slightly over my nipple, and I jerked in his lap.

His hands pulled me over him, dragging my core up and down his length. It felt, it felt so—

I grabbed the back of his head and gasped. "Don't stop—don't stop—"

Nick hummed and kept sucking at my breast, sending little shocks of pleasure down to my core, and flicked his thumb over my other nipple. I was going to—

His teeth grazed my nipple again, and my whole body tensed. His hand dragged me over his lap, my core rubbing just right...

An orgasm raced through my body, and I shuddered against him. My mouth opened into a silent 'o' and I flexed my fingers sporadically. He held onto me, curling his arm around my back to help me feel safe, help me feel held. He ran a hand soothingly up my back as I twitched.

After a moment, after the waves of pleasure had receded slightly, I put a hand over my mouth. "Oh, my god."

I had just come without barely anything, just Nick's mouth on my tits. I'd never come so quickly, not with anyone, not even with myself. I couldn't believe—

Nick brushed a hand over my face, bringing my eyes down to his. "You're okay."

His voice shook me out of my shock spiral, and I laughed into my hand. A fresh flush came up on my cheeks. "I've never just—"

Nick's lips curled into a satisfied smile. "But did you enjoy it?"

My legs twitched. "What do you think?"

He smoothed a hand over my hair, curling his fingers through the strands. "I think… I'm glad you enjoyed yourself. Maybe a little smug, too, if I'm being honest."

My cheeks were still bright red, and I gave him a soft look of reproach.

Nick drew my head down and whispered into my ear, "It's really hot, knowing I can make you come so quickly."

The flush crept over my chest, and my desire came roaring back, barely minutes after my surprise orgasm. Now wasn't the time to be ashamed. Nick was right here with me, and his erection was still pressing against my inner thigh. I gave him a sly smile, suddenly wanting to even the playing field.

I wanted to see how quickly I could get him to come.

I pressed his shoulders back so he was leaning fully against the couch, and he gave me a questioning look.

Which quickly turned to desire when I slid myself off his lap and settled myself on the floor between his legs. God, I loved the power kneeling before him made me feel. It was odd how much an act of submission made me feel so powerful. But it was. With Nick, I felt totally safe, totally free to be everything I was in front of him. And right now, that meant I wanted to make him feel good, the way he had just done for me.

I wanted to taste him on my tongue, to know what his pleasure felt like sliding down my throat.

"Are you sure?" Nick clenched a hand against his knee, and I tried to hide my smug smile. He was holding himself back for me, I could tell.

"I wouldn't be on my knees in front of you if I wasn't."

He swallowed, his eyes going dark with desire. "Good. I don't want you to do anything you don't want—"

"Believe me," I said, eyeing his clothed erection. "I want to."

I slid my hands up his inner thighs and slowly undid his jeans. God, I was salivating already—I'd never been so excited about going down on a man before. But Nick had me hungry for everything, and I pulled his zipper down with zeal.

His hand flexed on his knee, and I looked up at him. It was possible he didn't want me to do this, so I needed to check. "Are *you* okay with this?"

"God, yes." Nick's jaw clenched, and he looked so hungry, just as hungry as I was inside—

I slipped my hand under his boxers, freeing his cock from his clothes. It was weeping, an angry red at the tip, and I immediately leaned forward to lap at the pre-cum. He tasted salty and warm and I moaned a little. I'd never liked the taste before, but this was Nick and he was looking at me with hooded eyes, his chest jerking with his breaths—

I wrapped my lips around his cock and slowly bobbed my head down, trying to fit as much in as I could. His hand came around my head, but he held me lightly. I could feel how careful he was trying to be. It made me want to see him unhinged, to see him overcome with pleasure.

I put my hand over his and urged him to hold me tighter, and soon I felt his fingers thread through my hair, holding me firm. I could still pull away if I really wanted, but he could guide me into a rhythm that he liked.

He groaned and threw his head back. "Christ, baby, that feels so good."

I hummed around his cock and looked up at him. The column of his throat was bare, and I pushed myself to take more of him into my mouth. I wanted his pleasure; I wanted him to explode—

His fingers flexed in my hair, and his hips jerked upwards a little. I whined when that pushed him further into my throat, but I didn't pull back. He swore and tried to apologize, but I hummed at him and gripped his thighs harder. I would do whatever I could to make him orgasm, and I squirmed a little in my position. This was the most powerful I'd ever felt with a man, making him come undone under me.

His hand tensed around my head, and he groaned again. "Elle—"

I looked up at him, and found him watching me with desperate eyes, and I knew he was close. I hummed and sucked harder.

He swore. "Baby, I'm gonna—"

I pulled off him with a pop, and mouthed at the tip of his cock. "I want you to. Please."

He groaned again. "Okay."

I plunged my mouth down on his, and I felt his whole body tense. God, he was so tense, held so tightly, I just wanted to feel him release all of it. I hummed around him, and his hand tightened against my hair. I wanted, I wanted—

He tensed, and his cock pulsed, and finally I felt a warm splash into my mouth, which I gulped down my throat. I pulled off him and leaned my head against his knee, watching him try to catch his breath. His fingers still stroked through my hair, and I smiled. "Alright?"

He looked down at me, mouth parted. "Alright? Christ, Elle, you just destroyed me."

I bit my lip and turned around, grabbed a glass of water from the coffee table, and took a few sips. He held out his arms and pulled me up into his lap, and I snuggled into his chest. He rested his head against my hair and sighed. We stayed there, silent, for a moment, and I listened to his heartbeat slow, his breathing calm down.

I closed my eyes and smiled to myself. I could get used to this.

ELLE

The next week passed quickly. I spent most of my time at Nick's house, and when I wasn't there, I was busy rehearsing with Deanna and the kids.

I tried not to notice the knowing looks she sent me whenever I arrived home from Nick's house, but she didn't ask questions, and I said nothing. He was her godson, after all. It was a little awkward for both of us.

He always waited after rehearsals with a cup of hot cocoa. My heart melted a little more each time, and my hunger for him grew with each day. I couldn't get enough of him. In his bed, in his shower, on the wall of his kitchen, on the floor of his living room. There was one time when we didn't even get out of the car after he picked me up.

With each passing second we knew how much limited time we had together. I was still leaving Mistletoe Valley after Christmas—and Nick was still staying. I tried not to think too much about that, happy as I was.

All good things had to end. I knew this. I just didn't want to face the truth of it.

꙳꙳꙳꙳   ꙳꙳꙳꙳

Deanna had invited Nick and me to Sunday dinner. Christmas was a mere week away, and the play was going on in five days. I didn't really want to think about how soon everything would be finished. The play, Mistletoe Valley, and Nick. I was due to leave the day after Christmas. My family weren't expecting me, anyway. My sister was busy with work, and she's the only one I would have wanted to spend Christmas with. So I'd spend Christmas Day with Deanna and Nick, and then it would all be over.

I took a sip of wine and felt it curdle in my stomach. I didn't want to think about my impending departure. Nick nudged me under the table, and I gave him a tight smile.

Deanna came into the room with plates full of roast vegetables, meat, and gravy. As much as I'd loved spending time with Nick, Deanna's food was a whole other level of delicious. I thanked her.

"It's my pleasure, Elle." Deanna served us and gestured for me to start. "You had a long day today."

"*We* had a long day," I reminded her. "You were there the whole time, too."

Deanna shrugged. "You were doing most of the work. I was just watching."

"How's it going, the play?" Nick interrupted us, looking between us both.

I gave him a sly smile. He already knew how the play was going, given that he saw me after every rehearsal, unwinding on his couch. I appreciated his attempt at pretending he had no clue for Deanna's sake. Nick gave me a subtle wink when Deanna couldn't see.

Deanna pointed her fork at me. "This one has been spectacular. The kids love her, and she's been getting the best out of them. I really think this year's going to be special."

Nick held my eyes, a soft look passing through his. "So do I."

I twisted my lips at him and looked at Deanna. "I've done barely anything. It's the kids. They're open and playful, and it's very easy to get the best out of them."

Deanna nodded. "Isn't it funny how encouraging kids to be creative and playful always gets better results than putting pressure on them?"

I blinked at the table. "I think I would have had a lot more fun if my acting teacher had seen it that way."

I thought about the draconian woman who had pushed me and pushed me towards perfection and performance and pretending. I hated her, a villain of my childhood. Since coming here, I realized how horrible she'd been, watching Deanna with the kids. I couldn't blame my parents, because they had just been doing their best, sending their kid to acting lessons because she kept telling them she wanted to be a star.

It became worse when I went to acting school, and I was told all the ways I was deficient, all the ways I needed to market myself and pretend and become a living brand. And for what? Shitty pay and poor opportunities?

Deanna patted my hand. "I'm sorry that happened to you. But I am glad that you can be a joy for the kids now."

Nick raised his glass to me, and I looked into his eyes—his caring, intelligent eyes. "To Elle, then. For bringing joy to Mistletoe Valley."

Deanna raised her own glass. After a moment, I did, too. Under the table, I nudged Nick's ankle with my own, a soft touch that spoke to all that I wanted from him, and every feeling of gratitude.

Deanna placed her hands on the table. "Actually, Elle, I have something to ask you while you're here."

I broke away from Nick's gaze. "What is it?"

Deanna took in a breath. "I'm getting older. The kids need someone to teach them, and they have loved you so much. Celia asked me today if you could stay forever."

The words felt like a punch to my gut, an external reminder of how much I wanted, so desperately, to stay. I could feel the dread building, suspecting what Deanna was about to offer me.

Deanna took a breath. "Pretty soon, I'm going to need someone to help me run the studio, teaching the kids. It's good pay, great hours, and year round. And I thought I would offer it to you, because…"

Deanna trailed off and looked between Nick and me, and I stiffened. Nick saw the look in my eyes and shook his head at his godmother. "Deanna—"

"Let me finish, Nick." Deanna told him sternly. "I just want you to think about it, Elle. This town has been good for you. You obviously love it, and it might be a good alternative—"

"Deanna." Nick's voice was low. "Enough. Look at her."

My heart was a hummingbird in my chest, and my breath was refusing to work right. It kept getting faster and faster, until I was nearly hyperventilating, until I was close to terror. The breadth of what Deanna was offering, the life I could have, that I could make for myself—

The wall of who I had decided I would be loomed high in my mind, threatening to suffocate me. I couldn't think. I couldn't breathe. I pushed myself out of my chair and ran from the room.

Even as I stumbled outside, even as I sat on the porch step and put my head between my knees, I couldn't get it to stop. I couldn't get the panic to go away, the sheer terror of realizing I was in real danger here, the real danger of losing everything I thought was true about myself.

I was Elle Sutton, the actor. I was the girl who did acting. It was my whole life, and I had promised myself I would never give it up.

It didn't matter that I hated it now. Because I really hated the whole rotten thing. I had committed to something, and I had no clue who I was without being the struggling actor everyone knew me to be—

Someone sat down beside me, and I knew it was Nick from the press of his strong thigh against mine. I tried to calm my breathing, and he cleared his throat. "Do you want to be alone?"

I shook my head, miserable. "Stay. Please."

He placed his hand between my shoulder blades, giving me reassuring pressure to ground me in reality. Slowly, surely, the panic abated until it became manageable, until I could control my breathing again.

I looked up at the night sky and winced. "Ugh."

"You're okay."

"No." I shook my head. "No, I haven't been okay for a while. And I'm so *sick* of feeling so lost."

I growled that last part at the sky, as if it had anything to do with my suffering. Nick said nothing for a moment, just kept applying gentle pressure to my back. "You're allowed to feel lost. Most people's twenties are a disaster. Half of mine felt like it was."

"Great." I closed my eyes. "Except I'm twenty-five, and I was hoping I would have my shit more together by now. I keep expecting to find myself, except I feel like I'm further away from *finding myself* now than I was as a teenager."

"I think the whole finding yourself thing is bullshit." Nick muttered. "We change and grow all the time. At least, we should. You just need to work out what you want, what you need *now*, to thrive."

I pressed a hand to my chest. "I have always been the acting girl. Always."

"But do you still want to be the acting girl?"

I put my head in my hands. That was the million dollar question, wasn't it? I couldn't answer that question, not when Nick was around. Because he made me want to give everything up, give up all my dreams and ambitions, just so I could be with him. *He* was fast becoming my new dream.

And that was the most dangerous thing of all. I couldn't give up my career, not for a man. It went against everything I'd ever stood for. Right?

I stood and gazed down at him. "I can't—I need to go for a walk. Alone. I'm sorry."

He shoved his hands into his pockets, and nodded.

I turned away from him and walked down the garden path. Fresh tears sprung up in my eyes, and I tried not to notice how hard it was to walk away from him. Every bone in my body was screaming at me to turn, to fold myself into his arms and have him tell me that everything would be okay.

But if I did that, then I would stay. I would stay in Mistletoe Valley forever.

I didn't know how I felt about that.

Several blocks down the street, I was too exhausted to continue. My mind was racing—it refused to shut up—and I didn't know what to do.

I blinked up at the sky, and a dark blanket of cold settled over my face. Suddenly, I knew what I had to do. There was only one person on this earth who could give me honest advice. My sister, Kat.

I pulled out my phone and wiped my eyes. I pressed a number and prayed she would pick up.

I sobbed with relief when I heard my sister's reassuring voice. "Elle! I know you said you were busy in December, but I would have thought you could call me back like... once. What's going on?"

I burst into tears. Again.

"Are you hurt? What's going on? Tell me!" My sister made a noise as if she was moving around.

"No—no. I'm okay. Really, Kat." I sniffled. "Actually, I'm not okay, but I'm not in any danger."

Silence for a moment. "Jesus, Elle. You can't just cry and say nothing."

I rubbed a hand over my eye. "Yeah. Yeah. I know. I'm sorry."

"I was about to ring the Mistletoe Valley police station and demand they send out a search party."

I chuckled. "That's really not necessary, Kat."

"I'll decide what's necessary for my little sister's safety, thank you very much." A pause, and I could almost hear her put her hands on her hips. "I've barely heard anything from you all month."

"Sorry." I bowed my head. "I've been... busy. It's intense. But I'm talking to you now, aren't I?"

"And crying. I can tell you've been crying."

"I'm fine. I just... wanted to hear your voice."

"Okay, now I know something's really wrong. You hate the sound of my voice."

"I really don't." I breathed.

A pause. "Right. Something's really wrong, isn't it?"

"I don't know what to do, Kat. I... feel so conflicted."

"Elle, you're confusing me. Is this about the play?"

I bowed my head in my hands. "No. It's... I've met someone."

Kat was silent for a moment. "Shit, Elle. Why are you sad?"

"Because he's staying here and I can't... I can't..."

"Can't what?"

"I can't stay with him!"

Kat tsked. "You've known him, what, three weeks?"

"I've never met anyone like him, Kat." I shot back, angry that she wasn't understanding me.

"I—okay. I need more details." Kat went into full problem-solving mode. It was one of the things I loved about her, how her mind worked so fast to come up with the best objective path forward.

I took a big breath and told her. I started with how I met Nick, that hilarious first meeting, and then how I came to Mistletoe Valley and fell in love with the town, with the life that people like Deanna had carved out for themselves. I told her about how much I loved teaching the kids, and then I told her about Nick. I told her about his apology, and his care, and the way he brought me cocoa after every single rehearsal.

"He sees me, Kat. I can't pretend around him." I sniffled. "I don't think anyone other than you has ever seen me like this in a long time."

"And what's the problem?"

I wiped my eyes. "The problem is that I want to stay, and I can't."

"Can't, or won't?"

"I don't know." I whispered. "I feel so lost, Kat."

Silence. "Right. Here's what we're going to do. You are going to go back to Deanna's, fix yourself a nice cup of cocoa, and go to bed. Tomorrow, I'm going to drive up—"

I gasped. "You can't, it's too close to Christmas—"

"Never mind that." Kat's tone brokered no argument. "You are more important. I'm going to meet this Nick guy and help you work out if he's fucked with your head or if he is the real deal. Then, you can decide what you do. Okay?"

I took a deep breath, feeling calmer. "Okay. Okay. You're the best, Kat."

"I know I am, Ellie." I could hear Kat walking around, and I was willing to bet she was hustling things to get ready. Kat's determination was unmatched, and I wouldn't be surprised if she arrived early tomorrow morning, driving through the night. "Text me your address now, okay?"

I sent it off to her. "Done."

"Good." A sigh. "Geez, girl, you never do things by half, do you?"

I laughed into the night air, a warbling sound. "Love you, Kat."

"Love you. I gotta go, chicken."

I scoffed at her old nickname for me, but left the call feeling much better. My heart felt lighter, and I felt less lost. My big sister was coming to help me. I hadn't asked for help this seriously in years, but I knew she wouldn't let me down.

Even if I had nothing else, I had her. I looked around at the winter streets of Mistletoe Valley and shook myself. I'd feel normal again, soon enough.

I just wasn't sure how I'd make it out of Mistletoe Valley without a broken heart.

NICK

Fuck. It was one of the hardest things in my life, letting Elle walk away. Her eyes were puffy from crying, and her shoulders tense from stress. It was unbearable—I just wanted to bundle her up in my arms and try to make everything better.

Except, the problem wasn't something I could fix. The problem was that she felt she had to go back to the city, back to that life she hated. And who was I to persuade her otherwise?

It looked to me like she was happy here, and any mention of her old life had her eyes shutting down, her shoulders slumping. It was clear to me—to anyone, really—that she hated her life in LA. But it wasn't my place to ask her to stay, or beg or plead or bargain my way into persuading her. The choice had to be hers alone, so I let her walk away.

I sat on the porch, and snow softly fell from the night sky. I could hear a dog barking down the lane, lights on in houses lining the street, and I had never felt more lonely. Because all I wanted was to be at Elle's side.

The front door creaked opened. Deanna shuffled out, sighed, and sat down next to me. She groaned as she settled down and pulled her coat tighter around her. "She's gone, then?"

I swallowed, looking out at the street. "She needed to walk. Alone."

Deanna nodded. "Good. She needs to make this decision herself."

I gave her a reproachful look. "She wasn't ready for that, Deanna."

"When will she be?" Deanna raised her eyebrows at me. "Maybe it was clumsy of me. But I have a feeling she's more ready to hear it than you think."

I stayed silent, grinding my teeth. I hated this, feeling so impotent when the woman I had begun to care for deeply was suffering. Elle had carved herself a place in my heart, but I couldn't help her. Not with this decision.

Sure, I could go to her and kiss her and beg her to stay, but that would make me the most manipulative asshole ever. She would give up much more than I would if I told her to stay, to take up Deanna's offer.

"You want to go after her, don't you?" Deanna cleared her throat.

I put my head in my hands. "More than anything," I groaned.

"Well," Deanna chuckled, "she's certainly got you smitten quickly."

I gave her a resentful look around my hands. "I don't need reminding of how much shit I'm in, thanks."

Deanna gave me a wry smile. "Love isn't something to be ashamed of."

Something clenched inside me. Was that what this was? Love? It had been barely three weeks, but I had to admit I was already head over heels for Elle, ready to drag myself through any amount of pain for her. "No, but given the circumstance, it's pretty fucking stupid."

Deanna crossed her arms. "What's life without a little stupidity? Some of the best things happen because of it."

"I'd love to hear an example." I pinched the bridge of my nose.

A pause. "I came here because I was pregnant. Unexpectedly."

I dropped my hands and looked at her. Really looked at my godmother, who had never let me in on this detail about her life. "You never told me that."

Deanna shrugged. "Your mother, bless her heart, was the only one who knew. I was forty, for God's sake. It should have been near impossible. But when I found out, it felt like such a monumental sign I needed a change that I up and left the city. I washed up here, because I'd visited once before and your mother had been kind to me."

I felt a fist around my heart, hearing her talk about my mother. Mom had always been kind, with a bigger heart than I had ever mustered.

Deanna squeezed my hand and went on. "When I came back, the second time, nursing an impossible pregnancy and a lost soul, I knocked on her door. And she answered. I remember you, a shy six-year-old standing behind her."

I remembered how my mom had welcomed her in like an old friend, and the rest was history. I cleared my throat, grief and confusion fogging it up. "What happened with the pregnancy?"

Deanna sent a sad smile out to the night sky. "I was barely into my second trimester when I lost the baby. But your mother helped me through it, and afterwards, I realized it was all for the best. But I couldn't go back to the city. I didn't want to."

"Why have you never mentioned this before?"

Deanna sighed. "I suppose because I don't like to talk about that time. If I can avoid it, I will. But I guess I ended up with a child, in the end."

She smiled fondly at me, and I squeezed my eyes shut, a tightness in my throat. "Why did you stay?"

Deanna gave me a calculated look. "Because the town welcomed me here. They showed me kindness, and support, and community. And your mother showed me unconditional love."

I gazed out into the street; the lamplight casting warm pools of light amongst the sea of darkness. I knew this street like the back of my hand, knew this house like it was my own. This town was part of me, and I would sign myself to the devil if I stayed in the city. But Elle wasn't there yet, and she might never be. "I don't think I can just sit around and wait for the hammer to drop. For her to leave."

"You don't solve anything by sitting there." Deanna nudged me. "And you will sabotage all your chances if you end it now, before giving it a shot. Before giving her a chance to decide."

I was silent, thinking of all the ways this could be agony for me, all the ways this could end badly. And yet, I knew what my godmother was saying was right. I couldn't end it now, not when I still had a chance. It didn't matter how small.

I blew out a breath. Something, somewhere along the path, would have to give. But I had no idea if that would be pain or happiness.

A guy had to hope, though.

Deanna stood and peered into the night. Who knows where Elle had walked to, but Mistletoe Valley was safe, thank God. Deanna patted my shoulder. "You know—something tells me she'll decide before too long."

She went back inside, and I sat, staring into the still darkness, for a little while longer.

꙳꙳꙳꙳ ꙳꙳꙳꙳

I called Matt the next morning. I'd already sent three texts to Elle, and it wasn't even mid-morning. I definitely needed to be stopped. I had a week left with her, if that.

Matt picked up on the third ring. "What's up, man?"

I pinched the bridge of my nose. "Wanna meet me in the town square? I've got some Christmas shit to buy."

A laugh. "Okay, hotshot, some of us have actual jobs."

"You never work on Christmas week. There's nothing to do." I reminded him.

A pause. "Alright man, I'll come if you tell me what the fuck's going on. You've never done this before."

I grabbed my keys and walked out the door. "Why don't I tell you when I see you?"

A sigh. "Fine. I'll be there in fifteen. And you better buy me a coffee."

ELLE

I woke in the morning to a headache, a dry mouth, and a loud noise—

Someone was knocking on my door.

I jerked upright, smoothing down my messy hair. "Hello?"

Deanna opened the door. I'd spoken to her, briefly, last night after I got back, and said I needed time to think about her offer. Deanna had nodded and passed me a cup of tea. I loved that woman. Currently, though, she was pointing to something behind her. "There's someone downstairs to see you."

I checked the time. 7:30AM. Fuck. I rolled out of bed and pulled on a dressing gown. "Sorry- I. It's my sister. I didn't think she'd be this early. Sorry."

Deanna reached out a hand to stop me from flurrying around. "You stay here. I'll send her up."

I baulked. "I—this is your house, we can go somewhere."

Deanna shook her head. "Whilst you're here, this is your house, too. I'll be downstairs if you need me."

"Okay. Thank you." I swallowed and smiled at her.

Deanna gave me a soft look. "I'm sorry if offering you the job last night put any sort of pressure on you. You don't need that right now."

I straightened. Despite the swirling maelstrom of panic Deanna's offer had kicked up, I didn't resent her at all for it. The problem was with me. "I… just have a lot of things to work out. About my life, I guess."

Deanna squeezed my shoulder. "I understand, love. You do what you need to do."

She left me alone, and I stared after her. Was it only three weeks ago that I had first arrived here? I couldn't believe how much had changed, how much had shifted inside me. Not only that, but I was a week away from leaving.

I heard footfalls on the stairs, and my sister appeared.

Kat had always cut an imposing, confident figure wherever she went, but she looked larger than life here in Mistletoe Valley. Her dark blonde hair was held back in a severe bun, and her black clothes made a harsh line across her long body. She always looked elegant. She also always looked ready to stab someone at any moment.

I smiled. I had missed her so much.

Kat eyed the room and crossed quickly to me. She gently touched the bags under my eyes, proof of my tears, and she sighed. "Hello, chicken. We'll sort it out."

It had always been me and Kat against the world. She had never abandoned me, not even when I went to college, not even when I graduated into acting failure. She had always encouraged my ambition, always encouraged me to keep going.

I threw myself into her arms, and she returned the hug with a tight squeeze. I pulled back and looked at her, noticing the extra boniness of her frame. She'd always been slim—she was taller than I was—but she became slimmer when she was stressed. "Have you been eating?"

Kat gave me a tight smile. "The new role's been giving me a bit of grief."

My smile dropped. "Kat. You shouldn't be here. You're too busy."

Kat had just been promoted to manager of a big department store in San Francisco. Christmas week was the worst for her, but she waved a hand, unbothered. "I've delegated. You're more important."

I opened my mouth to protest and then shut it. I was really grateful my sister had come to help me, but I worried that she always dropped everything for my sake. Even if I asked her not to. "I've missed you."

Kat's lips twitched into a small smile. "Just as well, I had a four-hour drive to get here."

I collapsed on the bed and patted the spot next to me. "I set my alarm for eight because I thought for sure you wouldn't get here by then."

"I'm an early riser." Kat sat down next to me and took off her shoes. "You know this."

"I do." I stared at the carpet, feeling soothed by my sister's presence. "But what do we do now you're here? We've got all day, then I've got rehearsals after school."

Kat leaned back and looked around. "Surely this town has plenty of things to do?"

I flopped backwards onto the bed. "It's too early."

Kat sighed and reluctantly lay down next to me. We stared up at the ceiling together, and the confused parts of my soul felt peace again. I'd found peace and safety with Nick, but I couldn't trust it. It wouldn't last.

I sighed. "I wish I had never taken this job."

Kat turned to me, and I could feel her eyes on my face. "Why?"

"Because…" I tried to find the reason, tried to articulate how deep the maw had opened inside me. "I wish I could go back to… normal life."

Kat rolled onto her side and looked down at me. "Elle, chicken, this is normal life."

"No." I murmured. "This is a fantasy land, where everyone is happy. It's not real."

Kat was silent for a while. "What do you mean?"

I blinked, then covered my face with my hands. "Because if it's real—if this is real, then—"

Then it was worth abandoning my old life and all my ambitions for. If this whole town—and Nick—was real, then I would have to face the truth.

I didn't want to go back to the woman I used to be. The idea of it made me feel sick. But that truth was something I wasn't ready for. I turned to Kat. "I need you to help me see this isn't real."

Kat was silent for a moment, and she pursed her lips. "I don't think I have all the information for that yet, Elle."

I looked away and took a breath. "Okay. Let's go get some."

I'd show her that Mistletoe Valley was a totally ridiculous, unrealistic fantasy for someone like me. And then she'd tell me I couldn't stay, and that would be that.

"And look! They have a Christmas shop. An entire shop for Christmas decorations and it runs the *whole year round*." I was leading Kat through the town square, both of us holding takeout cups of coffee against the cold winter air. It had snowed lightly overnight, coating everything in a thin carpet of white.

Kat hummed as we peered into the shop. "That's not a bad business gimmick."

"Exactly." I snapped my fingers, feeling giddy. "This whole town is a *gimmick*. That's exactly why I can't stay."

Kat gave me an unreadable look. "Elle, don't get ahead of yourself. You were crying to me last night about how much you wanted to stay."

My phone buzzed in my pocket. It had done that a lot this morning, but I had ignored it. I waved my hand dismissively. "I was feeling overly emotional. I'd had an intense few days."

By intense, I meant fucking Nick on every available surface at every available moment, but I didn't need to tell Kat that. I swallowed, knowing the text messages I'd been getting this morning were probably from Nick checking in on me after last night.

Even though I desperately wanted to answer his messages, fear stopped me. I knew my feelings for him would override my fear of staying, would override my fear of the unknown. I didn't want him clouding my judgement.

I couldn't change my whole life for a man. I couldn't.

Kat waved a hand in front of my face. "Elle. Elle. Okay—you know what? Answer the goddamn phone."

"What?" I croaked.

Kat slid her hand into my bag and brought out my phone. "This buzzed for the third time in an hour. Answer him."

"But—"

"I thought I taught you to never avoid something out of fear." Kat put her hands on her hips. "Or are you really a chicken?"

I sent my sister a dirty look, but relented. She was right. I was running on fear and adrenaline, and I couldn't avoid Nick forever. He didn't deserve that.

NICK: I hope you're okay.

NICK: I'm sorry if anything I said or did last night made it worse.

NICK: I know you're going back to the city, and
I don't want you to change that for me. Or for
Deanna. Or for anyone. If you don't want to see
me, let me know, otherwise I'll pick you up after
rehearsals? Deanna told me you were busy today.

I gripped my phone—hard—and blinked a few times. Jesus,
why did he have to say all the right things? But even as I
wanted to, I couldn't bring myself to respond. Not yet. Not
yet.

Kat flipped her hair out of her face. "Okay. Either put him
out of his misery, or put the phone away, chicken."

I nodded and furiously typed out a message. I couldn't leave
him hanging for any longer. Not Nick.

ME: I'm feeling okay, thank you. My sister's
traveled up though—bit of a long story.

NICK: I see. Want me to give you space to spend
time with her?

I bit my lip. This was a stretch, asking him to meet my
family. Maybe he didn't even feel the way I did. Maybe this
really was just a casual thing for him—

I shook myself. I couldn't say no to him out of fear.

ME: I'm going to have lunch with her at the Hollyoak. You're welcome to join. If you're free?

I bit my lip as I waited for him to reply, the text bubble hovering for a full minute before he did. He was probably busy, he probably couldn't—

NICK: I'd love to. Anything I need to know?

ME: My sister is… protective.

NICK: I see. Can I bring backup?

ME: Who do you have in mind?

NICK: Matt's with me right now.

ME: Great.

We can feed him to her as an offering.

NICK: I'm sure he'll love that.

As easy as that, Nick was meeting my sister. I had no idea how to feel about that. It had been so long since my sister had met any of my intimate partners, because I... hadn't dated anyone seriously in a long time. All of them had been false starts, or unlabelled nightmares that fizzled out and went nowhere.

I sighed and locked my phone. "Done. We're going to lunch with him in an hour."

Kat was watching me intensely, her lips pursed. "Alright. Show me the rest of this illustrious town."

Mistletoe Valley was filling up with holiday makers, and I imagined it would be packed by the end of the week. This perfect town, with its perfect vibes, was a siren call to more than just me, judging by the amount of visitors arriving. I showed Kat some of the boutiques and stores, and even she was impressed by the artisan deli.

Although I couldn't think of someone who wouldn't be impressed by an artisan deli. Those places were magical. With barely a thought, I pulled out my phone.

ME: Just out of curiosity, what's your opinion of the artisan deli?

NICK: I'm ambivalent. Why?

ME: You're strange.

NICK: I'm aware. What's going on with the deli?

ME: My sister is cooing over a limited edition wine label.

Kat wasn't exactly cooing, but she was eyeing the rack with something like religious zeal. The sharp gleam in her eye was her equivalent of squealing in delight. Who knew what would happen if she ever actually smiled at something.

I tapped my finger against the side of my phone. Even now, with my most beloved family with me, I still wanted to text Nick, to banter with him, to listen to what he had to say. My phone buzzed again.

NICK: You know, you could send me a photo so I could BYO it for lunch and really impress her.

ME: That's smart.

It's almost as if you went to law school or something.

NICK: Correct. I learned two things at Stanford:
how to act like an asshole and then how to win
people back over.

ME: No wonder the whole town adores you.

NICK: It's a real skill.

ME: It worked on me, didn't it?

NICK: All part of my evil machinations. Send
me a photo of the wine.

ME: You're not actually…

NICK: Yes actually. I'm not above bribery.

ME: Sent a photo.

What are you doing this morning?

NICK: Sorry, can't talk. I'm working on my evil machinations.

I desperately tried to suppress my smile and looked up to see my sister examining me. There was something in her eyes, something considering. I hadn't seen her look at me like that for a long time.

"What?"

Kat shook her head slightly and ran a hand along the shelf of gourmet pickles. "You really like him, don't you."

It wasn't a question. My sister's eyes were calculating when she faced me again, and I felt… protective of the thing between Nick and I. "Yes."

Kat held my gaze for a long, agonising moment. Eventually, she nodded, frowning.

God, who knows what that even meant? As close as I was to her, I still struggled to understand my sister's expressions sometimes. They were so different to my own, because I had worked so long at making my face expressive, easily readable. Yet another thing to add to the pile of reasons Elle Sutton was only an actor, nothing else.

That was the crux of it. Who was I if I wasn't Elle, the actor?

I drifted after Kat, letting her inspect the artisan goods and me out of the corner of her eye when she thought I couldn't see. But I knew my sister, and knew she wouldn't offer her opinion until it was well planned, until she knew for certain she was right.

Most of the time, she was right. Sometimes she could be wrong. Rarely.

"How's Winterbourne's going?"

Winterbourne's, the department store that Kat managed, was one of the oldest in the state. It was a tough job, but she was capable. Capable, and paid handsomely for the stress. Kat shrugged, eyeing a jar of organic chocolate spread. "Hell. But that's expected."

Particularly around Christmas. I felt another surge of guilt rise, knowing how busy she must be.

Kat beat me to it. "Nope. Don't get that guilty look. I don't do things I don't want to do."

I swallowed my apology and nodded. "Yes, ma'am."

Kat checked her watch and nodded. "Time to check out this Hollyoak Hotel, don't you think?"

She linked her arm with mine, and we walked together through the streets of Mistletoe Valley. Even if I felt like an utter mess inside, I had my sister by my side. For now, everything was okay.

ELLE

The moment we entered the Hollyoak, I was hit by the comforting smell. Mike had really stepped up his game for Christmas. The whole place was decked out, with tinsel and mistletoe strewn everywhere. Even Kat stood still for a moment, a slightly impressed expression passing across her face as she took in the place. Kat slid her gaze to me. "I can almost see what you mean."

I looked around the room. "Exactly. Too perfect."

Kat hummed. "I'm not sure there is such a thing, but yes. Everything is... welcoming."

I could tell by the gleam in her eye that she was evaluating everything, calculating and cold. Possibly storing away decoration ideas for Winterbourne's. I pulled her towards the bar and smiled at Mike.

He saw us coming and leaned on the bar. "Miss Elle! How's the play going?"

I rapped my fingers against the wood. "Great. Although you'd hope so, given it's on very soon."

Mike tipped his head back and barked out a laugh, then turned to Kat. "Glad to hear it. And who's this?"

"My sister. Kat." I nudged her. "She surprised me with a day visit."

"Ah, good. Hope you enjoy your visit, Miss Kat. Elle here's been a real treat to have around."

Kat turned a surprised eye to me. "Has she now?"

I felt a flush coming up on my cheeks. "Do you have a table for lunch, Mike?"

Mike nodded and pointed at a spot in the corner. We were early, so the place wasn't busy, but it would probably fill up soon. "For our illustrious director, you can have the corner spot. Just the two of you?"

"Um." I cleared my throat. "Two more."

Mike gave me a curious look, but said nothing. "Rightio. Any drinks to start off with?"

Kat snapped open her wallet. "Savignon Blanc, thanks."

I caught her eye. It was unusual for her to go so strong with alcohol this early in the day. She shrugged. Given that she'd already driven over four hours this morning, I decided not to comment. Kat sent me a grateful look, and we headed to our table.

Before we got there, however, Nick and Matt walked through the door. Nick's eyes immediately met mine, and I felt something soften inside me, at ease.

I waved at him, and Kat sent me a strange stare. "He's brought a friend."

"I told him to." I gave her a polite smile. I knew it was a gamble, telling Nick to bring a friend, but Kat was overprotective to a fault.

Kat held my gaze for another moment, her lips tightening. My sister didn't like surprises, but she'd just have to deal with this one. Nick needed backup. She pursed her lips. "He looks like a gym bro."

Her eyes dragged over Matt, and I nearly snorted into my glass of water. If there was one type of guy Kat hated more than anything, it was a gym bro. I didn't bother correcting her, because it certainly looked like Matt spent a lot of time in the gym, but I didn't want her hackles raised before she even met him. "He's nice enough. They both are."

Kat made one last suffering look, and smiled tightly at them just as they reached us.

Nick quirked his lips at me before turning his attention to my sister. "Hi. I'm Nick."

"Kat." My sister gave him a once over with calculating eyes. "You're the lawyer, yes?"

"I am." Nick nodded, sending me a quick look. "Although I wouldn't say I'm *the* lawyer, usually I'm just a lawyer."

"Do you often use semantics to be annoying?" Kat quipped, putting her finished glass back on the bar. God, she'd finished that fast—she must have been more tired than I thought.

Nick, to his credit, just smiled at her. "Sometimes. I am a lawyer."

Kat set her viper eyes on Matt. "So I've heard. And you are?"

I blinked at my sister, and shared a look with Nick. "Kat—"

"Matt." Nick's friend slid his hands into his pockets and eyed my sister like she was a new challenge. "Nice to meet you, Kat."

Kat smiled, and looked like she wanted to flay Matt alive. "Call me Katherine."

"When did you drive up, Katherine?" Nick asked politely.

Kat reluctantly looked away from Matt and gave a bland look at Nick. "You can call me Kat."

Nick cleared his throat, and his eyes caught mine. I shook my head a little, watching Matt react to Kat. My eyes darted between them, slightly confused. I'd never seen my sister look so...vicious. Maybe with assholes, but not with someone she'd just met.

Matt was staring at my sister with amusement. "You drove up this morning? You must be tired."

Uh-oh. Kat hated men telling her how she must feel.

Her eyes swivelled back to his, and I could feel her take a breath preparing to eviscerate him—

"Why don't we sit?" I interrupted, and started walking towards the corner table.

"Sounds like a great plan." Nick came with me, and I could feel my sister and Matt following. As we walked, Nick's finger brushed against mine, and I felt a flush of warmth unfurl in my chest. When he was around, I felt centred, like the answer to a question I'd been asking my whole life.

A little terrifying, that realisation. As we sat next to each other, I murmured quickly to him, "I'm sorry about last night."

He sent me a quick look. "You have nothing to apologise for."

I turned away so I wouldn't be tempted to do something ridiculous, like climb into his lap and kiss him hard. Matt and Kate were just sitting down, and I watched them strategically angle themselves away from each other. It was hilarious. It was like they'd both—wordlessly—decided they were about to battle each other.

I shared a small look with Nick and could tell he was seeing the same thing. I pressed my lips together and he cleared his throat again.

"I hope you don't mind, Kat, but I brought a gift for lunch."

Kat eyed Nick with a gleam in her eyes. "I like gifts."

Nick pulled the wine bottle from a paper bag and presented it to Kat. "Not sure if you've had a chance to visit, yet, but the artisan deli down the road stocks some great wine. I thought you might like it."

My sister's eyes lit up, and she tapped her finger against the table. "I thought lawyers weren't allowed to make bribes."

"Sure." Nick flashed her a smile. "But we're not above giving gifts during the week of Christmas. Elle mentioned you liked wine."

She flicked her eyes to me and mellowed out at Nick. "That's clever of you. I accept."

My sister reached for the bottle and opened it straight away, pouring the wine into her wineglass and then each of ours. Matt's eyebrows raised slightly at her abruptness, and I noticed a curious gleam in his eyes when he looked at her. Interesting.

"What do you do for a living, Kat?" Nick interrupted my observations and brought me back to the conversation.

"I'm the Executive Manager of Winterbourne's." Kat answered, her voice sharp.

"The big store in San Francisco? I bought my first suits there when I went to Stanford."

"Then you have good taste." Kat said simply. "Elle led me to believe you lived here, in Mistletoe Valley."

"I grew up here, did law school at Stanford, then moved to LA for work."

"And you're back because?"

"I like it here. It's my hometown." Nick flashed her another winning smile. "I'm setting up a new law firm here. My own."

Kat looked at me briefly. She hummed. "Why now?"

Nick inhaled. "I've waited long enough."

"So you have no love lost for the city?"

"None."

Matt chuckled. "Yeah, Nicky's the golden boy of the town. He couldn't stay away long."

"Remind me why I invited you?" Nick asked Matt.

Matt spread his hands. "You'd already dragged me out of bed."

"And what do you do?" Kat turned her eagle eyed attention to Matt, and he smiled lazily at her.

"Real estate."

Kat raised an eyebrow and took a sip of her wine. Matt looked like he was going to say something else, but Mike interrupted us to take our food orders. The place was filling up with the lunchtime crowd. Mike quickly took our order, and I didn't miss the way his eyes shifted between Nick and I.

My sister looked ready to needle Matt a little more, so I tried to intervene. "Kat, what's the Christmas display look like this year?"

Kat leaned back and gave me a dirty look. "Christmassy."

Nick snorted into his drink.

I looked at them both, then turned to Nick. "Hold up. Do you not like Christmas?"

I knew Kat hated Christmas, but Nick? He'd never given me any sign he hated it. Nick pressed his lips together. He seemed torn, and I could tell that he was trying to be polite.

I raised my eyebrows. "That explains the elf thing."

Matt nearly choked on his drink. "The elf thing?"

"Nick hates elves." I explained. "Figures he would hate Christmas, too."

"Wait," Matt pointed between us, "how do you know he hates elves?"

I turned to Nick, a smug smile on my face. I had long since forgiven him for his rudeness when we first met, but it was fun to tease him a little. "I think you'd better explain."

He crinkled his nose and shrugged at the rest of the table. "I bumped into Elle in November. In LA. I may have been rude to her, and she *happened* to be dressed as an elf."

Kat put her drink on the table. "You already met each other?"

I shrugged. "Yeah. It was a weird chance meeting, which was *hilarious* when I came and saw him here."

"I'll bet." Matt muttered into his drink.

Nick leaned back in his chair. "I just want it on the record that I don't... hate Christmas."

"Oh?" I said.

He made a sheepish smile at me. "No."

"Bullshit, bro." Matt interrupted. "You hate everything about it."

"Correction." Nick glared at Matt. "I *used* to hate everything about it."

"Right. And gold grows on trees." Matt shook his head at Nick.

"It's money." Kat gave Matt a sickly smile. "Money grows on trees."

Matt flashed his canines at my sister and puffed his chest out a little. "I prefer mine. A little more imaginative."

What the fuck was going on? It was like I was watching a tennis match between two incredibly vicious players.

Thankfully, our food arrived, and we could eat in relative peace. Relative being the operative word in that sentence, because I'm fairly certain I caught Kat and Matt glaring at each other several times.

I snuck glances at Nick myself. But they were very different to the ones Kat was sending Matt. I felt my eyes drawn to him, reassuring myself he was there. After my meltdown last night, today I noticed how much being around him helped me feel grounded. I felt like me when I was with him.

I felt like the version of myself that I wanted to be, calm and grounded and *happy*.

Even so, a part of me raged at that truth—that I couldn't possibly find my happiness with another person—that I couldn't rely on someone else like that.

Under the table, Nick's hand brushed against my thigh. It was a gentle, reassuring touch, and I melted inside. Kat and Matt were bickering about something, but I ignored them. I focused on the gentle touch of the man beside me and slid my hand into his. His hand was warm and encompassed mine. His thumb brushed soothing circles against the back of my hand, sparking my nerves.

I looked up and caught Kat observing us.

Suddenly, all I could see in front of me was a future where I kept holding Nick's hand, where everything was calm and peaceful and we carved out a space in the world where I could work out *who the hell I even was*—

I couldn't do it. I became distantly aware of how I was spiting myself—spiting my own happiness. But I couldn't. I couldn't just abandon everything I used to want, could I? Throwing my lot in with someone I'd only met a month ago? That would go against everything I stood for, every bit of independence I wanted to cling to. It didn't matter how miserable I was, at least I could be miserable alone. I was afraid that if I stayed in Mistletoe Valley, Nick would realize how much of a *mess* I was inside, and then where would I be?

I pulled my hand out of his and felt my heart break a little. He took his hand back to his lap, and I could feel a subtle hint of hurt radiating off him. God, I was the most wretched woman in the world, but I couldn't...

I couldn't let myself be happy. I had spent so long without it, so it felt like a lie when I had found it again.

My sister was looking at me, taking in every detail, every single emotion that ran across my face. She placed her napkin on the table and stood abruptly. Thankfully, we were finished eating, so she wasn't being outrightly rude. She cleared her throat and checked her watch. "We'd better go, then."

"Leaving so soon, Katherine?" Matt murmured sarcastically.

Kat gave him a spiteful smile. "I came here for my sister. You'll have to forgive me for wanting to have her to myself for a little longer before she has to work, and I have to leave."

Nick stood. "I'll get the—"

Kat was already moving to the till to pay for our meals. Matt shot up and followed her, grumbling as he went. It obviously affronted him that she was trying to pay for all of us. I allowed myself a moment to smile at the scene. No one could convince my sister to change her mind. Matt could try to get in the way, but I doubted he'd succeed.

That left me standing with Nick, alone, for a few moments. I turned to him. "I'm sorry—"

"You really don't need to apologize." Nick sat softly, but his eyes were shuttered. I'd pulled away from him, effectively rejecting him. My heart wrenched again.

I opened my mouth, trying to find the words to explain the absolute mess that was inside of me, but I couldn't. Nothing came out in time.

My sister returned to my side. "Well, it was a delight to meet you, Nick."

Matt cleared his throat.

She ignored him and linked arms with me, dragging me out of the Hollyoak. I locked eyes with Nick one last time before the doors shut behind me. His eyes were carefully blank.

Kat began walking fast through the streets, but I pulled my arm from hers and stopped. "What are you doing?"

She barely looked back at me. "Not now. We need to get a few blocks away."

I followed her in silence, and after a few minutes, we were far enough away.

Kat crossed her arms and sat on a bench next to the footpath. Her eyes searched my face and she shook her head. "What are you doing, Elle?"

I slowly sat down beside her. "There are many answers to that question depending on what you're actually—"

"What do you want for yourself? From life?" Kat interrupted.

I tipped my head to the sky, watching the clouds drift. It was an unusually sunny day, at odds with my stormy emotions. "That's a very broad question."

"Fine." Kat sighed. "Then what do you want for yourself in your career?"

"Success."

"Bullshit."

"What?" I blinked at her. My sister was a highly successful manager, and she was trying to tell me I didn't want to be successful? "Kat—"

"If all you wanted from life, chicken, was financial success, you would have done a business degree." Kat gave me a sharp look. "But you didn't. You chose a career in the arts. Professional pretending."

I jolted back softly. Kat had never criticized my choice to be an actor before. "Don't make fun of it that way."

"I'm not." Kat insisted. "I'm laying out my thinking. Why did you choose it?"

"I… You encouraged me to do it." I gave her a sharp look. "You told me it was a good idea."

And that had been true. My big sister, my fierce and competent sister, had encouraged me to pursue acting as a career, when the only other people who did so were my acting teachers. She had supported me, bolstered my ambition and my hopes, and encouraged me to see it through. So why was she questioning me now?

"I only encouraged you because I thought it was what you wanted." Kat sighed.

"I wanted it." God, I hoped that was true, that I did actually love acting at some point in my life.

"But you don't anymore. Elle, these past few years you've changed. You have no light left in you." Kat stared at me, her eyes calculating. "Until today. This is the first time I've seen genuine joy on your face. For a long time."

I squeezed my eyes shut. Panic was tightening my throat, so I swallowed it down. "It doesn't matter."

"Chicken, cut that shit out."

I was shocked at the way Kat was speaking to me. She'd never been angry with me like this before. "What?"

Kat stood and put her hands on her hips. "Joy matters. Happiness matters. God knows most of us fall short of it sometimes, but you have found a place, and a person, who makes you light up again. What the fuck are you doing, thinking you have to go back to your miserable life?"

My sister's words echoed in a hard place in my heart, piercing through the last part of my resistance. Tears fell down my face. She was right. I had found something here, a town, and someone I was beginning to love. And my default reaction was that I had to suffer instead?

God, *that* was a lot to unpack with a therapist.

"What am I doing?" I chuckled at the sky, dark humor bubbling up from inside me. "What am I doing?"

Kat made a noise and pulled me into her arms. I clung to her and sobbed softly into her shoulder. I hated how lost I had been, but I was finally feeling like something was being forged inside me. This feeling of being lost was the only way I could find out what actually made me happy. Kat stroked my hair. "I'm sorry, chicken. I'm sorry for not seeing it earlier."

I pulled back from my sister, who had always been so ready to take the fall for me. "This isn't your responsibility. It's my life."

"I know. So, what are you going to do about it, then?"

My shoulders hunched up to my ears, but I felt something fall into place inside me. This entire month had felt like I had taken a wall down, brick by brick. This was what I knew:

it didn't matter that I was lost. It didn't matter that I didn't have all the answers about what I wanted to do. I had found something here in Mistletoe Valley that had awakened the real me—the one I had locked inside and forgotten.

I wasn't about to let that go.

I straightened and nodded to my sister. "Thank you."

Her eyebrows raised. "That wasn't an answer."

A laugh burst out of my throat. "I don't have one. I know what I want to do today—but I have no clue what I'm doing next week, or the week after, or after that." Another delirious chuckle. "I have no plan. Nothing at all."

Kat frowned. "I feel like I haven't actually helped you, then."

I clutched her arm, shaking my head. "No. You have. I promise you, you have."

Kat had helped me to work out a fundamental truth about how I wanted to exist in this world: I *didn't* need to have a plan. I didn't need to worry about what was going to happen in the future. If I was unhappy anyway, who the fuck cared? Anything was better than the life I had been living.

Kat's eyes roved over my face, and whatever she saw in my expression made her nod. "Good. You've got the sparkle back."

I smiled at my sister and gave her another hug. "You're the best. Thank you for coming to my rescue."

Kat put her arms around me. "I don't think you needed rescuing as much as a smack over the head."

I huffed out a laugh. "You've got to go, so you're not driving through the night."

Kat's lips twitched. "Any idea when I might see you again?"

I gave her a wry smile. "No clue."

Kat hummed, and we began walking again. "You know, he seems like a good one."

"You barely talked to him." I nudged her. "You were too busy bickering with Matt. What was that all about?"

"You know I hate those gym bro types." Kat looked amused. "Besides, I noticed plenty. I'm an excellent read of people."

I was silent for a moment. "You're right. He is good."

Kat just hummed, and we kept walking into the distance. I smiled. The path ahead of me was murky, but I was happy about that. For the first time, it felt like a deliberate choice, like I had taken power back into my own hands.

Tonight, I needed to talk to Nick.

ELLE

Nick didn't come to see me after rehearsal. The realization jolted through me as Deanna and I packed up, and I kept watch on the door. The last of the kids left, and he was not there.

I felt like an idiot. It made sense that he might want to give me space, especially after I pulled away from him yesterday. And yet here I was, still sneaking glances at the door, waiting for him to arrive. It was unsettling how quickly Nick Corrigan had slipped into my life.

But I was done running from things because they unsettled me. I was done being scared, and I was done being a coward.

Rehearsals were going well. We were doing dress runs tomorrow night, and then only three days before the performance. The kids were really excited, and I was confident it would be a good show. It had been so easy, this whole process. I'd discovered I was much happier as the person in the chair directing than I was onstage. Funny.

Even after the long hours of rehearsal, I didn't feel tired. Instead, I was jittery, nerves pulsing through me. Because Nick hadn't come to see me, and I knew that meant something.

I needed to see him. I needed to tell him what I had decided, what I had realized about myself and what I wanted. I needed to apologize for pulling away, and I needed to reassure him I wanted him.

I pulled my coat on and nodded at Deanna. "I'm going for a walk. I might not be home tonight."

Deanna nodded. "Alright. I'll see you tomorrow if that's the case."

I went out into the cold night air and headed towards Nick's house with purpose. After spending most of the past week there, I was sure it would only be a ten-minute walk.

I pulled my coat closer around me. Ten minutes in the near freezing cold. It would be my penance for running away from him yesterday, penance for pulling away from him at lunch. Slogging through the snow and the cold was what I deserved.

Great.

Twenty minutes later, my nose was running and my ears were burning from the cold. But I'd made it, and I marched up the steps to Nick's front door, knocking five times. There were lights on inside, thank goodness, so he had to be home.

It was another minute before he answered, and he blinked down at me when he opened the door. "Elle."

"You didn't visit me after rehearsal." The word blurted out of my mouth before I could stop them. I had a plan, that I was going to apologize and explain myself and—

Something flashed across Nick's face, and he glanced over my head. "Yeah. I wasn't sure—I wanted to give you space."

"You—you thought I didn't want you to?" I sniffled. The cold walk had made my nose drip. I looked at him, really looked at him, and saw the guarded way he was holding himself, like he wanted to flee at any moment. By pulling away, I had done that. I could see it had shut him down, closed him off to me.

"I don't really like pursuing people who don't want me to, so yes." Nick gave me a tight smile.

"I want you to." I breathed out. "I don't want space."

Nick clenched his hand around the door. "I didn't want to get in the way, especially with your sister—"

"She's already left to go back to the city." I took a breath. "I'm sorry I…pulled away."

Nick's hand clenched again, but he kept his face blank. "You don't need to apologize, Elle. You have your own things to figure out, and I shouldn't have—"

I couldn't stand letting him dismiss himself, rationalizing his way out of the situation. "My sister was angry at me."

"Oh?"

"Yeah." I cleared my throat, shoving my hands in my pockets. "She was angry, because being here is the happiest she's seen me in a long time. And she's worried I'm going to just throw it away."

"Throw what away?" His expression nearly broke me, half guarded and half hopeful.

I knew I had to ask him. I had to know. I wanted it all out in the open now, not just sideways looks and avoiding talking about the truth.

"What would happen if I took Deanna's offer and worked here?" I gestured at the space separating us. "What would happen with this?"

Nick sucked in a breath. "Why are you asking?"

"Because it's a stupid decision to make until I know that detail. Because I really like you, Nick. I like you a lot, and it's come on really quickly. That terrifies me. But I need to know—is this just a casual thing for you?"

Nick blew out a breath, suddenly looking frustrated. "You're really asking me that question?"

A flush came up on my cheeks. "Yes."

"Of course not." He replied, almost angry.

I inhaled, but words were stuck in my throat.

Nick went on. "It hasn't been casual for me since about ten minutes after I met you."

The ground was going to fall out from under me, the way his words hit me. I knew, deep down, that Nick felt strongly for me. God knows I felt something strong for him. But hearing it out loud, after weeks of carefully skirting around the issue, made my heart beat faster, squeezing in my chest. "Really?"

"Really." Nick gave me a wry smile.

I swallowed. Now was my chance to be honest with myself, to be honest with him, with what I wanted, with my own vulnerabilities. "I want to—I want to stay a little longer after

Christmas. I don't know if Deanna will have me, but I'm going to ask—"

"Stay with me." The words fell out of Nick's mouth, and he looked a little shocked that he'd said them so quickly.

I gave him a surprised look. "Really?"

"Really, Elle." Nick's eyes were bright, but then he shrugged a shoulder. "But if you don't want to, I'm sure Deanna would—"

"I'll stay. With you." I blurted out. This entire conversation was a mess, but I could tell by the look in Nick's eyes that he was right there with me.

This felt right. This felt like the best decision I'd made in my whole life. Nick's eyes took me in, and he opened the door wider. "Do you want to come in? Sorry. You look cold."

I laughed, surprise bubbling out of my throat. "I'm freezing."

I stumbled through the doorway, but my foot caught on the threshold. I tripped forward, right into Nick. He caught me, cradling me firmly in his arms, and I just… melted. Distantly, I was aware of the door shutting, and then Nick's warm, glorious arms closed around me. I wrapped my arms around his waist and snuggled into his chest. Nick rested his chin on my head, and he chuckled gently. "Did you actually walk all the way here in the freezing cold?"

"I was…" My teeth finally caught up and chattered slightly. "I thought an evening stroll would be nice."

"I'm sorry I didn't show up after rehearsal. I said I would." Nick sighed, his breath rustling my hair. "I just didn't want to go in case I wasn't... wanted."

I squeezed him tighter. "You're very wanted around me, thank you very much."

"Yeah." He ran a hand over my hair. "I'm getting that now."

I tilted my head up so I could see him and rested my chin on his chest. It was comical, the near foot of height difference between us. But he made me feel safe, and he made me feel warm inside. I scanned my eyes over the column of his throat, to the softness in his warm eyes. He really was gorgeous—masculine and pretty in equal parts. I bit my lip. "What were you doing tonight?"

"Nothing important." His eyes flicked over my face. "Are you hungry?"

I gave him a sly grin. "Always."

He laughed, the vibrations echoing in my body. He pulled away softly and grabbed my hand. "For food."

I hummed and let him pull me into the kitchen, where he picked me up and sat me on the countertop. He stepped into the space between my legs, and I pretended to consider. "I guess I could also go for some food."

Nick's lips curved into a sly smile, and his pupils widened. "Maybe you could try the virtue of patience."

"You keep saying that, and I keep having to tell you that patience is overrated." I huffed, running my fingers over the hem of his olive sweater.

He pulled away with a smile. "And what if I said that it would please me to feed you right now?"

I rolled my eyes and crossed my legs. "Alright then."

I looked down and saw that he had been right in the middle of making dinner. Homemade pasta was strewn across the counter, flour dusting the surface. I laughed in surprise. "You were just making pasta for yourself?"

Nick smiled and shrugged. "It's relaxing for me. One of my roommates got me into it in college. I freeze the pasta I don't cook."

I put my chin on the heel of my hand. "You're so weird."

"So you *don't* want some fresh pasta?"

"No, I absolutely do." I leaned back on my hands. "I just like teasing you."

Nick hummed, and I watched him work. His strong hands deftly handled the thin ribbons of hand cut pasta, dropping them into the boiling water. He had a sauce already simmering in a pan, and after what felt like only a minute, he pulled out the pasta and put it straight into the sauce.

The smells were incredible, and I realized how hungry I was. My stomach gurgled, and he gave me an amused look from the stove. I could get used to this. Coming home from work, sitting with him in the kitchen, watching him cook and reveling in the peace and joy it gave me.

The old familiar panic rose at the thought, but I swallowed it down. With time, I hoped I could get rid of those fears altogether.

We ate together; me sitting on the counter and Nick standing close next to me. Neither of us wanted to be separated by a table. I liked it this way, casual and comfortable and so *domestic*. It was like I belonged in this kitchen, in this house.

"Do you want to know something about me?" I put my fork down on my plate, watching him.

Nick nodded, his eyes warm. "Always."

I cleared my throat. "My full name is Eleanor. But I stopped using it when I was a kid because I thought no one would hire an actress called Eleanor. No one but my family knows that."

"Eleanor." Nick rolled the name around on his tongue, and I felt a lick of heat roll in my stomach. It sounded good in his mouth. "It suits you."

I laughed, shaking my head. "No, it doesn't. Don't lie."

"I'm not lying." Nick put down his plate. "It's a beautiful name."

"I still prefer Elle."

Nick's lips twitched. "As you wish."

"Okay, Westley." I pushed his shoulder. "Thank you for dinner."

"My pleasure." Nick cleared our plates away, and I watched the muscles in his back work as he did. A whole other type of appetite was working up inside me again. "I'd be a poor host if I didn't feed you."

"Oh, you're my *host* now?" I teased him, desire unfurling in my belly. "Would my host be able to show me to the bedroom?"

"What for? I've got a whole night's activities planned, including chess, whist, catching up on the latest news—"

"Nick." I said roughly.

He turned. "Elle."

"Come here." I widened my legs slightly, but it frustrated me when he stayed in place.

He shook his head. "Patience, remember?"

"I've been fed." I insisted.

"Yeah, but what if you need something else? Water? Some tea?" He walked closer to me, brushing his hand over my knee. "I don't want my *guest* to be left wanting."

"Your guest is already *wanting*," I whispered.

Nick's eyes darkened, and I could tell he wanted me just as much. But for whatever reason, he was holding back, resisting the urge to give in just yet. "Are you sure?"

"Nick, I'm about to beg—"

"Are you sure about staying? After Christmas—with me?" There was something vulnerable in his eyes now, and I softened.

"I'm sure." I said quietly. "I don't know if I want to stay… forever, yet. But I'm sure about now."

Nick sighed and slid a hand into my hair. "That's all I need."

He picked me up and carried me to his bedroom.

NICK

S he was here, in my arms. And she was *staying*. It didn't matter to me if she couldn't commit to anything concrete. She had made the choice to try, to stay for a little longer, and suddenly the noose that had been tightening around my neck loosened.

Because now I could hope for something that lasted a little longer than just December. I squeezed her tighter to me, her legs wrapped around my waist as I took us upstairs.

She felt like she was made for my arms, and I had an urge to never let her go again. For now, at least, I wouldn't have to.

Elle was nibbling at my jaw, and I groaned against her hair.

"I've missed you," she whispered into my skin.

I felt her words settle into my heart, burrowing her way further into it. "Me too, baby."

I felt like a teenager again, shaky and unsure. Every time I touched Elle, she undid me. Her hands brushed over my hair, and I shook with need.

Finally, finally, I reached the bedroom and laid her down on the bed. She held on to me, and I settled between her thighs. She looked like a goddess lying like this. Her golden blonde hair was haloed around her head, and her dark lashes brushed her cheeks as she smiled coyly at me. "What is it?"

I pressed a kiss to her lips, then pulled back. "My full name is Nicholas, which you can probably guess."

She smiled, and it lit up her face. I was so far gone for this woman. "It's ironic you hate Christmas, then. Good old St. Nicholas would be sad."

I huffed and pressed another kiss to her cheek, working my way down her jaw and onto the delicate skin of her neck. "I don't… hate Christmas."

She squirmed under my tongue when I found the spot she liked. "You—totally do."

"Do not." I pulled the hem of her dress up, revealing her creamy skin to my touch. Elle was partial to dresses, I had noticed. I didn't mind at all, because it made it so much easier for me to do this. She gasped a little when my knuckles brushed along the front of her panties, and I watched her face, memorising the pleasure I could wring from her. "You did so well, being so patient for me, baby."

Her eyes flashed, and I knew I'd hit the mark. She liked praise, and her brows pulled together.

I loved so many of the facets of Elle Sutton, but this one right here, under me and panting with pleasure, was burned behind my eyes.

We'd had sex so many times over the past week, but this time felt different. Now, every time I touched her skin, I got a shock of energy reminding me she was staying, that she was *choosing* me, even if it was just for a little longer—

I pushed my fingers inside her wet core, and I felt her pussy clench around me. She was so wet, so worked up, already. Her body responded so well to mine, like they had made her just for me.

She clutched at my shoulders. "Nick—"

"Are you all wet just for me, baby?"

She clenched her eyes shut and nodded, whining a little when I brushed my thumb gently over her clit. It was like playing an instrument—her body—strumming it until I got just the right sounds from her, just the right reactions.

It didn't take her long to come. She was so pent up, so tight, and I whispered dirty things into her ears to help her along.

"So good, baby. You gonna come just for me? Come on my fingers, like a good girl?"

She gasped and tensed, and I knew the last phrase had done it. I filed the information away and watched her writhe on my hand, her inner walls spanning from her orgasm. I grinned into her neck. "That's a new one."

She shoved my shoulder playfully once her breathing evened out. "Shut up."

"Alright." I quickly took off our clothes, kissing her whenever I could. Her lips were a drug to me, especially now. She was staying, she was staying, she was staying—

"Nick." Elle's voice broke through my frantic thoughts. "Are you okay?"

I touched my forehead to hers and forced myself to take a breath. "I'm really glad you're staying. A little longer."

A smile broke out on her face, and I fought the urge to collapse against her. "Me too."

"Good." I surged forward and captured her lips with mine, wanting more of her, wanting all of her—

"Nick." Elle broke away, a strange light in her eyes. I had the feeling whatever she was about to say was going to destroy me. "I'm on the pill."

I blinked. What did she mean?

Elle gave me a meaningful look. "And I'm clean. I haven't been with anyone since my last test."

I clenched my teeth together, hard, so I wouldn't gape at her. Was she seriously asking me if I could fuck her raw? "I'm clean too," I ground out.

Elle's eyes glinted in the low light, and she smiled slowly at me. "So?"

I pressed my face into her neck so she wouldn't see my tortured expression. "Fucking hell, baby, you're going to kill me."

"But like… a good death, right?"

I snorted. "Are you sure?"

"I wouldn't mention it if I wasn't." She replied.

As a lawyer, I knew of all the reasons I shouldn't risk it. Rationally, there were many. But I trusted Elle, and I knew she trusted me. And fuck it, I'd never wanted to do something so bad in my life. Something went feral inside me at the idea of getting to come inside her. "You want me to fill you up, baby?"

Her eyes went half lidded, and she bit her lip. A flush spread across her pretty tits, and I knew that I'd just turned her on again. "Uh-huh."

I held her legs wide and slowly pressed in, and we both groaned together. Without a condom, this felt so much better. It felt like I was becoming one with her, and I never wanted to leave—

It felt like coming home.

She clenched hard around me, and I felt her soft hands grabbing at me, pulling me further in. "Nick—"

"I know." I could hear the emotion in her voice, the need and desperation and want. "I'll give it to you, baby."

I pulled out and plunged back into her, creating a rhythm that said something. It was like with every thrust; I was saying what I couldn't voice. Not yet. She was everything; she was home; she was the answer to every question I'd been asking myself my whole life.

Elle clenched around me, and I groaned into her neck. I wanted her to clench around me again, I wanted to feel her pant and moan and writhe under me, so I whispered in her ear, "You're such a good girl, taking me so well."

Her inner muscles fluttered around me, and she whined. "Jesus."

"Not quite." I smiled into her neck, and then I lost myself to the pleasure of thrusting deep inside her for a moment.

I couldn't remember the last time I'd enjoyed sex this much, or that I'd cared about the person I was with as much. And judging by the look in Elle's eyes—because she had agreed to stay—I knew it wasn't just me.

I shuddered, my own climax approaching alarmingly fast. But I wanted to feel her clenched around me, wanted Elle to have her own before I found mine.

Her hands clutched at me, and I knew it wouldn't take much to tip her over. So responsive. I grabbed her jaw firmly, directing her attention to my face as I kept pushing inside her. "You want me to fill you up, baby?"

Elle whined, going soft and pliant under me. "Y-yeah."

"Need you to show me how much you want it, Elle. Need you to come around my cock, okay?"

She clenched around me, and I knew that my soft command had nearly pushed her over the edge. "Please, Nick, please—"

"I'm not stopping." I slipped my hand down to the apex of her thighs and rubbed my thumb over her clit lightly. "I want you to come around me, okay? Then I'll fill you up."

"Please, please, I want it—I—" She thrashed under me, and I locked my eyes onto her face. I wanted to watch every moment of her coming undone. I wanted to see every expression on her perfect face. "Nick—"

"I've got you, baby," I leaned in closer to her and kissed her temple. "Just want you to show me how badly you want it."

"I want it, I want it—" She threw her head back, and I doubled down on my thrusts, keeping my rhythm relentless, wanted to push her over—

Every muscle in her body tensed, and I soaked in her expression, her perfect lips open, her brows puckered together. Then she shuddered around me, and I groaned. Her internal walls were squeezing me hard, and it was like heaven and hell. My balls tightened, and I wanted to fall right over the edge with her. "I'm gonna—"

"Please. Please, Nick, fill me up." Elle groaned, still in the throes of her own climax.

All it took was Elle saying those little words, and then I was barreling into my own orgasm, my cock jerking inside her. She whimpered and softly bit into my shoulder. I had to close my eyes for a moment, because it felt too perfect. It felt like I would move heaven and earth to never give this up.

She was everything.

We caught our breaths, and I rolled off her. She sighed and curled into my side, and I stared at the ceiling. My heart was beating fast from exertion, but also a realization.

I loved her.

I'd felt it coming on for a while, but I think I had been holding myself back, not allowing myself to admit it. But now that she had come to me after deciding to stay, I couldn't hold it back any longer.

She hummed in my arms, and I pressed a kiss to her head. It was paltry compared to the emotions raging inside me, but at least it was something.

"You good?" I asked her.

She hummed again, her eyes still closed. "Very."

I pressed another kiss to her forehead and slowly, gently, pulled away from her. Before we fell asleep, I had to get her comfortable and clean her up. I wanted to take care of her so well, so she never left. "I'll be back in a minute."

Elle let me go with a soft sound, and I padded away. It only took me a minute to find a clean washcloth, wet it and return to find her watching me from the bed. "I could have—"

"It's okay. Stay there," I repeated, then kneeled down beside her and helped clean her up. The sight of my spend oozing out from inside her nearly had me hardening up again, but sleeping next to her sounded more appealing right then.

I threw the washcloth to the floor when I was done and lay back on the bed with her. She snuggled straight into me, and I wrapped my arms around her.

I took a breath. "Elle?"

"Yeah?"

"I'm really glad you're staying."

She was silent for a while, and I thought she had drifted off. I closed my eyes too, preparing to fall asleep. But right before I did, I heard her whisper, "You feel like home, Nick. Of course, I'm staying."

I had the best dreams of my life that night.

ELLE

I t was the day of the Christmas play. The kids were running
  around screaming, and I was trying not to freak myself
out. It would be fine. Deanna had reassured me many times
that the play was in good shape, so I had to trust her. I'd never
done this before, had always only been on the other end of
it, acting on the stage. Not that I'd done much of the acting
thing for a while.

It didn't matter. I was proud of the work I had done with this
play, proud of what the kids had done, too. They were all so
open and joyful, and I could tell that the families of Mistletoe
Valley were going to really enjoy the show.

Only three hours to go before the curtain opened. I was
standing in the Town Hall trying to calm the kids and help
organize the setup of the audience chairs. I was only half
successful.

My phone buzzed in my pocket, and I pulled it out. I needed
a moment's break, anyway.

NICK: Everything going okay?

ME: I mean, there's no fire and no broken bones, so we're going well. Celia's been doing laps of the room for the last fifteen minutes, though.

NICK: I'm looking forward to it.

ME: Save me a seat, will you? Deanna told me to watch from the audience, so I get to 'revel in my achievements' or whatever.

NICK: Of course. Want some hot cocoa beforehand?

ME: You know I'd never say no to that :)

NICK: I'm aware. I'll see you in 30, then?

I put my phone away, smiling like a madwoman. It was ridiculous the amount of joy that Nick gave me. I'd spent the last few days grinning from ear to ear, and even the kids at rehearsals had asked me what was going on. Nick Corrigan was what was going on, and I was staying for a while longer, and I was happy.

Incandescently happy—one could say.

I focused on setting up the chairs for the next thirty minutes and watching the kids run amok. When Nick finally arrived, they screamed and swarmed him. He fought his way through and smiled at me.

I cleared my throat at Celia, who was clinging to him like a limpet. "Celia, why don't you go find some more chairs for the corner? Your grandmother would want a good spot."

Celia raced off, and finally Nick and I were mostly alone—one of the teen girls hovered nearby like she wanted to eavesdrop, and I raised my eyebrows at her and chuckled. "It's almost like you're a celebrity."

"They just know me well." Nick handed me the cup of cocoa with a soft smile. "I got extra chocolate sprinkles tonight."

I hid my smile behind the cocoa cup as I took a sip. "You know me well."

"Yeah." Nick looked around the hall, taking in the rows of chairs. I watched him inspect the decorations the kids had placed around the walls, the mistletoe and tinsel and fake snow. "It looks…"

"Like your worst nightmare?" I teased him, nursing my cocoa between us.

"Pretty. I was going to say it looks pretty." Nick looked down at me, and his eyes were warm. "How much time have you got?"

My smile turned sly. "Not enough time for *that*, Nick Corrigan."

"That's not what I meant, but thanks for putting the idea into my head." Nick shuffled closer, and my lips twitched with the urge to lean forward and kiss him. "Now I'm going to be thinking about that for the next few hours."

I huffed and took another sip of cocoa to restrain myself from pouncing on him in front of all the kids. I checked my watch. "I've got another five minutes before I need to wrangle the kids."

"Are you nervous?"

"About the show?" I shook my head. "No. The kids are great, and it's not really about me, is it? That's kind of the big relief, really."

"Good." Nick looked like he was about to say something, but we were interrupted by Deanna rushing out from backstage. Something was clearly wrong.

I braced myself for bad news, and Deanna flapped her hands, "I've just had to send Katie home. She fainted backstage."

I swore. Katie was fifteen, and she was playing the narrator. If she was out of the picture, someone else would have to step up. The only problem was I couldn't think of anyone who could fill it without—

"I was thinking you could read the part. The kids agree with that idea. They'd love to see you up there with them."

I blinked. "But, shouldn't one of the other kids—"

"It's too much work for any of them to take on right now. I think it's a good solution."

I was silent for a minute and took a breath. I could feel Nick observing me. Over a month away from performing, here I was being asked to *pretend* again. It filled me with dread, but I needed to step up for the sake of the play. It was my job. "What about you?" I asked Deanna.

Deanna gave me a wry smile. "I don't go onstage anymore, love. I hate it."

This shocked me. Deanna hated performing? I had no idea she felt that way. I took a breath and cleared my head. That left me as the only option. The only saving grace was that I had memorized all the lines from sitting through them in rehearsals. I nodded and swallowed. "Okay. I guess we're doing this."

Deanna headed backstage and gestured for me to follow her. "You're about the same size as Katie, so the costume should still fit, but let's tell the kids about the change of plans and then—"

I looked behind me briefly, back at Nick. He gave me a wry smile and a nod, and I shrugged back. I mouthed 'bye' to him and let myself be led backstage, trying to ignore the anxiety igniting in my stomach.

I wasn't lying to Nick earlier. When I was just Elle the director, I wasn't nervous at all. But the thought of standing in front of an audience again, being an actor… It was terrifying. Not for the usual reasons of stage fright or nerves; it was terrifying because it represented everything I hated, everything I didn't like about myself.

But we had a show to put on, and I would be damned before I let the Mistletoe Valley Christmas play down. I'd suck it up for a single night, and then it would be over.

Then I'd get to enjoy Christmas with Nick.

I looked down at the script in front of me, reminding myself of the first line of the play for the forty-second time. I adjusted my hat, making sure it was secured firmly on my head.

I was dressed as an elf.

The irony wasn't lost on me. Here I was, dressed similarly to how I had been when Nick and I had first met. I was holiday cheer embodied. Funny how, somewhere along the line, acting had become synonymous with everything I dreaded. Except, this play wasn't about me. I might have directed it and was now narrating it, but it wasn't for me. It was for the town.

It didn't matter if my hat was perfect, or my face pretty enough, or if I stumbled over a line. It was about the kids, and it was about people enjoying it.

I could hear the chatter of the audience. The curtain would go up in less than three minutes, and I was the first thing they were going to see. But nothing, except for the old ghosts of my acting teachers past snagged my brain.

I could do this. This wasn't about me. That realization freed me up, helped me feel lighter. Nick would be watching. Nick, and the rest of Mistletoe Valley, the place that had become my home these past weeks. And I was staying, for now. God knows for how long, because I couldn't commit to that yet, but I was staying. That had to count for something.

I had a job to do, so I swallowed my nerves, took a deep breath, and walked onstage.

The play was a huge success. The kids were delightful, better than I had hoped, and I could tell the audience was enjoying every minute. They laughed, they gasped, they cheered in the final act when the lovers overcame their obstacles and committed to each other. I was just the narrator, guiding them through the story.

I'd never had more fun in my life.

It was Christmas, and I was dressed as an elf—and I didn't even care about that. I didn't care, because I finally felt like I belonged in a community again.

When we took our bows, all I could feel was relief. Pride—in the kids and their achievements—but also relief that I had done it. I'd come here, to this strange job, knowing I needed a change. And I'd found it.

I hugged every single kid backstage, praising them and telling them how proud I was of their work. Deanna was there, and she squeezed my shoulder. "Brilliant work. Everyone loved it, I could tell."

I hugged her, swiping my hat off. "Sure you're not biased."

"Of course I'm biased." Deanna nudged me and took me aside. "There's someone who wants to meet you."

Who could want to meet me? I blinked. "I already know Nick's in the audience—"

"It's not Nick, love." Deanna gave me a meaningful look and beckoned me to the corner of the backstage area, where a smart-looking woman was standing. She looked vaguely familiar to me, but I couldn't place her. Deanna cleared her throat. "Elle, this is Maria Munroe, the artistic director of the Chapel Theatre Company."

I resisted the urge to gape. I'd wanted to audition for Chapel for years, but Leslie had never got me a spot. They were an incredible company, ethical and experimental and *cool*. All the best new works went through Chapel. Why was the artistic director of the company standing here wanting to meet me? I clenched my hand around my elf hat, suddenly feeling ridiculous, but smiled my best smile at Maria. "Nice to meet you. What brings you here?"

Maria waved a hand and shared a smile with Deanna. "Mistletoe Valley is one of my favorite holiday spots, after Deanna introduced me to it many years ago. I was her first director here."

"You directed the first Mistletoe Valley Christmas play?"

"I did." Maria gave me a smile. "And it taught me a lot more than my training ever had. Wouldn't you agree?"

I swallowed, slowly easing into the conversation. "That's… exactly how I'd describe it. It's probably the best experience I've had in years."

"Elle reminds me a lot of you, Maria." Deanna interjected. "She wasn't afraid of being experimental."

Maria's eyes tracked my face, and she smiled. "You work in LA, right?"

"Yeah." I nodded, nervous about where this was going. Was I about to be blacklisted? Deanna wouldn't do that to me, and besides… I didn't even know if I cared about that world anymore. Right?

"Interesting." Maria crossed her hands. "Why haven't we seen you audition for us at Chapel?"

"I've begged my agent for a while, but she never got me a spot."

Maria's eyebrows rose. "We see anyone who has an agent. Invites go out to everyone each year. Who's your agent?"

"Leslie." Deanna answered for me, saying the name like a curse word.

Maria made a face, then winced at me. "Sorry. She's had a vendetta against the company ever since I yelled at her publicly."

I nearly snorted, suddenly liking Maria much more. "I wish I could have seen that."

"I'm sure." Maria gave me an appraising look. "Would you say you enjoyed creating theater? It can be hard for actors to pivot."

I looked back at the stage, as the last kids sidled out to their waiting families. I hadn't expected to enjoy it—had just wanted to do the job, get my paycheck and go back to the city—but I'd found much more than I'd bargained for with the experience. "I loved every minute."

"I'm really glad to hear that." Maria smiled at me. "I have a... slightly odd proposal for you, Elle."

My breath hitched in my throat, and I tensed. "What is it?"

Maria shared a look with Deanna. "Would you be interested in working with Chapel?"

"What—" My eyes darted between Deanna and Maria. "What do you mean?"

"We've just had one of our artists pull out of our first show next season from illness. We need a replacement. It's a collaborative show, an unknown work, and we need actors who know their stuff, who can add their own voice to the piece. After seeing you tonight, I feel you're the perfect person for that."

Something clunked in my stomach. Shock raced through my system, and I blinked at Maria. "Do you... want me to audition? I'm..."

"Maria doesn't particularly like the audition process." Deanna interjected, somewhat wryly.

"Rehearsals start first thing in January." Maria brushed away my concern and fished something out of her pocket. "If you're interested, take this and text me after Christmas. I'd need to know Boxing Day."

I stared at her extended hand, at the tiny rectangle of paper in it. It was everything I'd ever wanted, my entire career. An offer of something real. Something big—falling right into my lap. God, I didn't even have to audition for it. This was every actor's dream. At the very least, I could reach my hand out and take the damn card.

So why wasn't I?

I thought back to every moment I'd had in Mistletoe Valley, realizing that I was done pretending. If I picked up that card, would I be agreeing to more of that?

Except… Maria didn't strike me as a woman who wanted pretense. Hell, she'd seen me perform in a kid's Christmas play and decided I was one of her next actors for a show at Chapel Theatre Company.

This felt like one of those moments that I would replay forever, would always wonder whether I made the right decision. The hesitation must have read on my face, because Deanna murmured to me, "Take the card now, Elle. Decide later."

I jolted and stretched out my hand. Deanna was right. It was just a card. It wasn't a commitment. So why did it feel like it was burning into my palm? I beamed at Maria, my old practised megawatt smile slipping into place. "Thank you for the offer, Maria."

Maria's eyes bore into mine, and I got the feeling she had seen my indecision. She nodded around the hall, smiling at the rafters. "It's a beautiful town, isn't it?"

"It is." I swallowed my confusion.

Maria looked wistful. "I nearly stayed here, you know. My career hadn't taken off yet, and I thought it might be better to admit defeat and live simply."

My heart stopped. "What?"

"I decided not to stay, which was a good decision for me in the end." Maria inhaled. "I imagine it will be hard to leave, but I suggest you try. Even just for a bit. There's something about this place that can cast a spell, but it doesn't last once you're out of it."

"There's nothing wrong with staying." Deanna asserted quietly.

Maria shot her an apologetic look. "Of course. Just some advice to someone in my shoes twenty years ago."

I clenched my fingers around the business card. "Thank you for the advice. And the offer."

Maria gave me another smile and stepped away. "I won't keep you any longer. I'm sure there are others who want to congratulate you."

The rest of the audience was milling about as I walked down the stairs and through the stage door. I slipped the card into my pocket and slipped on my smile, ready to find Nick and get out of there. I didn't want to chat, anymore, didn't want to bask in anything. I just wanted to curl up beside the fire with Nick, and forget the rest of the world existed.

Unfortunately, the rest of the world had other plans.

Families immediately swarmed me—parents of kids in the play—hugging, kissing, and congratulating me. It was near-ly overwhelming, but every interaction was positive, every person had something nice they wanted to say. The tide of congratulations swept me away for several minutes, and I got lost in the swell of bodies. I hadn't even seen Nick yet. Maybe he wasn't even here anymore—

A hand pressed against my back, and I relaxed. I knew who it was, had felt his hands on my body enough in the past weeks to recognize his touch. Nick. I tore my attention away from Sally's mum for a brief moment to give him a smile, and he pressed soothing circles into my back. A part of me went warm and fuzzy inside, instantly at ease in his presence.

The card was burning in my pocket, but I ignored it. Nick cleared his throat to interrupt an eager parent. "Sorry Theodora, but I've got to steal Elle for a moment."

Sally's mum, Theodora, nodded and blinked, but I was grateful when Nick pulled us to the side, against a wall. Nick pressed a paper cup of water into my hand. "Drink."

I sighed in relief and drank the whole cup. "I haven't drunk since before the show."

"I had a feeling." Nick slid his hands into his pockets. "You did spectacularly, by the way. Although I don't think you need me to say that." Nick gave a meaningful look around the room.

My heart warmed, the empty paper cup light in my hands. I leaned against the wall and gave Nick a searching look. "Your opinion matters to me. If I'm being honest, I'm not a big fan of the general congratulations."

"I thought you would have loved it."

"Not really." I crinkled my nose.

Nick nodded, and I knew he understood. It was so rare for me to be able to say so few words and feel understood implicitly. Nick subtly brushed a finger down my waist, and I belatedly realised I was still dressed as an elf.

A laugh bubbled up from my throat, and I gestured to my ensemble. "I swear, this was not my idea."

Nick chuckled. "I was just about to say that the outfit is growing on me."

"Oh really?" I stepped a little closer, and was keenly aware of the crowded hall. I wished we were back home. Back at his home, I corrected myself. "And why is that?" I crooned.

"You know why." His lips curled into a dark smile. "But I need to correct a wrong assumption you just made."

"What's that?"

"I never hated the costume on you." He smirked down at me.

"Oh?" I felt my curiosity pique. "You certainly seemed unimpressed that day."

"Incorrect. I was frustrated that a gorgeous woman—dressed in a ridiculously hot elf outfit—had disrupted my already busy day. And I knew, the moment I saw you, that I was going to be thinking of you in that outfit all day." Nick admitted.

"You were angry because I was…attractive?" I couldn't help it, I laughed. "That is the most ridiculous thing."

"I was also in a rush and you'd messed up my paperwork." Nick conceded. "But you were gorgeous to me, even then."

"So…the elf outfit stays on?"

"I was going to take you out for a drink first, but we could always find a dark alley round the back if you're that desperate."

I resisted the urge to punch his shoulder, and bit my lip as a flush of heat went through my body. "We're in public."

Nick flashed his teeth at me. "Just a thought. Drinks?"

"Please." I peeled myself away from the wall. "But I guess I'd better get changed first. Wouldn't want to be tempting any lawyers around the place."

I smiled and walked away, and caught him looking at the view as I went. I shook my head, still not used to feeling so damn *happy* all the time.

But as I got changed, the business card fell from my pocket. I stared at it on the floor, knowing I would have to make a decision, sooner or later. It wasn't just stay or leave anymore, it was choosing who I wanted to *be*.

I tucked the card into my actual pocket once I was dressed, and decided to deal with the problem later. Tonight, I could let myself be happy, and celebrate. Tonight, and then tomorrow, and then the day after. I was safe for now. I could be happy for now.

ELLE

I couldn't tell him. I couldn't tell Nick about the job offer in the city. Not even when we got back to his house and made love, not even when we woke up on Christmas Eve and he kissed me fully awake.

I would tell him after Christmas was over, I promised myself. For now, I wanted to keep it tucked away, deep in my mind, because then I wouldn't need to face it. I could stay happy, safe, and content, if I pretended for a little while longer.

Nick and I spent most of the day in bed on Christmas Eve. I was exhausted after the play, and he said he had nothing else to do because it was the holidays. He made me hot cocoa, and we watched a movie in bed as snow fell outside. It was a bubble of happiness I refused to ruin with the offer I'd received. As far as Nick knew, I was staying.

"Something's on your mind." Nick murmured beside me, his finger idly drawing circles on my knee as it rested against him.

I took another sip of my cocoa and shook my head quickly. "Nope. Nothing in this head."

Nick chuckled softly, his finger pausing. "I don't know if I believe that."

I sighed and clenched my hand in the sheets. "I… I'll tell you after Christmas, okay? I just want to spend these holidays without worrying."

"So it's something to worry about?"

I looked out the window, unable to meet his eyes. "It's… I don't know. It's not something you need to worry about."

"Except it's worrying you, so now I am worried."

I stood up, needing to be away from him if I was going to spill the details. I couldn't see how I could get out of it now—Nick had that gleam in his eye when he would not let something rest. I began pacing at the foot of the bed and avoiding his eyes. "Deanna introduced me to someone yesterday. The artistic director of Chapel Theatre Company."

"Is that a good company?" Nick's voice was even, not betraying any of his emotions. He'd slipped into rational mode, and I hated that I was the cause.

"Yeah. It's one of the best." I paused and looked out the window. "Apparently, one of their actors has pulled last minute from the first show of their season next year. And she offered me the job."

Nick was silent for a moment, and I looked over to see him staring at his hands in his lap. He nodded once and looked out the window. "I'm not surprised. You were… shining onstage last night."

I barely registered the compliment, my stomach churning. "She wants an answer on Boxing Day."

"So you're saying yes." I hated how even Nick's voice was, how carefully he was trying to hide his emotions from me.

I shoved a hand through my hair and paced to the window. "No. I don't know what I want to do. It's all so fast, and I don't know—"

"You shouldn't let me stop you from accepting it." Nick crossed his arms.

"It's not all about you." I snapped the words before I could stop them, and then I winced. "I'm sorry, I didn't—"

"No, I agree with you. It shouldn't be about me." Nick's neck tensed, but he was being perfectly rational. "I shouldn't be giving you advice. You didn't ask for it."

His words deflated me, and I sat on the bed. "I just… I don't want to decide yet. I want to enjoy Christmas with you."

Nick slid his hand across the sheets and grabbed mine. "Okay."

I lay down on the bed again, flopping over the bottom of the mattress. Our outstretched hands still joined, I could feel Nick thinking.

Eventually, he spoke. "Can I ask one question? Then we'll drop it."

I sighed at the ceiling. "Sure."

"This is the kind of job you've dreamed of getting, isn't it? And it's fallen right into your lap."

I squeezed my eyes shut. "Yep."

Nick brushed his thumb on the back of my hand. "Okay. We'll deal with it after Christmas."

And then he was pulling me back into his arms, into the circle of his warm body, and I felt safe again. He kissed my forehead, kissed the tip of my nose, and pulled me into him again so I was snuggled into his warm chest and could hear the rhythm of his beating heart.

I didn't want to think about it, but I knew I'd eventually have to make the choice. I'd already decided to stay, but it seemed the universe wanted to tempt me to change my mind. I didn't know what to do with the information. Being with Nick, being in Mistletoe Valley, was the easiest thing I'd ever done. But didn't everyone always say that you needed to choose the hard stuff sometimes?

Nick was right. This was everything I'd ever dreamed of, and it had fallen right into my lap. Surely I couldn't brush that off as easily as I desperately wanted to. Because if I was being honest with myself, all I wanted to do was stay here. I didn't want to go back to the city.

But what if what Maria had said was true? What if this place was a trap, a pretty fairytale that breaks the moment you leave and go back to the real world? It would be stupid to not at least try.

Nick's hand brushed my hair away. "I can still hear you thinking."

I sighed into his shoulder. "I'm trying to stop."

"I see." Nick's hand curled around the back of my neck, pulling me up to face him as I sat on his lap. "How about I distract you?"

And then he pulled me in for a searing kiss, and he was right. He distracted me—thoroughly and mercilessly. We ended up spending the rest of the day in bed, but I couldn't complain. It was the perfect way to spend Christmas Eve, sated and happy and distracted.

❯❯❯❯❯   ❮❮❮❮❮

I woke on Christmas Day with a feeling of foreboding. Snow was still falling in gentle flakes onto the ground, and Nick was still with me. But he was quieter than usual, and so was I. It was as if our agreement to say nothing about my impending decision meant we couldn't think of much else to say.

The present I'd bought for him was sitting under Deanna's tree, and we were going there for an early lunch. The annual Mistletoe Valley Christmas ball was tonight, and I knew it was the moment that Nick would announce his firm. I would stand there, smiling and happy for him, knowing I would have to decide what I was going to do.

I couldn't stand the silence as we drove to Deanna's and was grateful when she opened the door. "Elle, you look lovely."

I was wearing a mint green sweater with burgundy jeans—one of my usual festive getups—but I hadn't put much thought into it. Today wasn't about that. It was about enjoying an easy Christmas morning with Deanna and Nick, the two people who had helped make Mistletoe Valley feel like home to me. I hugged Deanna and gave her a beaming smile. "Merry Christmas."

Deanna smiled back. "And to you. You both hungry?"

My stomach growled, and Nick chuckled. We'd worked up quite an appetite given our morning… exertions. I nodded and stepped through the door.

It was funny to me—how little time I'd spent in this house since that first date with Nick. But it still felt like home: welcoming, cozy, smelling of roast meats and spices and pine needles from the tree. His hand brushed mine as we walked through the hall, and I nudged his back.

Deanna handed us steaming mugs of eggnog, and we settled down on the couch before the fireplace. She passed us our presents, and we took turns opening them. Deanna gifted me a hand painted landscape of the Mistletoe Valley mountain line, and I hugged her again. "To always have this place, no matter where you are," she explained. I blinked away tears at her thoughtfulness.

Deana opened her presents, a timber cutting board from Nick, and a handcrafted knife set from me. Nick cleared his throat. "I noticed your knives weren't very sharp last time you had me over for dinner. So we coordinated a little."

Deanna pressed a hand to her chest and hugged us both. It was mostly Nick's idea, after I'd asked him if he had any hints of what I could get Deanna for Christmas. I was more than happy to give Deanna a gift worthy of her and the help she'd given me.

Then it was Nick's turn, and my stomach flipped. It had taken me so long to find something for him until I'd stumbled across this gem in the antique shop. As he unwrapped it, he slapped a hand to his mouth and roared with laughter. I was puzzled—I didn't think it was that funny. He pulled the gift from the packaging, revealing a DVD copy of Pride of Prejudice, the 2005 version, still in its original wrapping. I'd had no idea what to get a man who had enough money to fulfill most of his own wants, so I had gone for sentimental value.

He tipped his head back and laughed again. "This is embarrassing."

"What do you mean?" I asked, alarmed.

Nick flashed a smile. "Open your present from me."

Confused, I slowly unwrapped the sturdy package, revealing…

A leather-bound special edition of Pride and Prejudice.

My jaw dropped. My shoulders shook and I quickly dissolved into giggles. I shook my head. "Did you… hear from someone that I'd bought this for you?"

"I swear to you, I didn't know." Nick held up his hands. "Even I wouldn't be able to plan something this clever."

I swallowed and gave him a soft look. How had we both thought of the same thing? It felt…

It felt a little like a sign, which was a thought I quickly pushed away. I didn't need to be complicating the situation with loaded expectations like that. I stood and smoothed down my sweater. "I'm just going to grab some water."

I trailed away to the kitchen and took a moment to look out the window. This all felt so easy, so peaceful, and it felt like I could fit in forever. Maria's words echoed through my mind, the way she had warned me against staying. I could tell this was going to be one of the hardest decisions of my life, because all I wanted was to stay in Mistletoe Valley forever.

But what if staying wasn't what I needed? What if I missed out on an incredible opportunity because of it?

Someone cleared their throat behind me, and I turned to see Deanna holding a glass of water out to me.

I gave her a sheepish smile and took it from her. "Sorry. I'm a little distracted today."

Deanna leaned against the kitchen bench. "You've got a big change ahead of you."

"What do you mean?" I took a sip while I waited for Deanna to answer.

She crossed her arms. "Forgive me. Nick told me you'd decided to stay for a little while, and then with Maria's offer, I just presumed—"

I made a face at the ceiling. "No, you're right. It is a big decision."

"I meant what I said a few days ago, that you could take over the studio from me if you wanted to stay."

I chewed my lip.

Deanna tilted her head, and I could feel her eyes scanning my face. "But you're not sure if you should do that, are you?"

I pressed my lips together and nodded. "I don't… how can I say no to something like that?"

"Easy. You don't text her back." Deanna joked, and then her face turned serious. "If you say no, what are you worried will happen?"

I put my head in my hand and whispered into my palm, "I'll spend my whole life wondering if I should have taken the job. Because what if…"

"What if you loved it and don't want to come back?" Deanna finished and shrugged. "It's a fair question. So why can't you say yes, then? It's only one job, and then you'd be done and come back here."

"It makes me feel sick, going back to that world." I admitted quietly. It was true. Whenever I thought of my life in the city, my stomach filled with dread and I got the powerful urge to cover my head with a pillow.

Deanna sighed. "You wouldn't have to be there for very long. The show would be over within two months."

"I know."

Deanna shifted. "Do you want to know my advice? As someone who has felt that feeling before—and knows how horrible it is?"

I looked up. I knew what her advice was going to be, but I wanted to hear her say it, anyway. "Yes."

What Deanna actually said shocked me. "I think you should do it."

I stared at her. "You… think I should do it?"

Deanna smiled wryly at the ceiling. "Because then you'll know, beyond any doubt, that you hate that world and you don't want to be a part of it."

"But…" I trailed off, realizing her logic made sense.

"You've seen the worst of being an actor, yes? So how can you be certain you hate it, doing the sort of work you've always dreamed of doing?" Deanna lifted her eyebrows at me. "If you do it and love it, that's your answer. If you hate it, you come back and set up a new life here."

I inhaled and nodded, but still felt conflicted. Deanna made it sound so simple, and I knew she was right, but still…

"What are you afraid of?" Deanna prompted.

I exhaled. "That when I leave, the magic of this place will disappear, just like Maria said."

Deanna put her hands in her pockets. "Then you shouldn't stay if this place is just a fairytale to you. This place should feel real to you."

I looked at Deanna, at this woman who had been so welcoming to me from the beginning, so wise and understanding. "I feel like I don't deserve the kindness you've shown me."

"Everyone deserves kindness." Deanna countered. "Unfortunately, the world tries to convince us we don't. Shall we eat?"

Nick came into the kitchen then, and I got the feeling he'd been listening to every world from the other room. I flushed, but he didn't look at me strangely, didn't show any sign that he thought differently of me after hearing my worries. I don't know why I was surprised. Nick seemed to take every part of me in his stride, even the messy parts.

I pushed off the counter. "What can we do to help with the food?"

Together, the three of us worked to set up a Christmas feast, spread across the dining table with enough food to feed ten people. Nick poured the wine and I cut bread and arranged the serving plates.

When we sat, Nick's hand touched mine, and I gave him a soft smile. I flushed across my chest, a warm feeling exploding in my chest. I loaded up my plate and caught Nick's warm eyes across the table. He raised a glass. "To Christmas."

It was the best Christmas lunch of my life.

⤖⤖⤖ ⬳⬳⬳

The old bank was totally transformed. I was used to the building standing empty and dark with some town memorabilia on the walls. But this was the Mistletoe Valley Christmas Ball, and they'd pulled out all the stops. I shuddered to think of what the tickets cost, but Deanna had told me mine was on the house.

The bank was decked out with red carpet lining the stone steps, holly and mistletoe garlands on every available hanging space. Strings of warm lights hung around the entrance, guiding us into a hall blazing with warm chandeliers.

As I got out of Nick's car, I stopped to take it all in. I adjusted my dress, a shimmering gold full-length a-line that Deanna had found for me in her studio's costume storage. For any other event, this outfit would be gaudy, but I hoped it would blend in for a Christmas ball.

"I know I've already told you, but I think it's worth repeating." Nick stepped to my side. "You look gorgeous."

I gave him a once over. "I'm still astounded that you found a golden pocket square at such short notice."

Nick's lips tugged up into a smile, and he shrugged. "I have my sources."

"Deanna, you mean?" I nudged him. "This whole thing is a lot fancier than you'd led me to believe."

Nick offered me his elbow. "It's Christmas. Why not?"

"Spoken like someone who is pretending to like Christmas." I slid my hand through his arm. "I don't think I've been escorted into an event since prom."

Nick chuckled, and we walked towards the entrance. "Yeah, well, traditions and all that."

I watched other people moving towards the building, all in similarly elegant clothing. It seemed like a much bigger event than I'd expected. "How did this thing start, anyway?"

"Not sure." Nick shrugged. "I remember Mike saying something about a fundraiser decades ago, but then it became a regular event that everyone looked forward to."

As we walked through the doors, I felt many eyes on us, and I caught the way some of them stared greedily at my hand in Nick's elbow. A juicy new piece of gossip. I suppose it hadn't been obvious to most of Mistletoe Valley that their golden boy had found a girl, but I guess after today everyone would know. I made a soft noise. "Lots of stares."

"I haven't brought anyone to this ball other than Deanna for a decade." Nick murmured to me under his breath.

Nick led me through the throng, showing our tickets before we entered the ballroom proper. It was even more stunning than the entrance hall, glowing lights and sparkling marble floors. One of the largest Christmas trees I'd ever seen sat in the corner, and I laughed. "That's got to be fake, right?"

Nick shook his head. "They chop one down from the mountainside every year. Honoring the old logging town origins and all."

A young waiter offered us champagne, and I took one for each of us. There were more curious looks angled our way, and I hid my smile behind my glass. "God, you really are the town's golden boy."

Nick took his glass and slid a hand into mine. "I'm surprised it took you this long to figure it out. Why do you think I wanted you at home all to myself?"

My cheeks reddened, but I squeezed his hand. An older lady passed by, and she leaned out of her conversation to whisper, "Loved the play this year, dearie. Such lovely stuff."

I smiled and made a grateful noise. Nick pulled me further into the room and nodded at some of the other guests. I'd known how popular he was here, but tonight was another reminder. It was like he had a connection with almost everyone in the room, knew them all by name. "Are you sure you want to break your silence with me on your arm? You'll never hear the end of it."

Nick gave me a serious look. "It's worth it, Elle."

"Why have you never shown up with someone until now?" I murmured to him, a piece of the puzzle I couldn't quite work out.

Nick scanned the room and inhaled. "I was in the city most of the time. And I didn't meet anyone to bring back here."

"No pressure, then." I breathed out, eyeing the room and the curious looks many of its inhabitants were slinging our way. I took another sip of the champagne, which was some of the best I'd tasted.

"You two scrub up alright." A voice teased behind us, and we turned to see Matt, looking suave in a gray suit.

Nick clasped hands with his friend. "So do you."

Matt chuckled and looked at me. "Your sister's a hellcat. How come you're so nice?"

I took another sip from my glass to hide my smile. I'd nearly forgotten Kat and Matt's hilariously biting conversation. "She's... very protective. She's the mean one, so I could grow up nice."

Matt's eyes softened slightly at that, but he shook his head again and turned to Nick. "Lionel was asking to speak to you, so I promised I'd find you."

Nick groaned softly and gave me an apologetic look. "Can I leave you with Matt? I really don't want to subject you to Lionel. I'll be quick."

"Sure." I waved him off. "Go do things."

Matt sipped his champagne and looked around the room. "I forgot how much I hated these things."

"You don't like it?" I raised my eyebrows. He looked like he was comfortable, fit right in.

"Nah." Matt shook his head. "Some of these folk are alright, but most of the ones who come here are uppity assholes, all rich upper lips who like to flaunt their money."

I took another look around the room, seeing the room the way he described, an exorbitant display of wealth and privilege. I imagined my shimmering dress was not even one tenth of the cost of some clothes in the room, and I caught one woman giving my outfit a critical eye. I took a sip of champagne to swallow down the bitterness of being judged. "And yet, you're here."

Matt flashed a sardonic smile. "I've got to cozy up to all the rich assholes if I want them to sell their houses with me."

"Then isn't this just an opportunity for you?"

Matt clinked my glass with his. "Exactly... I don't always have to like it."

"I guess there's always things in life we don't want to do," I spoke into my glass.

"Speaking of, can you tell Nick to hurry and sign his lease papers?" Matt winked and nudged me. "He's been so distracted with you he's forgotten."

A stone sank in my gut. "His lease papers? For the new firm?"

Matt nodded and gave me a curious look. "He didn't tell you?"

I looked across the crowd, finding Nick's head standing out above the mass of bodies. "No. I thought he'd signed them."

"Like I said... I think he's been distracted."

"He shouldn't be." I looked back at Matt. "Did he say why he's delaying?"

Matt eyed me, something hesitant in his eyes. "You know why, Elle."

I swallowed, my heart pounding. Was he really putting off signing the lease because of… me? "I… he shouldn't be doing that."

"No." Matt murmured. "He shouldn't. He might miss the place he wanted if he waits much longer."

The walls felt like they were closing in on me, every signal from the universe telling me I needed to make a choice, and I needed to make it now. My breathing picked up, and I looked around. "I need to—"

"Elle." A hand landed on my back, and I realized Nick had returned. "Are you okay."

I looked at Nick, really looked at him. "When were you going to tell me?"

Nick gave Matt an angry look. "What the fuck did you say to her?"

"I thought she knew, man." Matt pressed his lips together.

"Knew what?" Nick demanded, but Matt didn't answer.

I pulled away from Nick. "You told me you already signed the lease papers for the new firm."

A conflicted look crossed Nick's face, and then he slowly shook his head. "I… haven't yet."

"Why not, Nick?" My voice raised slightly, but I tried to keep it low enough to not draw attention. "You told me you'd wanted this for the longest time."

Nick just looked at me, and I could see the conflict in his eyes. His jaw muscles clenched. He was holding himself back from confirming what we both already knew: He had been putting it off because of me. Because he wanted to follow me back to the city if I went.

The string quartet began playing, and the MC announced the first dance of the night.

And suddenly, all my worry left me. Nick had been holding off on his firm because of me. He cared about me that much—to jeopardize one of his biggest dreams—on the off chance that I might leave for the city. I handed my glass to a surprised Matt and jerked my head to the middle of the floor. "Dance with me?"

Nick seemed surprised at my abrupt change, but wisely didn't comment. He also handed his glass to Matt and took my hand. "I would love to."

We glided onto the floor, and other couples settled around us. There was no set dance, just people twirling around the space. I settled my hands on his shoulders and looked at him. "What are you doing, Nick?"

His eyes searched my face, and he pressed his lips together. "You know what I'm doing."

"Yes." I nodded, looking away from him briefly. "But I want to hear you say it."

Nick sighed. "I… If you left, I wanted to follow you. If you wanted me to."

I closed my eyes briefly, my heart flip-flopping in my chest. "But this is what you've wanted for years. You've prepared for it for years. Haven't you already handed in your notice?"

"I have," Nick admitted reluctantly. "But that's nothing a bit of groveling can't fix. And I'd do it, Elle. I—You were willing to stay longer for me. Why can't I be willing to put my own plans on hold for you?"

I blinked back tears. He was right. I was prepared to shift, so why was I so angry when I heard he was prepared to go back to the city for me? I plucked at the only reason I could think of. "But you hate it there."

"So do you." Nick reminded me softly. "But I could find happiness there, Elle, if it was with you."

"You'd really do that for me?" I asked, my voice trembling. "If I said right now that I was going and didn't want to come back here, you would do that?"

Nick nodded slowly, his warm eyes soft. "Without question."

"Why?" I had a feeling why.

Nick froze, then he nodded. "I love you, Elle. I think I loved you the moment that you ran into me and yelled at me for being an asshole."

I laughed, the sound almost getting caught in my throat. "You love me?"

Nick made a mock suffering sound. "Unfortunately, yeah."

"Against your better judgement and all that?" I teased.

Nick smiled again at the reference. "Something like that."

My smiled faded, and I frowned. I felt happy, and I think I'd known for a little while that Nick loved me. But what he was offering, what he was willing to do… "You can't put it on hold, Nick. You have to sign the lease, you have to go forward with your firm. You know why?"

Nick's eyes flashed in alarm, and I squeezed his shoulder to reassure him. "Why?"

"Because I love you too much to ask you to do that for me." I said simply, the admission making my chest feel lighter. "I can't ask you to be unhappy, for my sake."

Nick pressed his forehead against mine. "I wouldn't be unhappy if I was with you, Elle."

But I could see that potential future, and it was grim. I could ask him, right now, to come back with me to the city, to postpone the firm and all his plans. And he would. I could see that in his eyes, could hear the honesty in his words. But what would happen when we got there, long term, when he was still working in a job he hated and I was still struggling to make it as an actor? Even if I took Maria's offer, that still wasn't any guarantee of regular work. I could blow it, and then I would still be Elle, the struggling actor. And Nick would still be the miserable corporate lawyer.

I couldn't do that to either of us.

I pulled away. "I can't let you do that. I won't let you do that. You have to stay."

Nick frowned at me for a moment, then inhaled. He seemed to come to a decision and nodded to himself. "Then you need to say yes to the acting job."

I reared back. "That's different—"

Nick shook his head. "I don't think it is. I heard what Deanna said, and I agree with her. How will you know if this is the right decision if you don't try it out?"

I frowned. "No. I'm going to say no, and then stay here for a bit, and you can open your firm—"

"You won't let me postpone my firm. I will not let you say no to this." Nick said firmly. His grip on my waist was firm, and suddenly I couldn't stand swaying to the music.

I pulled out of his arms. "You can't tell me what to do."

"Of course I can't." Nick breathed. "But if you don't take the acting job, I couldn't live with the guilt of knowing you'd said no to such a great opportunity because of me. If you say no to the job, I'm not starting my firm."

"I don't—" I wanted to scream. I was so confused. "Why can't you just start your firm and I stay here for a bit while I decide…"

Nick gave me a sad look. "Because you're giving up too much. If we're going to do this—if you and I are going to be together, Elle, because I want that more than anything—I need to know that you're certain. You've been so conflicted in the last few days. I couldn't bear it if you came to resent me for saying no to acting. I couldn't bear it, Elle."

A tear fell down my face and I angrily brushed it away. "And I can't bear leaving you. Don't you see, you idiot? I don't want to leave."

"I see it, I see it, Elle." Nick wrapped his arms around me, and I softened in his embrace. He twirled us softly around, and I sobbed into his jacket. "I don't want you to leave either."

"Then why are we still talking about this?" I whined. I couldn't understand how I felt like my heart was breaking and Nick was *right there*.

He stroked a soothing hand down my back. "Elle, listen to me. You have to say yes to the acting job, and I'll sign the papers to the firm. If this thing is meant to work, it will. I believe that."

"And if it doesn't?" I looked up at him.

"It will." Nick gave me an encouraging smile. "I know it'll work out. You'll only be away for a month or two, right? That's nothing."

I was seeing the sense in what he was saying, but still… "I'm going to hate every minute."

Nick brushed his hand over my face. "Selfishly, I hope you hate it. I hope you're thinking of me the whole time, and want to come back to me at the end of it. But you have to find that out for yourself, Elle. Because I want all of you, without hesitation. I couldn't live with it if you came to regret your decision."

I swallowed, and something bittersweet settled in my stomach. This wasn't the end, it didn't have to be the end, but I felt the truth of what he was saying in my soul. He was right. So was Deanna. I couldn't just hide away here, pretending my old life didn't exist.

I needed to face it, confront all the facets of who I was and who I used to be, and decide with a rational mind. Nick's words, the way he was encouraging me to do something for me, made me love him even more.

Nick read these decisions on my face and nodded. "You know what you need to do. This job is what you've always wanted, right?"

I smiled, tears still pooling in my eyes, and laughed wryly. It wasn't what I wanted anymore, but I had to *know.* I had to know I hated it, had to know that Nick was my new dream, that Mistletoe Valley was my new home.

I told him as much, and Nick responded by pulling me closer and spinning us around. "I'm going to hate this just as much as you, you know."

I sniffled into his shoulder and smiled. It was agony because I knew I had to leave him, and hopeful because I thought it was only going to be for a bit. I could deal with a little bit.

"So what now?" I looked at him.

"For now, we dance. Then, you need to send that message. I'll tell Matt I'll sign the papers."

I looked at the ceiling, watching the sparkling chandeliers above us. "This feels horrible. It's Christmas, for God's sake."

"It's the best Christmas I've ever had." Nick looked at me, his eyes serious. "Because you're here."

A smile spread across my face. "For a lawyer, you can be really sappy."

"For you, I'll be anything, Elle Sutton." His warm eyes stared into mine.

My heart squeezed, and I twisted my fist into his collar. "This isn't goodbye, right? You're not just trying to get rid of me?"

Nick's eyes met mine, and they were full of light. "Sorry, but you're not getting rid of me that easily."

I smiled again. "Okay. Let's try it."

Nick spun me around the room for the rest of the night, until I was dizzy, until all my sadness had been wrung out of me, and I was at peace.

The next morning, I left his bed and said goodbye to him, walking out the door without looking back. I knew if I looked back, I would never leave.

NICK

I was the biggest fucking idiot to ever exist. I hadn't just let Elle Sutton slip through my fingers; I had *told her to go.* Why the fuck had I done that?

I knew, though. I was terrified that if I persuaded her to stay—saying no to this amazing opportunity—that one day she would look up and resent me for it. Because if I asked her to stay, to choose me, to choose Mistletoe Valley, she would give up a hell of a lot more than I would.

So I had to be okay with it and let her go. Boxing Day, I got drunk on the couch, swallowing the pain with too much whiskey and drunken scrolls through her Instagram account. I was so in love with her. I hoped, against all the odds, that she would hate every minute of her time in the city and come home to me.

Days passed, then weeks. I signed the lease for the firm, barely able to stomach it. I sent her a photo when I did, and she sent me one back of her in the rehearsal room. We'd barely spoken since she left, but I knew she was busy. Hell, I was too, trying to launch my new firm.

Those weeks were the most miserable of my life. I worked—harder than usual—helping people out in town however I could. I even visited some of the neighboring towns to consult, visiting people who'd heard of me from friends. I spread the word about my firm, ignoring the squeeze in my heart whenever I thought about Elle.

If I'd ever been in any doubt that I was in love with Elle—that December had been some sort of spell—I wasn't in any doubt now. She was what I thought of when I woke up, finding the other side of the bed empty. She was what I thought of when I used the kitchen, when I turned around and half expected her to be sitting on the counter, smiling at me. She was what I thought of when I visited Deanna, expecting to see her come round the corner and greet me, too.

Deanna noticed how miserable I was and tried to comfort me. "She's doing what she wanted to do."

"Yeah." I chewed through the word slowly, knowing that I logically agreed with Deanna.

"If she's meant to come back, she will." Deanna sighed and looked out the window. "I think she'll come back."

"She better." I answered.

I spent a lot of time with Matt, drowning my sorrows with drinks at the Hollyoak. Even Mike noticed my mood and wisely said nothing. Only one night in mid-January, he broke and said, "Elle was a really good one, Nick. I'm sorry."

I had only nodded and ordered another drink, unable to say anything else. How could I explain she had gone, but I was hoping for her to hate her dream job and come running back to me? There was no way to say it without sounding like an idiot. I scrolled through her Instagram again, finding a new post of her with the other cast members, smiling and looking happy. My heart seized.

Matt took my phone from my hands and placed it on the bar. "That's enough, bro."

I glared at him and nursed my glass. "I can be miserable if I want to."

"She wouldn't want you to be miserable, man." Matt shook his head. "If what you told me is true, she's going to come back to you."

"She might not."

Matt gave me a hard look. "She won't want to come back to someone who's been a mopey asshole for two months. It's tough, I get it. But you've got shit to do, so focus on that."

I swallowed my drink and nodded. Matt was right. My firm needed as much work as I could throw at it, and moping wouldn't fix that.

So I threw myself even more into my work. I couldn't stand sleeping in my bed anymore, but that suited me just fine. I worked until the early hours of the morning and fell asleep on the couch instead. It was better than stumbling home drunk and miserable.

As much as I was missing Elle, I couldn't ignore the fact that I knew she was right. Opening this firm, moving back to town permanently, these were all things I needed to do. Despite how much I missed her, I was more fulfilled than I'd been in a long time. The work I was doing with my new firm made me feel satisfied. I was helping people, just like I'd always wanted, helping them solve problems and make sure they had someone to help assert their rights.

I only hoped that Elle wasn't slowly forgetting about me back in LA. My hand itched to text her, to call her, but we'd both agreed that a bit of space would be better for both of us. Otherwise, how could we know it wasn't just convenience pushing us together? But Christ, it sucked. I couldn't believe how badly I wanted to hear from her at every moment of the day, how I wanted her presence in my life.

I knew my feelings for Elle hadn't waned at all. The distance had made it greater. I could only hope that Elle felt the same, otherwise I was well and truly fucked.

>>>>>>> <<<<<<

I got a text from Elle in early February. It was simple, and to the point.

> ELLE: I hope you're going okay :) My show starts performances soon.

> ME: I'm busy with the firm, but okay. Dare I ask how it's going?

ELLE: …

ELLE: The cast is lovely. It's a good show. Tickets are already selling out.

ME: Would it be a good or a bad idea for me to come watch?

ELLE: (Sent a photo)

ELLE: Too late, I already got you a ticket to our last show :)

I checked the date and time on the ticket. It was a Saturday, so it should be fairly easy for me to get myself to the city. My stomach clenched at the thought of seeing her again.

ME: I'll be there.

ELLE: Good.

ELLE: …

ELLE: I'm really looking forward to seeing you.

My heart unclenched, and I leaned back and exhaled in relief. So she did still want me, after all. Now I just had to hope that actually performing in this show didn't totally change her mind.

ME: Me too, baby.

ELLE: :)

ELLE: I've gotta go. We're in tech and I have almost no time for anything other than work and sleep. Bye :)

I clenched my hand around the phone, flipping the photo of her I'd saved on my phone. It was a cropped shot I'd stolen from her Instagram, one from a recent cast shoot. In it, she was smiling and happy, and it had made my heart sink when I'd seen it. But now, I could see behind the smile, to the woman who still missed me, who was being courageous and working hard, and *still missed me*.

Some of the worry that had been gripping me eased. Because when I saw her again, I was certain I would move heaven and earth to make sure she stayed by my side.

Elle Sutton was it for me.

I just had to hope she felt the same.

ELLE

I had never missed anything more than I missed Nick Corrigan. I wanted to be back in his arms, back in Mistletoe Valley. I wanted to see the students again; I wanted to walk along the river; I wanted so many things.

But I'd done it. I'd finished the show. As I sat in my dressing room, the sounds of people moving through the theater found me, but I couldn't move. Nick had been in the audience tonight. He'd watched, and even though I couldn't find him in the darkness, I knew he was there. I had felt his eyes on me all night.

I looked at myself in the dressing room mirror, the lights around the mirror illuminating my face. I looked utterly unlike the person I had been in Mistletoe Valley. Here, an actress sat before the mirror, dramatic makeup painted on her face and perfectly styled hair. Even my costume looked melodramatic, deliberately ripped and torn to symbolize my character's last moments onstage.

Hilariously, my character died onstage in the last act. Which was fitting, because I felt like I had died every single day I had been away from Nick.

It hadn't all been torture; I had to admit to myself. I'd loved rehearsing, loved the cast of people around me. All of them were delightful, and I'd seen a much better side to the acting profession. Some of them had even become friends, of sorts.

After the shows in the past weeks, I could barely stomach going out the stage door to meet with people. No one was here for me, the breakout actor of the show. Anyone who had wanted to talk to me just wanted to wax lyrical about how amazing the show was, which I had to accept graciously. After a few days, I started waiting in my dressing room until everyone had left to go home. I couldn't stand the small talk, couldn't stand the networking that my castmates did naturally.

I had to admit I enjoyed being onstage again, in a distant, dull sort of way. The play was a drama, with a streak of humor running through it that was delightful to play with. When I was onstage, playing against the other actors, I was enjoying myself. But the moment I came off the stage, I slumped in a heap of exhaustion.

It was such an odd thing, watching the death of an old passion right before my eyes. But I was done. I'd finished.

I smiled to myself in the mirror. I knew it had been the right decision to try it, to say yes to Maria and leave Mistletoe Valley and Nick. Just as I knew now that all my former passion for acting was gone. It was dead, much like my character in the play.

That led to only one path forward. I was going back to Mistletoe Valley. If Nick would still have me.

A tiny fear threatened to squash my hope, but I pushed it down. He had to still want me. And if he didn't, then I'd stay miserable in the city, doing what I had always done.

A knock sounded on the door, and I tensed. This was it, this was him—

"Sorry, El, but I thought I'd drop this off to you." The voice wasn't Nick. It belonged to Lily, another actor in the cast—a friend of sorts. She smiled sheepishly and held out a water bottle. "Also, I hope you don't mind, but Michael Cornish asked for your number, so I gave it to him."

Lily was younger than me, so it didn't surprise me she'd just handed out my number without checking. I brushed a hand across my face. "Who is he?"

Lily gave me a strange look. "He's the new casting director for HBO."

"Why did he ask for my number?" I tensed.

Lily shrugged. "Dunno. But I figured it was something good. By the way, I let someone in who was here to see you. See you later for drinks?"

Lily barely listened to my answer before rushing off, and I blinked at the spot she'd left. Okay, so I'd said she'd become a friend, but it was more like watching a tornado whip around me. I don't know if anyone could get close to someone like Lily, with her flighty energy.

My phone dinged, and I forgot about the conversation with Lily. I hoped it was Nick, but it was from an unknown number.

UNKNOWN: Hi Elle, Lily Thorne gave me your number. I was hoping to speak to you after the show, but you must have had other commitments. I'm casting a new HBO show, and would love to see your audition tape for a specific role we're having difficulty casting. The project is quite secretive, but I can say that it would be a BIG deal for someone at your stage of career. The tape would need to be submitted by tomorrow midnight, so please respond ASAP and I'll send through the sides.

I slammed my phone onto the bench, face down.

What the fuck was going on? I felt a laugh bubble out of my mouth. I'd been struggling for years, and suddenly every director and their dog wanted to work with me? I could keep saying yes, keep following this path, but then what? I would end halfway up a ladder I had no interest in climbing.

At least this time, the decision was easier. I wouldn't do it. I dropped my head in my hands. I wouldn't do it.

The more I repeated this to myself, the calmer I felt. I just needed to see Nick, needed to feel his grounded energy around me—

"Elle."

I whipped my head up, locking eyes with Nick in my mirror. He was standing at my door, looking just as handsome as I'd remembered, and relief choked its way up my throat. My bottom lip wobbled. "Nick."

I watched his eyes take in the room, landing back on me. "You look like you belong here."

I could hear the question in his words, and knew what he was really asking me. I shook my head, still rooted to my chair. "It's pretend, Nick."

"You were incredible out there."

"Smoke and mirrors." I reminded him.

Nick inhaled. "I've missed you."

And suddenly I was flinging myself out of the chair, flying across the small space so that I could throw myself into his arms. Nick caught me and spun me around.

I sighed into his shoulder and felt him nuzzle my neck. "Nick."

He breathed me in, his hands spanning my waist. "Elle."

We stayed like that for a long moment. A part of me that had been missing for weeks was finally back, and I closed my eyes.

Eventually, Nick spoke again. "Are you okay?"

I looked at him. "I am now."

His eyes crinkled, but then he looked at my phone on the desk. "You were glaring at that. What happened?"

I withdrew from his embrace and began pacing. "It's… a casting director just asked me to audition for a TV show. A big one."

"Sounds like a big deal." Nick's face had gone back to that horrible neutrality, and I knew he was hiding his genuine feelings from me. "Do you want to?"

He had always been asking me what I wanted. Not what I should do, or what was rational. What I wanted. I sunk into my chair and put my head in my hands. "No. I—don't."

I heard Nick moving around the room, and looked up to see him eyeing all my decorations, the little pieces of me I'd spread around the room. His eyes landed on the painting of Mistletoe Valley that Deanna had gifted me, and he paused for a moment.

I held my breath, unsure of what to say. It felt like he was making his mind up on something.

Nick turned around, his eyes burning with intensity. "You could do it, Elle. Say the word—right now—and I'd follow you anywhere."

I sat straighter. "But—your firm, haven't you already?"

"Fuck the firm." Nick crossed to me in two large strides and kneeled down in front of me. "The firm matters to me, but it can wait. These past two months have been torture, Elle."

His hand curled around the back of my knee, and I leaned forward into him. "What are you saying, Nick? You can't just—"

"I can. I will." Nick pressed a kiss to my knee, the soft affection ruining me inside. "Say the word, Elle."

I shook my head. I'd already decided I wasn't doing it, so why was he—?

Nick went on. "You could do it, you know. Stay with me in Mistletoe Valley sometimes, and work as an actor here the rest. Or I'll work remotely and follow you anywhere. I would do it, Elle. Tell me to do it, and I would."

I looked down at the phone, the audition call still open. I could do it. But did I want that life? I looked at Nick, the man I loved, kneeling in front of me. I slowly shook my head. "Nick."

His eyes were so beautiful as he looked at me. "Elle."

"You idiot." I breathed. "I don't want to do that. Do you realize how miserable I've been these past months?"

"You have?" He breathed, blinking. "All of your Instagram posts, you looked so—"

"You've been watching me on Instagram?"

Nick nodded, a little sheepishly. "I… needed to see how you were doing. You looked so… happy, and I was worried—"

"How many times do I need to tell you it's an act, Nick Corrigan?" I grabbed his hand and pressed it to my chest. "This, right here, is the real me. And it belongs to you. You've brought that out in me."

Nick was still, as though he couldn't believe what I was saying.

"I don't want to stay here, or be an actor, or anything like that." I laughed, something in my chest lighter now that I was finally *free*. "I want to be with you."

Nick collapsed his head on my lap. "Thank Christ."

I tipped my head back and laughed. "How could you ever think I would want anything else?"

Nick smiled wryly at me. "Sorry, but I still struggle to believe that someone like you would want me."

I scoffed. "If there's anyone in this relationship who is out of the other's league, it's me. You are way too good for me, Nick."

"Funny," Nick brushed a hand down my cheek, and softly dragged his thumb over my bright red lips. "I think the same thing about you."

"I guess we're both idiots, then." I murmured under his thumb.

Nick inspected my face, and I knew he was looking at my stage makeup, my costume. "You look so different."

I turned slightly to look at myself in the mirror and knew he was right. The sight of me, all dolled up and uncomfortably polished, wasn't the real Elle Sutton. She belonged in a comfortable knit sweater, sitting beside a fire in Mistletoe Valley. She belonged in a tiny drama studio filled with gorgeous kids. She belonged with Nick Corrigan, a man who gave her sweet kisses and searing touches. I sighed. "It's not me, is it?"

Nick held my gaze in the mirror for a moment. "I guess that's up to you."

I pulled over the makeup wipes and began de-caking my face, baring the real, raw me. Nick stood and began unpinning my hair, helping to take down my facade.

One by one, every lock of hair fell down. Bit by bit, I ridded myself of the actress.

I stood and pulled at the top of my costume. Nick helped me unzip it, and he handed me my clothes. With every inch of skin that I bared, I could feel the heat of his gaze, but he made no move to touch me until I was me again.

Until I was Eleanor Sutton, the woman he'd helped me find again.

He put my coat around my shoulders and leaned against the door, crossing his arms. "What do you want to do?"

I smoothed my hand over my hair and smiled. "I want to say goodbye."

Nick's eyes flashed in alarm.

I rushed forward and grabbed his hand. "Not to you. To this."

I gestured above us to where the stage sat. Nick helped grab my bags, and I dragged him upstairs. The lights were still on, but there was no one around. Not even the technicians in the lighting box.

I walked to the middle of the stage. "You know, five years ago, I would have murdered myself to know I was giving this up."

Nick walked around me and looked out at the empty seats. "And what do you feel now?"

"Freedom." I tipped my head up and bathed in the glow of the lights for one last time. "Relief. I don't know when, exactly, but I think my joy for this thing died a long time ago."

A hand touched my cheek, and I opened my eyes to see Nick standing over me. "I think you're braver than most people ever will be, admitting that."

"Not brave," I smiled. "I can't even take credit for it. I had the help of an amazing man who helped me see what I really wanted."

"And what do you want now?" Nick prompted, a smile blooming on his handsome face.

I crowded further into his space. "Right now, I want a kiss."

Nick leaned closer and stopped right before his lips touched mine. "And then?"

I smiled and brushed my nose against his. "I'll decide when we get there."

Nick smiled against my lips. "Sounds good to me."

I pressed up on my toes, and we were kissing. For a time, we forgot the rest of the world existed. Standing on the bones of my old dream, I had discovered my new one, and he was standing right in front of me.

I couldn't wait to see where he led me.

Epilogue

When I woke up on Christmas morning, the other side of the bed was empty. The sun was barely peaking over the mountains, and I pulled Nick's pillow to me so I could snuggle into it. It wasn't unusual for him to have to leave early, but I thought today would be different.

After all, it was Christmas. He didn't have any work to do.

Nick's pillow smelled exactly like him, like fireplaces and fresh snow. He couldn't have gone far, probably just working out in the basement, and would be back soon. I snoozed, on and off, and smiled into his pillow, knowing he would be back.

Christmas in Mistletoe Valley was my favorite time of year. It was only my second season in the town, admittedly, but it was special to me. I'd always loved Christmas time, but my experience in Mistletoe Valley last December had changed my life.

The biggest change being that I was actually happy now.

A sound came from downstairs, and I snuffled into the pillow. Definitely Nick, downstairs. Except when he padded into our bedroom with a mug in hand, he wasn't wearing his gym clothes. He was still in pajamas, and sat down next to me with a lazy smile. "Hello, gorgeous."

I rolled over and stretched my body out, sleep still softening everything with a hazy sweetness. "Good morning. Where'd you go?"

"I made you this." Nick helped me sit up and handed the mug to me.

I leaned into him and took a deep breath, realizing he'd made me a hot cocoa. "This is very Christmassy of you."

Nick kissed my temple. "I told you last year, you converted me."

I hummed into my mug and took a sip, warmth spreading inside my belly. God, I loved him so much. "You were still reluctant to let me decorate the porch with fairy-lights," I reminded him.

Nick coughed into his shoulder, clearly trying not to laugh. "I came round, though, didn't I?"

I took another sip of my cocoa and leaned back into the pillows. "You did. I'm very persuasive."

"I'm aware." Nick was looking down at me, his eyes soft and warm. He always looked at me like I was a treasure, but there was something more in his expression today.

I cocked my head at him and smiled. "What is it?"

Nick's eyes flicked down to my lips. "You've got... a little—"

I raised my hand to touch my lip, but he beat me to it. He swooped down and kissed me, licking the extra chocolate sprinkles off my top lip. I pulled away and laughed. "I guess that's one way to fix it."

Nick hummed and looked out our large window. The sun was halfway risen above the mountains, and I settled in beside him to watch. We sat quietly for a few minutes, basking in the growing glow of the early morning sun. I loved the moments like these that I spent with Nick, enjoying the quiet life with each other. I knew he'd felt the same over the course of our relationship.

But today, I could tell there was something on his mind, something keeping him from being fully present with me. I put my mug on the bedside table and nudged him. "What is it?"

Nick looked at me and smiled wryly. "Sorry. I didn't mean to be thinking of something else."

I huffed and ran a soothing hand over his brow. "Don't apologize for that big brain of yours. It has a lot of things to be thinking of."

Nick grabbed my hand and entwined it with his. "I'm not—I wasn't thinking of other things. I was thinking about you, actually."

"Me?" My lips twitched into a smile. "All bad things, I hope."

"Yeah. Horrible, terrible, deplorable things." Nick chuckled at his lap.

I was silent for a moment, waiting for him to speak. I'd learned this past year that it was much easier to wait for him to formulate his thoughts instead of pushing him before he was ready. He would always tell me important things when the time was right.

Nick took a breath and squeezed my hand. "I'm thinking about last Christmas. About the day you left."

I squeezed his hand back, my chest seizing with the memory of me walking away from him. "It wasn't fun, was it?"

"It was the hardest thing I've ever done, Elle." Nick said softly, his eyes haunted. "Watching you walk away and being okay with it."

My heart seized in my chest, and I knew I'd cry if I thought too much about that time, that decision. I cracked a joke instead. "You really want me to believe it was harder than law school?"

"Yes." Nick answered instantly.

I took a breath and looked out the window. "I'm here now, aren't I?"

"You are." Nick sighed, and I put my chin on his shoulder, waiting for him to continue. "Elle—"

"The answer's going to be yes, by the way." I interrupted him, still on his shoulder.

Nick pulled back and gave me a look. "You don't know what I was going to say."

"You idiot." I climbed onto his lap, kissing his nose. "I love you. Of course, I knew what you were going to say."

Nick's eyes brightened, and he rested a hand on my hip. "You sure about that?"

I pretended to consider for a moment, but I was almost certain I knew what he was going to bring up. I'd been able to see it in his eyes for the last month, maybe longer. I'd seen it when he eyed my ringless finger. I'd seen it when he'd casually asked what size rings I wore. I'd seen it whenever I came home from the acting studio, the tight way that he hugged me, like he never wanted to let me go.

Nick Corrigan was getting proposey. I didn't know when he was going to do it, or even if he definitely was, but I was fairly certain that's what he wanted to check with me. As if I could give any answer other than yes.

The old version of me would be in shock at how calm I was at the thought. I wasn't nervous and excited and tying myself into knots about the possibility. But our love wasn't like that. It didn't give me frenzied butterflies, or make me worried, or cause me stress. Our relationship had grown stronger than I had thought a partnership could ever be.

It was peace, and it was safety, and it was passion. Of course, I was going to say yes if he asked me to marry him.

I smiled down at him from my spot on his lap and brushed some of his ruffled hair out of his eyes. "I know what it's about, Nick. It's going to be yes."

Nick's eyes flicked between mine, and he seemed to read something in them that made him satisfied. His hand tightened on my hip. "Good. I just wanted to check, before—"

"I know." I kissed his lips, barely brushing my lips against his, before pulling away. "We're on the same page, Nick."

He sighed and smiled at me, his warm brown eyes bright. "Yeah. I know."

I wound my arms around his wide shoulders and arched my back a little. "I've got an idea about what would make this morning even better?"

"Oh, yeah?" Nick smirked—knowing exactly what I was implying—and asked, anyway. "What's that?"

"Sex, Nicholas." I deadpanned. "Some sex would be a fun way to start the day."

Nick tipped his head back and laughed, and I gloated a little, the same way I did whenever I could make him laugh like that, unrestrained and joyful. Gah, I just loved him so much. It would be slightly annoying if he didn't bring me so much joy and contentment.

Nick nuzzled my neck. "I think that can be arranged."

I pressed myself onto his body and rode him as the sun came up, soft licks of pleasure running up my spine and my heart full of love.

⤜⟫⟫⟩ ⟨⟨⟨⟨⤛

"We're going to be late." I pulled on my boots in the hall, trying to check the clock in the living room for the time.

Nick steadied me and offered me my coat. "No, we're fine. I sent her a text, anyway."

I groaned. "I don't like being late."

Nick pulled on his own coat and opened the front door. "From the sounds of it, we're not the only ones who are late."

"What? Why?" I looked at Nick as he bundled me out the door. "It's just us three, right?"

"Mike is going to be there. Matt's coming, too." Nick shrugged. "His family's out of town, and Deanna invited him to have Christmas with us instead."

"And Mike?" I waggled my eyebrows. Nick and I had both talked about whether Deanna had a thing with Mike, but we'd never been able to work it out.

Nick flashed me a smile and reversed out of the driveway, heading towards Deanna's. "I guess we'll find out, won't we?"

I laughed and watched the trees and snow pass us by. "I guess we will."

⟩⟩⟩⟩⟩ ⟨⟨⟨⟨⟨

Christmas lunch was no less merry for having two extra people. I liked Matt, and I was really fond of Mike, so they were both welcome additions to the party. Deanna was lovely as ever, and she looked even better this year after retiring, rested, and happy.

Her garden, in particular, was more beautiful than ever. I said as much to her when I entered, the winter blooms catching my eye.

Deanna pulled me into a hug. "You're looking much better, too. I'm glad you got some rest after the play."

I brushed off her concerns. I'd directed the play again this year, but hadn't gone onstage. Next year, I'd look at starting up Deanna's tradition again, but I had wanted to find my feet first after taking over the studio. "I've been practically bed bound."

Nick made a sound from behind me. "I can vouch for that."

I elbowed Nick lightly in the ribs, and I heard him laugh as he went to hug Deanna. I turned to the others in the living room.

Matt, who I'd grown friendlier with over the year, was wearing his usual cocky grin. "Elle."

"Matt." I punched his shoulder as I passed. "Your parents abandoned you, did they?"

"Nah." Matt shrugged off my punch and poked me in the ribs. "I told them to go, bought them tickets so they could have Christmas in Italy."

I blinked at him. "That's very nice of you."

Matt shrugged. "I had some extra cash, and they deserved it."

Deanna walked passed. "Just like a good son, he is. You hear that, Nick? Buy me some plane tickets sometime."

"You hate plane travel." Nick reminded her.

Deanna put a hand on her hip, her silver hair piled elegantly on her head. "Oh. I suppose you're right."

"Smells good, Dee," Mike piped up, nursing a beer in the corner.

Nick and I made a face at each other at the nickname, but restrained ourselves. We'd get the answer to that in time.

"Thank you, Mike." Deanna swept her hand towards the dining table. "Shall we, everyone?"

I waddled out of Deanna's house with a very full belly, several presents, and a big smile. As expected, the lunch had been a feast. Nick held my hand as we walked down the front path, and he tugged me to a stop, looking up at the sky.

"Do you want to go for a walk with me?"

I looked up at the sky, and saw that the snow might hold off for a little while. Given my belly was stuffed with food, a walk was a good idea. We rarely had the chance to walk together in winter, now that Nick always picked me up from the studio himself, saving me from the cold. I squeezed his hand. "I'd love to."

We wandered through town, peeking into festive windows and listening to the sound of snow crunching under our feet. I felt totally at ease, totally content with my life now. I thought of who I had been, just over a year ago, miserable and desperate for something I didn't even want, but was too scared to admit it.

I wasn't that girl anymore. Elle the actress was long gone, and I was glad of it.

"I can hear you thinking." Nick's voice rumbled, snapping me out of my spiraling thoughts.

"Nope." I flashed him a smile. "Sorry, but I've got absolutely no thoughts in this silly little head."

Nick huffed and squeezed my hand. "It's a wonder you've got a grasp of the English language, pea-brain."

I giggled at his dry comeback, my heart squeezing. "Pea-brain, is it?"

"Sure." Nick shrugged. "It's gotta be the size of a pea in there, if you have no thoughts."

I laughed out loud; the sound rippling through me. I pressed a hand to my side and bent over. I wiped my eyes and tried to stop the fit of laughter. "It's—a wonder you can stand to be seen with such an airhead."

"It's an embarrassment, truly." Nick's lips curved into a smile, and he stepped closer. "Everyone I know has no idea why I'm around such a ditz."

I crinkled my eyes at him. "Poor Nick, having to date such a vapid woman. I heard she's bottle blonde and a former actress."

"A deadly combination." Nick's warm eyes were bright. "It's a shame he loves her so much."

"A real shame." I whispered.

Nick tilted his head at me. "What were you really thinking?"

"Sometimes I get the feeling if you could open my brain and read my thoughts, you would." I teased.

"Selfishly, I would." Nick took a breath and kept walking, grabbing my hand and taking me along with him. "But I suppose we've got to keep a small air of mystery between us."

I hummed and listened to the crunch of our footsteps. "A lot has changed in a year. That's all I was thinking."

His thumb brushed over my palm. "I know what you mean."

I pulled him to a stop beside a streetlight, the lamp already lit despite it being mid-afternoon. I brought his exposed hand up to my mouth and breathed on it, trying to keep it warm. He'd given his gloves to me, just another thing in a line of things Nick did for me, all the time, to show he cared. "Do you, though? I sometimes feel you've changed my life for the better, much more than I've changed yours."

Nick's eyes softened, and he cupped my cheek. "That's an outright lie."

I blinked up at him, waiting for him to continue.

"There's not a single moment of my days that you don't influence, where I'm not thinking of you, or our life together, or coming home to your arms." Nick stepped closer to me, and he looked almost angry. "If you weren't in my life, I wouldn't be half the man I am today. I was a robot before I met you, just going through the motions. Now, I look forward to waking up every single day because of you, Elle."

My heart seized, and a single happy tear fell down my face. Nick delicately brushed it away with his finger.

He kissed my forehead. "Don't ever think that I've changed your life more than you've changed mine. It's not a competition, gorgeous."

I swallowed and looked up at the sky. "I just—I'm so *happy*, Nick. I'm happier than any person has any right to feel, and I—"

"Marry me, then." Nick said the words, then looked taken aback.

My breath stopped, and my heart squeezed tight. A warm feeling bloomed in my chest, growing with every second since he said those two words. "Are you—"

"I—Christ." Nick shoved his hands through his pockets, and he frowned. "I didn't even bring it—"

I covered his hands with mine, trying to stop him from stressing. "Nick."

He slowed and looked at me. "Elle."

A laugh bubbled up from my throat. "Were you being serious?"

"Of course I am." Nick grabbed his hand in mine, looking solemn. "I've never been more serious in my life."

"You want to marry me?" I repeated, wanting to hear him say it again. I knew it was coming, dammit, we'd even been talking about it vaguely just this morning, but hearing him say it made it *real*.

Nick cleared his throat. "Marry me. I'm asking if you want to marry me."

"Of course I will, you idiot." I squeezed his hand in mine.

Nick tipped his head back briefly, looking relieved. "Thank fuck."

I nudged him and laughed again. "We literally just talked around this thing this morning. What did you think I was going to say?"

"People can change their minds." Nick reminded me, solemn, and then he winced. "I'm sorry, I should have brought the ring—"

"Stop." I put a finger over his lips. "I don't need or want anything flashy. You asked, and I said yes. In the perfect spot, too."

I gestured around us to the snow-covered trees, the warm streetlight illuminating us under the snow clouds.

"I love this place. I love Christmas. I love you." I shook my head at him, smiling. "I don't need anything else."

Nick's eyes burned into mine, and he smiled. "I love you, Elle."

"That's a good thing, I guess, given you just asked me to marry you." I quipped. "Otherwise we'd be—"

I couldn't say anything more, because Nick pulled me in and pressed his lips firmly against mine, and I melted into him. The kiss was a pledge, and a reassurance, and an invitation all in one. After a few moments, we broke apart and smiled at each other.

"Why don't we go home and you can show me that ring?" I whispered.

Nick huffed out a laugh and stepped back, lacing his hand with mine. "Alright."

We walked, hand in hand, through the streets of Mistletoe Valley. I felt like the luckiest girl in the world to have found this—like the last piece of the puzzle had fallen into place. A warm feeling bloomed in my chest.

With the man I loved at my side, and a perfect town around me, I had found a life with joy. I hadn't chosen 'success', or suffering, or infamy. I had chosen love, and I had found peace.

The snow fell around us like a promise, and I smiled at the sky.

Afterword

Thank you so much, dear reader, for picking up this book from a debut author. In some ways, Elle's journey in this book is like my own. I graduated from acting school a year ago, into an industry that had been absolutely ravaged by the pandemic, and realised that I hated the thing I'd worked towards for years. I did one professional gig onstage, and then realised that was it, and I needed another career. I know I'm not alone in this, that this feeling isn't exclusive to the performing arts, because burnout and career pivots have been increasing throughout the world.

I hope Elle's journey rings true to your own path of self-discovery, even if it does not exactly mirror your own. We all deserve to find peace and happiness, no matter what we once wanted, and I hope you can find that in your own time, too. Even if reading this book only gave you some amount of joy to tide you through, I'm grateful I could help. Books have always been my safe place, and I hope my own stories can be one for you.

To my parents, who supported me through the worst of times, and housed me when I decided to throw caution to the wind and give the writing thing a go, I owe you everything.

Anna xx

About Author

Anna has been swooning over love stories ever since she can remember. Her debut romantic comedy, THE MISTLETOE PROBLEM, is her first step in writing love stories herself, and she couldn't be happier. She loves writing about grumpy, clever men and determined, feisty women. When she's not writing, she's taking her dog for walks along the beach in sunny Australia, or shouting into the void about her latest fictional obsession.

Find her at www.annabarlowauthor.com

Instagram: @annabarlowauthor

Twitter: @annabarlowbooks

TikTok: @annabarlow

Want more of Elle and Nick? Get a free bonus epilogue as a welcome gift when you sign up to my newsletter!

Katherine and Matt's story coming Jan 2023….

Printed in Great Britain
by Amazon